THE PENNINGTONS

A tale of family, friendship and secrets, from a well-loved author

1902, Bath. When the housekeeper suddenly resigns, seventeen-year-old housemaid Daisy is left to cope alone with the almost bedridden owner of the house, Montague Pennington, Esq. Monty's unpleasant relations begrudgingly search for a new housekeeper, as lively Daisy takes charge. However serious problems arise as a mysterious stranger begins to target the entire family. It seems that the Penningtons hold dark secrets, and the past can-not be suppressed for much longer...

THE PENNINGTONS

Pamela Oldfield

Severn House Large Print
London & New York

This first large print edition published 2012
in Great Britain and the USA by
SEVERN HOUSE PUBLISHERS LTD of
9-15 High Street, Sutton, Surrey, SM1 1DF.
First world regular print edition published 2010 by
Severn House Publishers Ltd., London and New York.

British Library Cataloguing in Publication Data

Oldfield, Pamela.
 The Penningtons.
 1. Housekeepers--England--Bath--Fiction. 2. Family
 secrets--Fiction. 3. Bath (England)--Social conditions--
 20th century--Fiction. 4. Large type books.
 I. Title
 823.9'14-dc23

 ISBN-13: 978-0-7278-9945-3

Severn House Publishers support The Forest Stewardship
Council [FSC], the leading international forest certification
organisation. All our titles that are printed on Greenpeace-
approved FSC-certified paper carry the FSC logo.

MIX
Paper from
responsible sources
FSC® C018575

Printed and bound in Great Britain by the
MPG Books Group, Bodmin, Cornwall.

ONE

On Friday mornings Daisy looked forward to the reading of the weekly letter from the housekeeper's mother whose name was Emily. This unfortunate woman, it seemed, was constantly beset by a variety of medical problems which provided fascinating information to the uninitiated – Daisy among them.

Emily Dutton suffered with her back and that was 'something chronic'; she suffered with her lungs – 'tight as a drum' or 'hack, hack, hack'; but, most dramatic of all, she suffered with her heart which gave her 'dreadful palpitations' and sometimes threatened to stop beating altogether. Presumably, Daisy thought, when the latter happened, Emily Dutton would be in no fit state to write a letter to anyone and poor Miss Dutton, the middle-aged housekeeper, would become an orphan.

But today was not Friday, it was Wednesday and Daisy had no idea that today's post would set in motion a change to the course of her own life. On this particular morning the postman had brought a small mixed bag which Daisy rushed to gather up from the mat. By considering the postmarks in conjunction with the handwriting she could often discover the name of the senders. Today she found one for Montague Pennington, Esq. (otherwise known to his small staff as Monty), and one for the housekeeper which was addressed in an unfamiliar handwriting. Definitely not from the housekeeper's mother, Daisy decided, narrowing her eyes inquisitively. The address was a scrawl, large and generously looped, with an odd splatter of ink in the lower left-hand corner of the envelope.

'Interesting!' Daisy pushed unruly ginger hair back under her lace cap and smiled with satisfaction. Their morning tea break would last for a few moments longer today and she might manage to sneak an extra biscuit from the tin while the letter, from whoever it was, was being read out.

The third and last item of post was a postcard from the local farmer reminding Mr Pennington that he could purchase kindling wood direct from a nearby farm at a reasonable price.

'We know that!' Daisy told the absent farmer, 'but Miss Dutton doesn't like your delivery boy since he trekked mud in on our clean floor and wouldn't apologize. She won't give you another order so you'd best save money on the postcards!'

She busied herself with the black lead, applying it to the stove with a practised hand then finishing it off with the brush.

Miss Dutton came into the kitchen, making no attempt to hide a yawn. 'I swear my bed gets lumpier by the day!' she grumbled. 'Think yourself lucky you can go home each evening.' She settled her ample body on a chair and poured herself a cup of tea.

Daisy said, 'There's a letter for you.'

Miss Dutton picked it up from the table and regarded it with suspicion. 'Now who on earth might you be?' she asked the absent sender, considering the letter unhappily.

Daisy said, 'Might be good news. I'd open it.'

'And it might not.' She reached for a knife and slit the flap of the envelope.

Daisy bit back a sigh of frustration. Satisfied with the stove, she stood up as the housekeeper began to read the letter silently.

Miss Dutton's expression changed and she gave a little scream and said, 'Oh my good Gawd! It's me ma! She's in the hospital. Fell and broke her leg!'

'She never did!' cried Daisy, thrilled by the drama of the moment. 'Then who's written the letter?'

'Miss Bligh, her next-door neighbour.' She stared distractedly at Daisy. 'That's it then. That's me finished here.' She clapped a hand to her chest and took a deep breath in an attempt to calm her nerves. 'I can't stay on a moment longer. I'll have to go and get her out of there. Take her home. She'll be relying on me, poor dear.'

Taken aback, Daisy asked, 'What's the rush? She'll be safe in the hospital for a few days.'

'Safe?' She stared at Daisy. 'In hospital? People *die* in those places. I shall have to get her home – she'll be terrified!' Gazing round the kitchen with unseeing eyes, she was already dealing with a variety of problems far removed from Montague Pennington's breakfast. She glanced again at the letter. 'She'll be bedridden for a week or two and Miss Bligh's going to lend me a commode. Now I call that very decent of her. I never really liked the woman but that is very decent.'

'Very decent.' Daisy was experiencing a frisson of disquiet. 'So when exactly will you be leaving?'

'As soon as I'm packed. Ma will be in a terrible state. I mean, *hospital!* All those doctors and nurses rushing about and people groaning – not to mention bed pans! Everyone's worst nightmare!'

'But when will you come back here to Park View? I mean, what about poor old Monty? Who's going to look after him? He's bedridden too!'

Miss Dutton rolled her eyes. 'But he's not *family*. He'll have to find someone else to run around after him. My mother comes first and if you had a grain of sense in your head, Daisy, I wouldn't need to be telling you so. Now let me think ... What time's the next bus into the town?'

'It goes past here at quarter to the hour which would be quarter to nine but ... you can't just abandon the poor old man!'

'Can't I? Just watch me.' She glanced at the wall clock. 'Ten minutes. I'll just about do it. I'm off upstairs to break the news, throw some clothes into the bag and run for the bus.'

Daisy's disquiet was developing into a feeling of panic. Surely she wasn't going to be left alone here with a creaky old man. 'But you ... aren't you supposed to give notice?'

'Too bad. He can pay me up to today and that's that.'

'But Monty must be turned seventy! The shock might be too much for him. You're always saying he can't manage without you.

Now you're going to "up sticks" and leave him helpless!'

'My ma's the one who's helpless. She's broke her leg, remember, and been carted off to hospital! Now I'll tell the old chap that I'll just take a few bits and bobs for now and I'll be back for the rest of my clothes in maybe a week. See how things go at home. Run upstairs, Daisy, and fetch down the small carpet bag from the box room. No one'll miss it and I'll bring it back when I come for the rest of my stuff.'

'So you are coming back to Park View, aren't you?' Desperate for reassurance, Daisy looked at her appealingly.

'Coming back? Course I'm not! Leastways not to work. You don't recover from a broken leg at the snap of a finger. It'll be weeks – legs are funny things. If it doesn't set properly she might be on crutches for the rest of her life! No, he'll have to find someone else.' She fumbled in a pocket, found a handkerchief and mopped her brow. 'I'll dash upstairs and tell him what's happened and then you can take it from there. Just find another housekeeper for him.' She snatched her apron from the back of the kitchen door and rolled it into a ball. 'Well, don't just stand there gawping, Daisy. Fetch the carpet bag. If I don't get that bus it'll be another hour!'

Daisy obeyed and when she came down

she found the kitchen deserted but a minute later Miss Dutton came downstairs with a bundle of clothes under one arm and a pair of shoes clutched in her hand.

Daisy said, 'I don't know how to get another housekeeper. I mean, who do I ask?'

'Put a card in the window of the village shop. Or better still, get in touch with Horrible Hettie ... or his sister, Dilys, Do them good to do something useful for a change. She's always got time for the Ladies Groups and Soup Kitchens but never time to visit her elderly brother.' She stared round distractedly. Now where's my purse? Ah! Got it.'

Stunned by the speed of the disaster, Daisy watched helplessly as Miss Dutton issued a few last instructions about the day's meals and then dashed out of the house. Just in time. The bus screeched to a halt for her and the conductor helped her aboard.

Daisy watched her departure from the front step, feeling slightly sick with shock. 'Get another housekeeper,' she told herself. 'Right then, that's what I'll do ... Bread and milk for Monty's breakfast ... order the Sunday joint, pay the window cleaner when he's done the windows – money's in the tea caddy ... fetch the coal...'

For a long moment she stood on the front step of the large elegant house, looking out over Alexandra Park and past that to Bath. How could Miss Dutton just walk away from her life here, she wondered. Housekeeper to Monty was an enviable position – at least Daisy considered it to be so. She closed the front door thoughtfully.

On the way back to the kitchen she remembered the mention of Monty's sister and felt a glimmer of hope – Dilys Pennington, now Mrs John Maynard, a widow for three years. She would know what to do. Miss Dutton had never liked her because she had tried on one occasion to interfere with the running of Monty's household, but Daisy was not proud. She would ask for help. And there was another family member – Monty's brother Albert who was married to the woman Miss Dutton had nicknamed 'Horrible Hettie'.

'Thank the Lord for small mercies!' she whispered. She would put everything in the capable hands of the Pennington family.

After Miss Dutton had gone Daisy sipped a cup of tea while she tried to gather her wits. There was so much to think about and she had no idea where to start. It seemed wise to notify the family as soon as possible but that meant using the telephone and Daisy had never been allowed to answer it let alone initiate a call.

'The numbers to ring must be in the telephone book,' she told herself. Not that she would recognize the Pennington women if they passed her in the street. They rarely came to call except at Christmas and on Monty's birthday when they arrived with gifts and departed within the hour. It was not what you would call a close family.

Her train of thought was broken by the jingle of a bell from upstairs and she jumped to her feet in alarm. The first bell of the morning usually meant that he was awake and Miss Dutton would jump to her feet and make her way up to the main bedroom with his breakfast tray. Today, however, was different because the housekeeper had already spoken to him and had told him the situation. The breakfast must wait, she decided. She would ask him for details of the family and suggest that she telephone someone.

Before she could change her mind she hurried upstairs, knocked on the door and went in. Daisy saw a small elderly man sitting up in a large bed. He had wild white hair, frightened blue eyes and gnarled hands which clutched the bedclothes to his frail body defensively. He eyed Daisy with a look of alarm.

'Good morning, Mr Pennington. I'm Daisy, the housemaid.'

They stared at each other for a moment,

each trying to adjust to the new state of affairs. Montague Pennington saw a young woman, barely seventeen, her hair pinned into an untidy bun below a small white cap. She was plump but not fat, wholesome rather than pretty and she smiled nervously. As she approached the bed he saw that her eyes were pale brown, her teeth were good and her apron was clean. He recalled vague memories of the occasional glimpse of her on the rare occasions when Miss Dutton was too busy elsewhere to answer his bell.

He relaxed slightly. 'Good morning, Daisy. We find ourselves in a bit of a pickle.'

'Yes sir, we do.' Her gaze took in his dressing gown thrown across the bedside chair and the small table which held a water jug (empty), tumbler, pills, crumpled handkerchief and a half hunter watch. A quick glance around the room presented closed windows with dingy curtains and dead coals in the fireplace. There was an upholstered armchair in one corner but it was piled with books, folded wrapping paper, board games and a pair of binoculars. Hardly a cosy room, she reflected. 'I think we should alert your family, sir. One of them could arrange for a new housekeeper. Miss Dutton says she'll never be able to come back.'

His face fell. 'Never coming back? But when her mother recovers...?'

14

'She seems to think it will take months and maybe the leg will never be healed.'

'I never thought she'd leave me.' He smiled sadly. 'She was very good to me. She looked after me.'

But not very well, thought Daisy. The lace curtains needed a wash, there was no smell of polish and a few dead flies decorated the window sill.

After an awkward silence he said, 'They won't be at all pleased – the family, I mean. They lead busy lives, all of them. My sister Dilys is on her own now, since her husband died. She is on various committees of some kind, to do with the poor and needy ... and Hettie plays bridge – she's very good – and I understand she and Albert entertain a lot. And she has Albert to look after and the house to run and always has trouble with the servants. Poor Hettie.'

'You certainly don't see much of them.'

'No.' He brightened. 'But they never forget my birthday.' He pointed to the dressing gown. 'That was a present from Albert and Hettie. It's from Harrods. When I commented on it Hettie said, "Only the best for you, Montague!" I thought that was very sweet of her.' His smile faded suddenly. 'Oh dear! There's the matter of the weekly housekeeping money. Miss Dutton always collected it from the solicitor for me. I gave her a letter to show to the cashier – an authorization. They will have to be notified.'

Daisy shrugged. 'One of the family could do all that.' He made no answer. 'Should I telephone them, sir? You could tell me how to do it.'

He sighed heavily. 'I'll have to give it some thought but in the meantime could you bring up my breakfast tray. Miss Dutton makes me bread and milk and...'

'I've watched her. I can do it. And a small pot of tea. Is that it?'

He nodded. 'And I need some more water for my tablets. I find it difficult to swallow them dry.'

Daisy picked up the water jug and the glass and made her way downstairs. She had an uneasy feeling about her employer. Had Miss Dutton been neglecting him?

Hettie Pennington was in the garden just before eleven that morning, talking to the gardener about the apple tree. 'I'm very disappointed, Mr Trew. The apples are so small this year.'

Mr Trew, short, and weather-beaten by years of outdoor work, shook his head. 'I did warn you, ma'am, back in April. They need thinning out. I told you at the time but you said no. You was quite definite about it.'

'Thinning out? You said no such thing, Mr

Trew.'

'Oh but I did, ma'am! Young Clarence was here at the time, making a bonfire, and he heard me. I said quite clear that it was going to be a bumper crop but we needed to...'

'Bumper crop? What nonsense!' Hettie tossed her head. She was tall and thin with cold grey eyes. 'Are you doubting my word, Mr Trew?'

'See, this is exactly what we got, ma'am,' he continued stolidly. 'A bumper crop of *small* apples. If we'd thinned them when I suggested it...'

A maid appeared at the back door and called 'Telephone!'

Hettie rolled her eyes. 'Will that silly girl ever learn?' she demanded of nobody in particular. To the gardener she said, 'Pick some. Fill the small wheelbarrow. Cook might be able to make apple jelly with them.'

Seething with what she considered Mr Trew's insolence, Hettie wished she could sack him but he had been with her for nearly three years and that was a record. Most of her gardeners left within a year.

In the hall she snatched up the telephone and held the receiver to her ear. 'Who is this?'

'It's Daisy. I'm Mont— I mean I'm Mr Pennington's housemaid. I thought you should know that...'

17

'Put Miss Dutton on at once. Housemaid indeed!' She sniffed.

'Miss Dutton's not here. She's had to...'

'What do you mean she's not there? Where is she?'

'She's left. Gone home to nurse her mother.'

'How very inconsiderate. Montague relies on her for everything. For how long?'

'Forever. Given in her notice. I thought you should know. I thought maybe you'd...'

'He'll have to replace her. Tell him to ask around. There's always someone who wants a job. Ask Miss Dutton. She might know someone who would step in ... Are you still there?'

'Yes. I was hoping you'd be able to sort out a few matters.'

'Naturally I would if I had a moment to myself but at the moment it's quite impossible. We have the decorators coming tomorrow to put up the new wallpaper for the third bedroom, not to mention four friends coming to dinner tonight and Albert and I have tickets for the Theatre Royal the day after tomorrow.' She gave a theatrical sigh. ''Twas always thus! You could ask Dilys. She's on her own and has plenty of time although she would like us to believe otherwise. Montague has her telephone number. Now you must excuse me ... What did you

18

say your name was? Maisie?'

'Daisy. Daisy Letts.'

'Thank you for letting me know, Daisy. I'm sorry I can't be more help.'

'But what about tonight and all the other nights? I'm a daily. Miss Dutton lived in.'

'A *daily?* Good heavens, girl, use your common sense. You'll have to stay full time for the moment. You can't leave my brother on his own during the night. Anything might happen. Make up a bed in one of the spare rooms.'

Hettie replaced the receiver. 'Sort out a few matters?' she repeated. 'What impudence. Daisy is going to have to explain herself. Sort out a few matters, indeed! I have better things to do with my time.'

She stood thoughtfully for a moment or two then made her way into the large sitting room where Albert, her husband, was settled in a deep armchair with a glass of malt whisky in his right hand.

'Before you ask,' she said, 'that was one of Montague's minions – Daisy or Maisie or some such – asking if I would help sort out their problems for them. And before you ask, "Which problems are they?" it's the disappearance of their housekeeper who has apparently left them high and dry to go and nurse a sick mother. The selfish nature of some people never ceases to amaze me.'

19

'Damned awkward for poor old Montague!'

'Most certainly but hardly our business.' She smiled. 'I referred her to Dilys. Let her play fairy godmother!'

Albert downed the last of his whisky. 'What could we do anyway?'

'Exactly. And why should we? What has he ever done for us?'

Her husband frowned. 'Now steady on, old thing. When have we ever asked Montague for help?'

'Exactly. But if we did he'd refuse.'

'We don't know that! He's my brother, Hettie, and I know him better than you do.'

She gave him a strange look, opened her mouth to speak then changed her mind and closed it.

Alerted, he said, 'What's that about?'

'Nothing.'

'Come on, old thing. Spit it out!'

'I've always suspected that there was something going on between those two – Montague and Miss Dutton – and before you protest I'll tell you why. One year when we called in on his birthday I went upstairs and caught Miss Dutton coming out of his bedroom. She didn't see me but I saw her...'

'And...?'

'She threw him a kiss!'

'Miss Dutton? Never!' He glowered at her.

20

'My brother and the housekeeper? I don't believe it.'

Hettie sat down on the arm of the opposite chair. 'Well, it's the truth. So then I wondered what she was playing at and I thought he'd probably promised her something in his will. We all know he's got plenty of money, thanks to your stupidity.' She gave him a venomous look.

'Now don't bring that up again, Hettie. Montague followed Father into the family business and I chose not to. We all understood what was at stake. He is the oldest child and was due to inherit. When he dies what's left will come to me.'

'It made him wealthy,' she said bitterly. 'And Cressida added to it!'

'Ah! Cressida.' He glanced down at his hands. 'No one expected her to inherit so quickly. No one could have known that her father's ticker was in such a state. Give her her due, Hettie, she was devoted to her parents. You've never been fair to Cressida. She nursed her parents, married Montague and ended up nursing him.'

Hettie tossed her head. 'She should have married someone her own age.'

'Montague was only twenty years older.'

'Twenty years' difference! My point exactly!'

'He was a good husband to her,' Albert

21

protested.

'No he wasn't. She wanted a large family – she said so many times. Your brother was too old.'

'What has age got to do with it?'

'Well then, the problem must have lain with Cressida.' She gave him a triumphant look.

'Not everyone is blessed with a family, Hettie. *We* only have one child.'

'*I* only have one child. You have two but your first attempt is nothing to boast about!'

Albert made no reply. The child by his first marriage had turned out badly and they rarely mentioned him. The child he shared with Hettie was a source of lesser disappointment but a disappointment nonetheless. George Albert, now in his twenty-fifth year, had left Cambridge University in his last term to marry a French student (against his parents' wishes) and was now farming in Brittany. Albert and George had once been close but Hettie had resented the closeness and George had responded by leaving them at the earliest opportunity – first to go to college and then to enter a hasty marriage with Monique.

The familiar recriminations never failed to upset Albert and Hettie, and they now lapsed into a cold silence until Albert remembered the mention of Miss Dutton and

22

his brother.

'As for Montague and Miss Dutton,' he blustered. 'He must have been lonely after Cressida died but really, if you are right ... that housekeeper! That is extraordinary. There's no way you could call the woman desirable. A suet pudding tied round the middle with string!' He shrugged dismissively. 'Good-hearted, maybe but, I mean, after Cressida...'

'Oh yes. I forgot.' She glared at him. 'You have always had a soft spot for the wonderful Cressida!'

'So you said, dear! It was news to me.' He gave her his practised innocent look.

Hettie went on regardless. 'And don't forget he's been housebound for years. You know what they say – beggars can't be choosers. It will be interesting to see whether or not he leaves her anything in his will – a "little something" for past favours!' She raised her eyebrows meaningfully.

Albert shook his head. 'You have a wonderful imagination, my dear. It has always impressed me.'

She recognized the sarcasm but ignored it. 'We shall see, shall we not?'

'Miss Dutton?' He shook his head again in disbelief. 'Not the Montague I know – and he *is* my brother!'

'And he has been getting rather vague of

23

late. We did pass comment about it on his birthday, if you remember.'

He frowned. 'Vague? No. I don't recall him being vague.'

'Forgetful then. You never notice these things.'

'I think I know him better than you do.'

'Rose-coloured spectacles, Albert!' Hettie laughed. 'Anyway. it may all be immaterial now because Miss Dutton has blotted her copybook by leaving him stranded. Left him in the lurch, so to speak. Ruined her chances of a bequest, I should imagine. Poor old Montague.' She watched him closely for a moment, anticipating a reaction but there was none forthcoming so she smiled sweetly and dropped the subject.

Daisy went back upstairs feeling very uneasy. Her employer had been right about Hettie. Would his sister be any better, she wondered.

Moments later she stood beside his bed, having told him the results of her telephone call. 'So shall I try the other one?' she asked.

The old man pursed his lips. He had finished his bread and milk and the cup of tea and waved them away impatiently. 'Dilys? Hmm. Yes, give her a call.'

Daisy retrieved the tray and made her way towards the door.

'Look in our telephone book under Maynard.' He instructed. 'John Maynard was a very decent sort of chap. Poor man. Called before his time, as they say. Still, he left Dilys well provided for. I did hope she would eventually remarry – she's a handsome woman in some lights although I shouldn't say so since she's my sister, but there. She's had offers and turned them down. That's the trouble with money, it makes a woman independent. Still, give her a call.'

As she reached the door he asked, 'What's for lunch?'

'Lunch? Lord knows, sir. I'll have to look in the larder. Miss Dutton never said nothing about lunch – nor supper, neither – but then she hardly had the time. So upset about her mother.'

He looked at her hopefully. 'You can cook, I take it.'

'I don't know, sir. I've never tried but it can't be that difficult, can it. I'll manage for a few days until the new housekeeper gets here.' She gave him a cheery smile. 'Don't worry. I won't let you starve.'

'I should jolly well hope not. What's your name? I did know it but my memory's not as good as it was.'

'Daisy. Daisy Letts.'

'Well, Daisy, when you have telephoned my sister, please bring up my hot water and

25

a clean towel so that I can wash while you remake my bed. We seem to have wasted a lot of time already with Miss Dutton's disappearance and you may need to telephone the butcher with the new order ... and has the newspaper come yet?'

'I don't think so but I've been too busy to notice.'

'Miss Dutton always brings it up about this time.'

Startled she said, 'Lordy sir! I'll need another pair of hands at this rate!'

He looked startled by her tone. 'Miss Dutton always managed without any fuss.'

'Of course she did, sir!' Daisy rolled her eyes. 'She had me to run about for her. I'm me and I've got nobody else.'

To show her disapproval she withdrew smartly closing the door behind her. 'What does he take me for?' she muttered indignantly. Downstairs she went straight to the telephone, found the number and rang the operator who then connected her to the Maynard's number. A maid answered and explained that her mistress was busy with the chiropodist. 'She suffers with her feet something terrible,' she confided in a half whisper. 'I reckon it comes from those fancy shoes they like to wear.' In a louder voice she asked, 'Will you ring back or shall I ask her to ring you?'

Daisy hesitated. 'Ask her to ring me, please, and say it's about her brother Montague Pennington.'

When she hung up the telephone she smiled, a cautious look of triumph. It wasn't so difficult – the telephone. A lot of fuss about nothing, she told herself. She had rather enjoyed speaking to the operator who had been very polite if a little abrupt. Perhaps they had been told not to chat to people.

Almost half an hour later the telephone rang and it was Dilys Maynard.

'I want to speak to my brother,' she said crisply. 'I have very little time and...'

'I'm afraid he's bedridden. I thought you knew.' Daisy stared at the receiver in surprise. Surely his family understood that their brother was no longer able to get around. 'This telephone is downstairs in the hall.'

'Bedridden? No. We thought him largely confined to bed from choice. A bit of a recluse, perhaps. He has no disability that I am aware of – unless something has been hidden from us. Is that the case?'

'I wouldn't know that, Mrs Maynard. I've never looked after him. That was Miss Dutton. She spent a lot of time with him. He's going to need a new housekeeper and...'

'A new housekeeper? What's wrong with Miss Dutton?'

'She's left. Given in her notice all of a sud-

27

den and rushed off to her mother who's in hospital. That's why I'm talking to you. Your sister-in-law thought you...'

'Ha!' There was a lot of expression in that short word. 'Now I understand. You've been talking to Hettie – to Mrs Pennington! Montague's housekeeper leaves him stranded and Hettie thinks she's going to burden me with the problem! That is so like her.' The silence lengthened. 'So Miss Dutton has left him after all these years. So much for devotion. I am surprised.' After a silence she asked, 'So what exactly am I supposed to be doing about it?'

'I think she was hoping you could find us a new housekeeper.'

'Find a new housekeeper? Just like that! That really is typical of my sister-in-law!'

Daisy stuck her tongue out at the absent Dilys and waited.

Mrs Maynard said, 'I wonder where Miss Dutton came from. Possibly an agency. You could look through the telephone book and see if there is anywhere in there that sounds like an employment agency. If there is ask them if they sent Miss Dutton and if they say "yes" ask them to send two or three names for us to consider.' She paused and Daisy heard her muttering to herself. 'In the meantime I may be able to come over and discuss the matter with your employer.

28

Montague will know what wages he paid and the hours and so on ... Yes, that will suffice for the moment.'

The line went dead.

TWO

For Daisy, time passed in a blur of unremitting activity. Monty (as she continued to think of him) was a demanding invalid and she began to realize why Miss Dutton had always appeared harassed and had considered herself unappreciated. The bedside bell summoned Daisy upstairs too many times and at last she ignored it.

'I'll come up when I'm good and ready,' she muttered.

Ten minutes later when that time came she went up to him and announced that she was going home to tell her parents what had happened and to collect some nightclothes.

'Mind you,' she warned, 'I don't know what my pa will have to say, me staying overnight with just the two of us. If he says "no" then that's an end to it and you'll have to be on your lonesome until first thing tomorrow.'

A look akin to horror dawned in his eyes. 'You can't do that!' he begged. 'Please! I'll pay you more money. I'll pay you another sixpence a night ... no, ninepence ... no, sixpence.'

'Ninepence,' she insisted, her eyes narrowing. 'Ninepence might do the trick. My pa's very sharp when it comes to money.'

He nodded. 'And as to it being just the two of us, tell your father, Daisy, that I'm in my seventies and have no interest in young ladies. He'll understand.'

Daisy nodded then smiled.

'So when will you be making supper, Daisy? It's nearly six o'clock already.'

'I don't rightly know but I'll ask my ma what I should cook for you. She'll know. Leastways she'll have some idea.'

When she left him she felt a twinge of pity for the old man. He was sitting up in bed and reminded her of a small and rather nervous schoolboy.

Watching the clock, Monty managed to stay in bed for forty-five minutes then, restless and uncertain, he slid carefully from the bed and tottered across to the window which looked across the garden to the lane which led to Arnsby Farm Cottage where Daisy said she lived with her father and mother. He stared from the window, through faded blue

30

eyes blurred with age, hoping for a glimpse of Daisy on her way back, but apart from a shepherd with a small flock of sheep, he saw no one.

Was she going to come back, he wondered, or would her father insist that she continue as a 'daily'. Should he have offered her more than ninepence per night? Would her father consider the offer derisory? And if he did allow her to return would her mother have told her how to provide a reasonable supper?

Perhaps he should telephone Dilys to tell her he was alone in the house. Perhaps his sister would take pity on him and hurry over to set things right? He tried to remember the last time he had seen her but the memory was vague and somehow disquieting. There had been a disagreement of some kind, he recalled – something to do with money.

With a deep sigh he gave up his vigil and stared round the bedroom. The photograph of his wedding caught his eye and he swallowed hard. Cressida. She had been such a catch. He smiled. Prettier than Hettie – his brother had been so jealous. Even his sister had resented Cressida's perfect complexion, naturally waved hair and beautiful grey eyes...

He sighed again. His wedding day was a distant memory. Suddenly, without warning, he was sixty-eight, a pathetic old man con-

31

fined to his bed, with no one to care. Even Miss Dutton had deserted him.

Another glance from the window showed no sign of young Daisy returning along the lane and on impulse, he crossed carefully to the door of his room and opened it. A few more slow steps and he reached the landing. Peering over the banisters he saw the stairs stretching endlessly below – or so it seemed. It was so long since he had even *seen* the stairs, let alone made his way down them to the ground floor. Clinging to the banister rail he wondered what he would do if young Daisy failed to return. He would need to go downstairs to find food. He would need to answer the telephone if it rang, and answer the door if anyone arrived to see him. The latter meant he would have to be fully dressed – if he could remember where his clothes were kept.

Confused and afraid, he took several deep breaths to try and steady himself but perched on the landing at the top of the stairs he felt horribly vulnerable. His legs were weak from years of inaction, he clung to the banister for support, and the thought of his bed was increasingly tempting. Perhaps, he thought, he should go back to bed and await developments.

At that moment he had another unsettling thought. If Daisy failed to return – he trembled at the very idea – how would he alert people to the fact that he had been deserted and was alone and helpless?

'Now then, Montague,' he told himself sternly. 'You would do what had to be done. You would find a way.'

He could write a message and wrap it round a brick or something and drop it from the window ... and the window cleaner would find it – wouldn't he? The postman might want to deliver a parcel and when nobody answered his knock ... but when did anyone last send him a parcel?

Slowly, his hands groping along the wall, Montague made his way back to his room and fell on to his bed with a gasp of relief.

'Safe at last,' he whispered.

As he slid back beneath the bedclothes he told himself that Daisy would return at any moment. *And she would stay overnight.* He would not be alone through the dark hours, listening to the odd creaks and groans of the house and wondering if any of them were more than that – the footsteps, perhaps of an intruder.

He was reminded of his first night at boarding school. Even though he was sharing a dormitory with other boys, he was only eight years old and far from home, and in an emergency his parents would not be there to help him.

'But you're too old now for monsters and goblins,' he told himself sternly, with a belated attempt to see the funny side of his situation. When night came there would be no ghosts hovering in the shadows; no malicious trolls hiding under the bed; no demons waiting in the shadows to pounce on him as soon as he set foot outside the safety of the bed. Nevertheless he would take no chances but would remain in bed until Daisy returned – and if she left it too long and found his dead body, she would have only herself to blame.

Almost an hour later Daisy left her home with a basket on her arm containing her best flower-sprigged nightdress (rolled up) and a small cloth and a tin of Euchryl tooth powder. A large slice of meat roll and some cold boiled potatoes were wrapped in a clean cloth and a large Kilner jar contained a rice pudding. There was also a slim bundle of simple recipes copied in her mother's almost illegible scrawl – sausage and mash, bacon and eggs and fishcakes.

Her mother, Martha, stood at the gate to see her off. 'And no nonsense from old Monty,' she reminded her daughter.

'He's over seventy, Ma!'

'And Dais, make sure you lock all the doors last thing...'

'I will, Ma!' She hurried a little, anxious to be out of her mother's sight and hearing. The last-minute warnings were starting to unnerve her.

'...and the downstairs windows – and sleep with the keys under your pillow.'

'I will!'

'Maybe see you some time tomorrow then. I'll make it all right with your pa ... and ask the old man about you-know-what!'

'I will. Bye!'

'God bless!'

As Daisy rounded the corner she let out a sigh of relief. 'You-know-what' referred to a request for more money for the nights she would 'stay over'. Part of a housekeeper's wages, her mother had reminded her. Her pa would never countenance anyone taking advantage of his daughter and Daisy, willing and eager, was already making plans for the extra money she would earn.

At five past six that evening Monty found himself sitting up in bed, eyeing his supper which Daisy had placed before him with a proud flourish. She had warmed up the roll in the oven and fried up the potatoes and was now watching for his reaction.

'What's this then?' he asked tremulously.

Daisy sat down beside him with a similar plate of food on his bedside table. 'Our supper,' she told him. 'Meat roll and potatoes and there's chutney if you want it.' To encourage him she reached for a jar of Miss Dutton's plum chutney and helped herself to a large spoonful.

'Meat roll?' He regarded her with dismay. 'I mustn't have meat. It's too difficult to digest. Miss Dutton insisted that...'

'She's gone, sir, so you'll have to get used to me until they find someone else. The potatoes are a mite burnt but they're still edible.' To demonstrate this, Daisy popped a large forkful into her mouth and chewed with relish.

'I have to have fish,' said Monty. 'Sometimes steamed and sometimes boiled, sometimes...'

'And what else?'

'Mashed potatoes or boiled potatoes, peas, runner beans...'

'I mean what else besides fish.'

'Nothing else. I have a delicate stomach.'

'Who said so?' She ate some meat roll. 'This roll's good. My ma made it. Try some.'

He pushed the plate away. 'I'll get indigestion. Or dyspepsia ... or heartburn. At my age...'

'Stop grumbling, sir. If you're hungry eat it. If you don't want it, I'll have it.' She gave him a stern look. 'If you're ill I'll send for the doctor. If you're not ill, you should eat. It's nourishment. I'm afraid Miss Dutton's been pampering you, sir. Giving you invalid food when you're not an invalid.' She sighed. 'Just try it, to please me. I've done my best at short notice. Tomorrow I'll send for some fish and make fishcakes. One of my ma's favourite recipes and I copied it out. Pa's very keen on...'

'Fishcakes? Are they steamed?' Tentatively he pulled the plate towards him and sniffed it. He lifted a forkful of meat roll to his mouth and closed his eyes.

'No, sir. Fish cakes are fried and very tasty. I shall put an egg in and some chopped parsley from the garden and something else – it may have been potato.' She smiled suddenly. 'There! You enjoyed that, didn't you?'

'It was ... better than I expected.'

'Now try the potatoes.'

Ten minutes later Montague had eaten everything on his plate including a small sample of chutney. He had actually enjoyed it in a somewhat fearful way, expecting at any moment to feel the first pangs of whatever disorder it was going to provoke. Nothing had happened, however, and he now felt pleasantly full. When Daisy had taken the plates downstairs, he settled himself comfortably in the bed and closed his eyes. He had survived the first few hours of Miss Dutton's disappearance and Daisy's first attempt to provide him with a meal. Cautiously hopeful, he told himself that it would only be a matter of days before Miss Dutton's replacement arrived.

It took very little time for Daisy to decide that she was not going to rush up and down the stairs half a dozen times a day. Somehow she must persuade her employer to venture downstairs for at least part of the day and she broached the subject with her usual lack of tact.

'You're wearing me to a shadow,' she told him next morning, 'so let's see how you get on with a trip downstairs.'

His look of horror was no worse than she had anticipated and she gave him an encouraging smile. 'You might trip if you come down in your nightshirt so you'd best put on some proper clothes. I'll sort some out for you and...'

'No, no,no!' he cried, genuinely alarmed by her suggestions. 'Miss Dutton warned me never to try the stairs because I'd fall head over heels and break my neck!' He stared at her, his eyes wide with fear, his lips trembling.

'But that's the trouble,' she insisted. 'That way you lose the use of your legs. My old grandmother went down that road and lost the use of her legs. So what if there'd been a fire? She'd have been burned to a crisp, not able to save herself by escaping down the stairs! You'd be in the same pickle, sir.'

Folding her arms she stared back at him, daring him to contradict. While he continued to mumble protests, she set about collecting his clothes and left them on the bed.

'I won't embarrass you by helping you put them on,' she told him. 'You take your time. Then we'll see how you go, sir, sitting on the stairs, one step down and then another. See that way you won't topple forward. No chance of you breaking your poor old neck!'

Ignoring the panic in his eyes she went down to the kitchen to wash up and then into the hall to telephone the butcher with an order for sausages, and catch the fish man to buy some cod for the promised fishcakes. Later she would walk along to Arnsby Farm where her father worked, and collect bacon and another half dozen eggs.

Monty's descent by way of the stairs worked better than she had dared to hope and by midday he was installed in the sitting room with a glass of Miss Dutton's home made ginger beer and looking distinctly nervous. While Daisy busied herself peeling potatoes he sat with the cat on his lap thinking about the turnaround in his life and hoping that when her mother recovered, Miss Dutton would reconsider and come back to him.

The next morning Hettie waited until she had the house to herself then telephoned her sister-in-law. Dilys came to the phone in an irritable frame of mind and said, 'Yes. What is it?'

Hettie bridled. 'What sort of greeting is that?'

'I'm sorry. The fact is I'm not very happy at the moment. I have a rather bad headache.'

'I don't feel too well either but I didn't snap your head off! It's Albert. I told him about Miss Dutton deserting Montague and he's now insisting we rush over to visit and make sure he's all right. Talk about a fuss about nothing. What can happen to him? Monty's not alone. He's got that maid.'

Dilys closed her eyes. 'Don't go over there,' she said firmly. 'We shouldn't do anything in a hurry. You know what your mother used to say about fools rushing in!'

'Don't worry, Dilys. Whatever my failings, I do not panic. As a matter of fact I was going to telephone you later to suggest that you and I meet and talk things over.'

'Tell Albert we both have things to do and we can't be expected to ... Talk things over? What sort of things?'

Hettie counted to ten and fixed a smile on her face in the hope that she would sound calm and composed. 'The point is, Dilys, that I think we should get together and think about Montague's future. He's getting to the stage where he might need help with ... with family matters.' She held her breath.

'Family matters? But he doesn't have any family. Cressida failed to produce an offspring. You know that as well as I do. What are you talking about?'

'I mean money matters, Dilys. He's a rich old man who is becoming rather vague. He has no children to inherit his wealth so ... what will he do with it? Has he made a will, for instance? Who will he leave it to?' She waited, silently urging her sister-in-law to understand.

In a changed voice Dilys said, 'A cat's home? Is that what you mean. Something like that.'

'A charity of some kind, maybe, or even Miss Dutton!'

She heard Dilys's sharp intake of breath. 'Surely not. After her defection...'

'She might change her mind. If her mother died, for instance, she might want her job back.'

'So are you suggesting we get together and...'

Hettie crossed her fingers. Dilys had always been a little slow on the uptake, she thought with an impatient sigh.

41

Dilys continued, '...and organize a new housekeeper – as quickly as possible?'

Hettie hesitated. 'That, yes, but I'm more worried about his money. Is he, do you think, still alert enough in his mind, to deal with such things? His solicitor, for instance, might need to talk with him and is he ... is he fit enough *mentally*?'

She heard Dilys sigh. 'Don't you think you should talk to Albert about this? He's always very defensive about his brother and he might say we're imagining it. I must say I hadn't realized that Montague was in such a state but then it's some time since we last saw him and even then, if you recall, Miss Dutton shooed us out very quickly saying he was tired and had had a sleepless night.' Her voice brightened suddenly. 'Should we talk to his doctor, do you think?'

'No!' It came out more forcefully than Hettie had intended. 'Well, later maybe but all I want for the moment is for us to go over there and maybe interview a couple of housekeepers for him and at the same time see how he is.'

'And bring Albert into the equation later if it seems necessary?'

'Naturally. Now we're seeing eye to eye, Dilys. I'm so glad we're of one mind and, as you say, we'll keep it between ourselves for the moment. No need to worry Albert.'

With the plan launched they agreed a date when the two of them would meet in Miss Maude's Teashop and move things a step further. Hettie knew of an agency which might provide a housekeeper and Dilys had agreed to apply there and see what transpired. As Hettie hung up the receiver she breathed a sigh of satisfaction. Dilys had taken the bait.

The offices of the Placewell Agency were small but meticulously tidy. It was owned by Mabel Gillworthy who attended each day until twelve noon when she was replaced by one or other of her two part-time assistants. On the following Monday afternoon at three o'clock precisely, a Miss Robbins turned from her typewriter to greet the next client.

'Miss Maynard?' she asked, smiling.

'It's *Mrs* Maynard. I explained to Miss Gillworthy that my sister-in-law and I are trying to find a trustworthy housekeeper for my brother who is...'

'Do please sit down, Mrs Maynard. I'm Miss Robbins. I have your notes and requirements to hand and have two people in mind who might suit your brother.' Her smile lit up an otherwise plain face which might have been improved by a less severe hairstyle. She looked about thirty.

Dilys Maynard narrowed her eyes. 'May I

43

ask how long you have held this position?'

'I have worked for Miss Gillworthy since the turn of the century – that is, for two years.' Her smile faltered a little at what she saw as a lightly veiled criticism.

Dilys sat down. 'I ask because the women you recommend must be of the highest moral calibre and I want to feel certain that I can trust your judgement. My brother is very frail, frequently forgetful, and suffers with his digestion so needs a delicate diet. He may also need help dressing as he is, I suspect, a semi-invalid. He's sixty-eight and has been alone for four years since his wife died. He's almost bedridden and...'

'Ah!' Alerted, Miss Robbins held up a tentative hand. 'We may have a slight problem, Mrs Maynard.'

'A problem?' Dilys asked indignantly. 'Miss Gillworthy appeared quite satisfied by our requirements. She seemed to think you could find a suitable...'

'The problem is the state of your brother's health, Mrs Maynard. Have you considered that a nurse might be better than a housekeeper? It sounds to me that your brother...'

'I know exactly what my brother needs, Miss Robbins. He has managed for years with a housekeeper. He isn't *ill* therefore a nurse would find very little to do.'

Miss Robbins bit back a sharp reply. She

was beginning to dislike the client but tried not to show it. 'We are properly trained to offer advice when we feel it is necessary.'

'But I haven't asked for advice. I have merely said that I want to be able to trust your judgement.'

'I see. Then let us investigate this further. We can now dispense with one of the names I had selected for you to look at.' Miss Robbins hid her sense of triumph at the immediate change in the client's attitude. Holding up the card she held in her hand she said, 'Miss Adams has specified "no nursing". In my opinion an elderly man who is already almost bedridden will need help dressing and maybe washing and possibly other bodily functions may prove problematic.'

'I've already told you that the last housekeeper...'

Miss Robbins intervened. 'Like you, our ladies rely on our judgement, Mrs Maynard. I would never recommend Miss Adams for the position you offer. I would feel I was deceiving her. No nursing. Never mind.' She replaced the card in her folder.

'I don't like your tone, Miss Robbins!' The client was reddening with irritation. 'Placewell Agency sent Miss Dutton to us originally and she has never complained that she had been misled. Not one word!'

Miss Robbins managed a frosty smile. 'Is

that so, Mrs Maynard? When did she first work for your brother?'

'She was with him for years. I don't know exactly.' The hands clutching her purse were white with tension.

'That explains it. When she first came your brother was almost certainly a much fitter man so Miss Dutton was simply his house-keeper. In the intervening years he has obviously deteriorated.' She made a great show of studying the second card. 'Now let's have a look at the second choice I found for you.' She held up the card. 'Mrs Amy Torrance – a charming woman in her forties. She's a first-class cook, used to complete household management including servants ... extra qualifications are floral arrangements, wedding catering...' She nodded.

'Wedding catering? How ridiculous!' Obviously exasperated, Dilys rolled her eyes.

'But with all that expertise she is naturally very expensive.' She turned the card over. 'Ah! I almost missed this – she is very emphatic about her church attendance every Sunday morning and no dogs or children.'

Dilys was breathing rapidly and her mouth was a thin line of repressed anger. 'You must have more than two people to offer me!'

'I'm afraid there are no others at present but we could give you a call if anyone else is added to the list. Good staff are always hard to find, Mrs Maynard – and just as hard to place.'

Dilys glared at her but Miss Robbins' professional smile was firmly in place.

'Perhaps your best option would be a nurse and a part-time housekeeper. I could show you...'

'No thank you! You have wasted enough of my time!' She stood up. 'I shall speak to my sister-in-law and we will direct our enquiries elsewhere. I think you have been less than helpful and I don't care for your attitude. I shall write to your employer to tell her so. Good afternoon!'

She swept from the office and Miss Robbins watched her go with mixed feelings. She muttered, 'God help your brother with a woman like you for a sister!' and turned back to her typewriter.

Dilys walked along the street in deep displeasure. The arrogance of the young woman, she thought. She was now on her way to meet Hettie at Miss Maude's Teashop and had expected to have the names and details of at least two housekeepers for them to consider. Instead she had nothing to show for her efforts and had been casually treated by an impertinent young madam. No doubt Hettie would have something scathing to say about her failure.

Miss Maude's Teashop had always been a favourite meeting place of theirs. The sandwiches were wafer thin, the biscuits homemade and not too hard for ageing teeth, and the selection of cakes so tempting that Dilys regularly succumbed and had two. When she reached the tea shop Hettie had not arrived so she chose a table by the window from which they could watch passers-by, and settled herself to await her sister. It was a small, cosy place in which to chat with polished wooden tables and chairs, walls decorated with shelves full of quaint pottery and half a dozen water colours painted by local artists.

Her thoughts drifted to the matter in hand and from there to the Pennington family in general. Not a very productive group, she reflected with some regret. Hardly a united family – two brothers and a sister and only two children between them. Yet their maternal aunt had had three children and their Uncle Henry, on their father's side, had married twice and fathered eight.

A waitress approached, complete with gingham apron and a neat cap. Dilys ordered a plate of mixed sandwiches for two and a selection of cakes. 'Including two cream slices, please.'

The waitress smiled. 'They are always a favourite with our customers.'

'I'm waiting for my sister and we both like

them.'

At the thought of the little feast to come, she felt marginally better and by the time Hettie arrived Dilys was smiling.

After their greetings, the pot of tea and the sandwiches arrived.

'You be mother,' said Hettie and they were soon enjoying cucumber sandwiches while Dilys explained what had happened.

'It doesn't matter,' her sister-in-law told her, 'because this morning Albert searched through the advertisements and found a woman who wants a job as a housekeeper and she sounds reasonable. I cut it out for you.' She produced the small slip of paper and handed it to Dilys.

Respectable woman, late thirties, seeks employment as housekeeper within Bath area. Good references and further details on application.

A telephone number followed.

Dilys looked puzzled. 'If she can afford a telephone, why does she need a job as a housekeeper?'

'Dilys! Trust you to pour cold water on it!'

'I'm sorry but ... doesn't it sound odd to you? We can't be too careful.'

'We can always telephone and ask her – in a roundabout way.' Hettie shrugged.

'We can certainly try her.'

Hettie leaned forward. 'There's something else. I don't want to mention this to Albert because you know how protective he is of Montague but–' she lowered her voice – 'if we're truly worried about him, there's such a thing as *power of attorney*!'

Dilys's eyes widened. 'Power of attorney? But that's only for people who've lost their reason. Montague's only a bit vague.'

'He is now.' Hettie's voice fell further so that Dilys had to lean forward to hear what she was saying. 'But what if he gets worse? If he refuses to talk to us about money matters now and then becomes senile later ... Do you see what I mean? We should bear it in mind for the future.'

'But only if it becomes necessary.' Dilys regarded her anxiously. 'There's been *none of that* in our family. Loss of reason, I mean – unless it has been kept from us. Hushed up, so to speak and I don't think it has.'

'"*None of that*". For heaven's sake, Dilys, I'm not suggesting Montague's going to go out of his mind but ... he might just get a little confused as he gets older and too con-fused to handle the money properly. Albert will never want to admit such a thing if he did but you and I might need to keep an eye on the situation. We ought to be ready if ... if he ever asks for our help.'

'But if he's confused, he won't know he needs help!'

'Exactly!' Hettie helped herself to the last

cucumber sandwich and eyed her sister knowingly.

Slowly Dilys nodded. 'We'll just bear it in mind,' she said uneasily, 'as a possibility.'

Hettie nodded toward the cake stand. 'You choose first,' she offered.

After a moment or two, while they ate in silence, Dilys said, 'Do you remember when Cressida's Aunt Maude was ill and she had to go out to Switzerland to look after her? I always thought it was all rather secretive. You don't think her Aunt Maude lost her reason, do you? Montague might have kept it from us. Cressida rarely spoke about her trip when she returned and she did seem rather quiet.'

Hettie hesitated. 'I don't think so. I'm sure Montague would have told Albert. They've always been close.'

'Close? How can you say that? To my way of thinking they have always been very competitive.'

'Well, you have known them longer than I have but I feel Montague would have confided in his brother.'

'Then why not in me? I'm his sister!'

'He *did* confide in you, if you recall – and in me and in Albert. He told us her Aunt Maude had gone into an "emotional decline" over a rather awful fellow. A climber. It was a clear case of unrequited love. Poor

51

old Maude! But then, Cressida was only a Pennington by marriage and she had no children so even if there had been ... instability of mind, it was never passed on.'

Dilys reached for a Bakewell tart. 'This will have to be my last or I shan't want any supper tonight.' Feeling that they had probably said enough about family matters she changed the subject. 'We're running another soup kitchen tomorrow evening and I'm contributing two quarts of ham broth with barley and that means an early start to get the ham bones simmering. So much of the goodness is in the marrow of the bones...'

At seven forty-five a.m. the following day the queue for the soup stretched outside the military Drill Hall and ten yards round the corner. It consisted of out of work men, homeless men, a few con men, probably more than one petty criminal and a sprinkling of destitute women – some with children and some alone. The ages ranged from an eleven-year-old runaway girl to an eighty-year-old man who moved at a snail's pace on two improvised crutches.

Dilys, standing inside the door, resplendent in an expensive apron, regarded them with compassion mixed with disgust. She headed the long trestle table and in front of her she commanded the large cooking pan which contained the ham broth she had made earlier. The alternative was vegetable stew.

Beside her Marguerite Wilson, ensconced behind a pile of roughly cut bread, sighed with exasperation and said in a low voice, 'How on earth do they allow themselves to become so dirty. A good wash would improve them and they would feel so much better.'

Dilys shrugged. 'I dare say they'd rather spend any money they have on food. Soap is hardly a priority if you have so little.'

Behind them there were tables and chairs but she knew that some of the hungry would choose to sit on the floor with their backs to the wall, ignoring the niceties of spoons, preferring to drink straight from the bowls. It was a defensive measure they adopted early on in their situation and it meant that they could not be attacked from behind and robbed.

They began promptly and the queue moved slowly. This was not because the supplicants were not in a hurry for their soup but because each person wanted to exchange a few words of conversation – a luxury they rarely enjoyed, due to their solitary lifestyle.

A quarter of an hour passed but the queue continued and for some reason Dilys glanced up at the next man in the queue. He was tall and gaunt and she imagined his scraggy beard and hair might have been nibbled by rats! Dilys shuddered. He wore shapeless worsted trousers and a collarless shirt and over both a long tattered coat that had lost all the buttons.

He held out a tin bowl that had seen better days and she dipped her ladle into the large pan of soup and emptied it into the bowl.

He whispered, 'Give us a drop more, missus.'

As she shook her head she caught sight of his eyes, a hard grey, narrowed and intense. 'I'm sorry. You know it's not allowed. One ladle-full per person.'

'You spilt some–' he lowered his voice – *'Dilys.'*

'I did no such thing!'

As he hesitated, Marguerite called sharply, 'Please move on. There are many people still waiting.'

He shuffled along, his face averted and, reaching the next table, received a large chunk of bread donated by one of the local bakers. He thanked no one, Dilys noted. As he moved further away he turned back to throw her a last spiteful glance.

Marguerite lowered her voice, 'People like him should be banned from the kitchen. He doesn't deserve a free meal.'

Dilys was struggling with a sick feeling in

54

her stomach. Shocked, she turned to Marguerite and whispered, 'He called me Dilys! I'm sure of it. How could he...?'

'Called you by name? Of course he didn't. You're imagining things.'

'No! He whispered it!'

'It was probably "missus".'

'Missus? Do you think so?'

'It rhymes with Dilys, doesn't it, and much more likely than knowing your name.'

'Missus? Could it have been?' Relief flooded her. 'I suppose so. A man like that could not know my name.' She forced a smile.

''Urry it up, for Gawd's sake!' A woman was next in the queue – small and old before her time. Her face was deeply lined and her wispy grey hair straggled from a matted woollen hat. She held out empty hands to show she had no bowl of her own.

Dilys recognized her, reached for a bowl and re-dipped the ladle. 'Good morning, Mrs Pegg.' The woman was rather deaf and spent most of her time begging beside the church porch. Dilys watched as, without bothering to find a seat, Mrs Pegg moved a few feet away from the queue and drank the soup down at once, alternately blowing on it and sipping it noisily. She then handed back the bowl and rushed on to claim her bread.

The queue seemed endless and before long Dilys felt the familiar ache developing in her back. It would be good to sit down when she reached home, enjoy a cup of tea and a biscuit and relish the solitude. Sometimes she wondered whether to give up this part of her charity work but then Hettie would gloat and say, 'I told you it would be too much for you!'

She dipped the ladle again, this time for a tramp she recognized. He went from house to house doing odd jobs for pennies. He had a skinny mongrel with him and Dilys knew that Marguerite would, as always, slip him an extra lump of bread for the dog. He and the dog would sit cheerfully together on the floor, sharing the small feast.

Five minutes later the supply of soup ended and the unlucky few were given two lumps of bread by way of compensation. Dilys carried the large pan into the small kitchen where she washed it out and made her goodbyes. As she left the hall the three male volunteers were folding and stacking the tables and chairs.

Fifteen minutes later she was back home, her feet resting on a footstool, enjoying her tea and biscuits.

She had finally dozed off when the telephone rang.

THREE

'Dilys, it's me, Hettie. How did it go this morning? I rang you earlier but there was no answer and I guessed you were running late. Same crowd as usual? Listen, I've been in touch with that woman who advertised as a housekeeper and she sounded reasonable. A Miss Locke. I suggested she meets us over at Montague's place so he can meet her too.'

'Hold on a moment, Hettie! You're rambling on so. You say the two of you are going to meet at Montague's? But when is this? You should have spoken to me first.' She rubbed her eyes, still slightly drowsy from her brief sleep.

'Sorry, Dilys, but I am rather rushed. It's this coming Friday at eleven o'clock. I've checked with that girl at Montague's and she says...'

'But suppose it isn't convenient for me to be there? I'll have to check my diary. I have a feeling there's something on Friday...'

'Then please do check, Dilys. If necessary I'll have to change the arrangements.'

Muttering under her breath about Hettie's lack of consideration, Dilys found her diary and discovered that the suggested date was not suitable.

Hettie was not pleased and immediately changed her mind. 'Then maybe we could go ahead without you and I'll find out what the woman's like and say we'll let her know when I've consulted with you. How would that be?'

Dilys hesitated, feeling that Hettie was somehow hustling her but on the other hand, she had things to do and wasn't particularly keen to visit Montague so perhaps she should let Hettie deal with it in her own way.

'As long as you tell her nothing is definite, Hettie,' she conceded, 'and you consult with me. As long as that's clearly understood I'm happy. And see what else you can find out about Montague's financial situation ... and make sure that girl's looking after him properly until the new housekeeper is in place. She's only a slip of a thing and might neglect him. Whatever Miss Dutton's faults, she did take care of him.'

'I'll see to everything and find out what I can but I'll have to be discreet. I'll ring you tomorrow afternoon and—'

'Will Albert go with you? To say a few words to his brother?'

'He may do, he may not. You know Albert. Now I must rush. Goodbye Dilys.'

Dilys replaced the receiver and stood for a moment or two, wondering uneasily if she had played into her sister-in-law's hands. Had she allowed herself to agree to something which she might later regret? Thinking back she decided that Hettie certainly had rushed her into approving her plan of action. Her sister-in-law had used that strategy before, she recalled, frowning. Dilys had never forgiven her for hurrying the choice of fabric for her wedding dress when she had married John. Every time she looked at their wedding photograph she regretted that she had not chosen the beige silk, but at the time, Hettie had grown impatient and accused her of dithering and had talked her into the ivory brocade.

If only Cressida had been her adviser, she thought with regret. She would have recognized that the beige silk would throw a soft warm colour into Dilys's face whereas the ivory brocade was cold and unflattering to her complexion. Cressida had been as different to Hettie as chalk is to cheese. Refined and discreet summed her up nicely. She had never been one to trample over another's sensibilities. John had admired her, she knew, but then most men were attracted to beauty. It was only to be expected.

As she walked back into the sitting room, her thoughts reverted to Hettie. 'Wretched woman!' she said crossly. 'Always so sure of herself!'

Still, that was water under the bridge. With a positive effort, Dilys allowed her equanimity to return. Hettie had agreed to consult her before making any commitment to the new housekeeper and probably that was enough. Dilys would like to have been there but she could not absent herself from the extra choir practice. There was always a shortage of altos and she would have been sorely missed.

That same evening Martha and Tom finished their supper and sat back, contented. Tom worked at Arnsby Farm, which was conveniently near, and he was valued for his work with the horses. While he would never be more than comfortably off from his wages, there was a little extra coming in each month and Martha was good at managing. Unlike many less fortunate, they mostly managed to pay their bills on time. Martha's nightmare was the moment when the farmer took it into his head to mechanize the ploughing and suchlike. If he bought himself one of those noisy tractors he would get rid of the horses and that would be the end of Tom's specialized work. He might even find himself demoted to general farm labouring.

Tom eyed the portion of minced beef pie that remained in the dish.

'Enough for tomorrow?' he asked, hoping she would say, 'No. You finish it off.'

She did not say that. She said, 'Just about, if I do a few extra spuds.'

He grinned. 'Not sharing it with Monty, then?'

'No. Our Daisy'll be cooking him fishcakes most likely. She's doing all right.'

'Let's hope so for his sake! We don't want her to poison the old boy!'

'Least she's picking up a bit of extra money, till the new housekeeper turns up.'

'I'm not complaining.' He sat back, patting his stomach then gave her a quick sideways glance. 'Did I see another jar of lemon curd in the larder?'

Martha nodded. Her mother was fond of anything with lemon in it and regularly made jars of lemon curd. When she wanted to visit she made a gift the excuse.

'Your ma's been round then, sticking her nose in.'

She shrugged. 'She heard about Miss Dutton going.'

'Oh yes? And what else?'

'The usual. You know what she's like.'

Tom rolled his eyes. 'Meddling in what doesn't concern her!'

'She thinks we should tell Daisy. She's her grandma. She's allowed to have an opinion, Tom.'

He leaned forward. 'Her opinion's fine but she should keep it to herself. And not come round with her jars of lemon curd, telling us what we should and shouldn't do! We'll tell Daisy when the time's right and not just to please your ma! You can tell her that from me.'

'She means well, Tom.'

'I expect Satan *means* well!' He sat back with a sigh. 'Anybody'd think it was the end of the world. Hundreds of kiddies are adopted and none the worse for that. In most cases a sight better off! At least they're wanted by their new parents.'

'I know but still...'

'No "buts", Martha. Daisy's ours, all legal and correct. Happy as a sandboy. She'll be told soon enough – it's not long now – and not a moment sooner. So tell your mother to stay out of it – or I'll tell her! And she won't like that much, I can promise you!'

Martha pushed back her chair and began to collect the plates, knives and forks. She knew Tom was right. She would have to have a word with her mother and warn her that Tom's patience was running out.

He said, 'What's for pudding?'

'Bramble and apple. Me and ma went out

and picked the last of the blackberries.'

She had made his favourite dessert and smiled as the irritation left her husband's face. It didn't take much to make him happy.

Two days later, on the Thursday, Miss Dutton reappeared and entertained Daisy for nearly twenty minutes with her account of her mother's progress – or rather, the lack of it.

'The food in that hospital!' she told her. 'Ma says she wouldn't give it to a starving dog and that's the truth! Boiled potatoes day after day, dried up minced beef, horrible steamed fish full of bones, mutton stew full of grease and gristle ... She couldn't eat it and was wasting away. I reckon I got her out of there just in time.'

'Dear oh dear.' Daisy took another biscuit. 'Poor soul!'

'And the doctor was Scottish with that funny accent they have up there and speaking so fast she couldn't understand him ... and now she's home and confined to bed so I had to buy a bed pan but Mrs Bligh's commode will come in handy later on.'

'You look very tired.'

'Tired isn't the half of it, Daisy.' She rolled her eyes. 'I'm worn to a shadow but she's my mother and at least I know she's being looked after properly with proper food. I made some rosehip syrup yesterday and now she can have a spoonful twice a day. That's full of goodness, Daisy. You should know how to make it ... and calves' foot jelly. A Mrs Bertram brought some round for her.'

'Mrs Bertram?'

'One of the many do-gooders, Daisy. Only the rich have time to make calves' foot jelly. It takes four hours, so they say. I can't abide the stuff myself but Ma's not fussy. If it's full of goodness she'll swallow it down, bless her.'

She stopped for breath and another mouthful of tea and Daisy stepped in quickly.

'Monty's doing fine and tomorrow there's another housekeeper coming and Hettie is coming to interview her and...'

'Does he ask after me? I expect he misses me, poor old boy. At his age he doesn't ask for much. I'll pop up and see him before I go.'

'He's not in bed. He's sitting in the summer house, reading the paper.'

Miss Dutton's jaw dropped. *In the summer house?* Lord sakes! What's he doing there? How on earth did he ... In the summer house? He'll most likely be getting a chill in his kidneys! Are you trying to finish him off?' She eased herself from the chair. 'I'll go out to him at once.'

'He's quite happy, Miss Dutton, and he's

warmly wrapped up. You'll see.'

Miss Dutton paused at the back door. 'What on earth made you drag him downstairs, Daisy? I can't believe you would be so heartless!'

'He was bored. He thought he was an invalid but he isn't.'

The ex-housekeeper stared at Daisy accusingly. 'And you thought you knew better than I did! What do the family think about this nonsense?'

'Mrs Pennington didn't say anything when she came to talk about interviewing Miss Locke.'

Momentarily distracted, Miss Dutton asked, 'And what, pray, do we know about this Miss Locke?'

'Not a great deal but they have talked on the telephone for a second time. She's a catholic. Roman.' Daisy shrugged. 'Mrs Pennington said she doesn't really approve of papists, whatever they are ... and she wants quite a lot of time off. Monty doesn't like the sound of her. He says she sounds like his grandmother who he hated when he was a boy.'

Miss Dutton shook her head disparagingly. 'She could be trouble,' she warned.

Daisy took another biscuit. 'The grandmother sounds horrid. She once stood him in the corner for a whole afternoon for poking his tongue out at her horrid little dog, and she used to suck cachous all the time – the grandmother, I mean, not the dog and now he can't abide the smell.'

'Cachous?'

'Little sweets that taste like violets and make your breath smell nice.'

Miss Dutton shook her head in despair at this folly then set off for the summer house, her back stiff with disapproval. Daisy took her time over the last three biscuits and put the empty tin away and by then Miss Dutton was back.

'Well, he *seems* all right,' she admitted reluctantly, 'but I hope you know what you're doing, Daisy. You might be storing up trouble for later though I hope not, for his sake. Now I must collect the rest of my things or I'll miss the bus home.'

Daisy waved her off ten minutes later, with mixed feelings. She herself believed that her employer's life was a lot richer since Miss Dutton had left him in her care. However, having someone to talk to reminded her how lonely it was being the only member of staff and she crossed her fingers that they would soon find someone who Monty liked and of whom the rest of the family could approve.

After Miss Dutton had gone, Monty folded his newspaper and set it aside. He was confused by his brief reunion with the house-keeper and it worried him. How could he have allowed himself to be kept in bed as a very bored invalid for all those years? At the time it had felt perfectly natural and sensible to have Miss Dutton fussing over him like a mother hen but now it seemed almost ridiculous. He could walk, albeit slowly, and it was much more interesting to come down-stairs and have the occasional word with young Daisy as she flitted to and fro, brush and dustpan in hand.

He smiled suddenly. Sometimes she put a cloth and a tin of polish into his hands and said, 'You do such a good job with the table, sir. I'll let you do it today. As a special treat!' And then she'd wink at him as though they shared a private joke. And he *did* make a good job of it even if he was a bit wobbly on the old pins and his arms and shoulders ached when he'd finished.

Sometimes he found himself in the sum-mer house exchanging views with the gar-dener, or in the kitchen, chatting briefly to the butcher's boy when he delivered the sausages or whatever it was Daisy had order-ed. His smile became a grin as he thought of sausages and mash with a spoonful of mustard. A really good tasty meal, that was – his favourite, in fact – even if the mashed potatoes were a bit lumpy and the gravy like brown glue! It was better than steamed fish day after day.

He eyed next door's tabby cat as it padded cautiously into the summer house, its paws crunching lightly over the fallen leaves that had blown in. Cats were not that bad, actually, he reflected, although Cressida had disliked them because their fur brought her out in a rash. Or so she'd said. They had never owned a cat so it was never proved.

'Damn!' he muttered. He had reminded himself of Cressida. A beautiful, sometimes secretive woman. A good wife but rather distant at times. He sighed. No, that wasn't quite fair. Not distant. Cressida was by nature almost reclusive and not relaxed in company. She hated parties and celebrations. Especially christenings, but weddings and funerals were also a strain for her. She 'kept herself to herself', as the saying goes.

'But good-hearted,' he said aloud. The cat seemed to take these words as an invitation and sprang on to his lap. Monty held his breath as the cat settled down and began to purr.

'Yes, Cressida was good-hearted,' he went on aloud. 'It couldn't have been easy in Switzerland, coping with that almost senile aunt.' Or was it melancholia? He couldn't remember. 'Anyway, it was a big responsibility for her but she didn't once complain.'

He looked at the cat. Was it listening? 'Months and months she was over there and came home as thin as a rake, looking drawn and wretched.'

He sighed. Poor Cressida. She had been denied the child she wanted but that was nobody's fault. One of those things, the doctor had said to comfort her. Dear Cressida. They had been so much in love ... and poor Albert had been so envious. Monty grinned at the memory. His brother's first marriage had produced that awful boy, Stanley ... and when his wife died he rather rushed into marriage with Hettie. Poor Albert. He was needy. Couldn't bear to live alone. Still, Hettie looked after him well but she couldn't compare with Cressida and Albert was jealous. The thought pleased him.

'Why is there always so much rivalry between brothers?' he mused then shrugged.

Cressida was long since gone. Gone but not forgotten, he told himself. Cressida was at peace now and he must soldier on alone.

Friday at quarter to eleven Hettie arrived at Park View and immediately began giving Daisy instructions. 'We'll start in the sitting room and will want a tray of tea and a plate of biscuits. You do have biscuits, I hope.'

'Yes, ma'am.'

'Don't put too many on the plate. She may

not be suitable and we don't want to waste money on her.'

'How many is too many?'

'Six will be enough.'

'Mr Pennington is wearing his best trousers and a corduroy jacket and I...'

'There is no need for him to be present, Daisy. I am perfectly capable of deciding whether or not Miss Locke is suitable.'

Daisy looked dubious. 'But it won't be any good if Mont— I mean, if Mr Pennington doesn't like her.'

'Liking doesn't come into it, Daisy. If she is competent and we can agree suitable wages...'

'But liking her *does* matter!' the girl insisted. 'It matters to Mr Pennington.'

Hettie gave an exaggerated sigh. Really, staff these days! The girl's too uppity for her own good, she told herself with growing irritation. When the time is right I shall suggest that Montague gets rid of her. Aloud she said, 'That is no concern of yours. You are simply a housemaid and I'll thank you to remember that. Now, where is my brother-in-law? I'll have a word with him and then I'll just have time for a quick look round to see that the house is in good order. No dust on the mantelpiece – that sort of thing.' She smiled thinly. 'I take it Miss Gray turned up yesterday. Dilys promised she would.'

Daisy said, 'She did – and Mr Pennington is in the kitchen, talking to the gardener.' She smiled. 'They like to chat about the government and put the world to rights. They're probably being rude about Mr Balfour!'

She has a nice smile, Hettie thought grudgingly, and lovely hair. She was suddenly reminded of her own youth when she was pretty with a flawless complexion, all of which had been snatched from her over the years. For a moment or two she was unhappily distracted from the business in hand but quickly returned to the present, pushed past the girl and hurried to the kitchen. Sure enough Montague was cheerfully ensconced on a stool while a middle-aged man leant against the jamb of the back door, a mug of tea in his hand. They both stared at Hettie – like two naughty schoolboys, she thought irritably.

To the gardener she said, 'You'd better get back to work, Mr...?'

'Everyone calls me Len.' He straightened up.

She stiffened. 'That may be but I would consider that a lack of respect if I were in your shoes! I assume you do have a surname.'

Before he could reply Montague said, 'Hettie! You're early.' He held his hands out wide, displaying his chosen outfit. 'How do I look?'

'Very nice.' It was still strange to see him up and about and not in bed and she reminded herself that this was not the frail, dependent man she had hoped for. A power of attorney suddenly seemed a remote possibility and she had the wretched Daisy to thank for that.

Len muttered something, touched his forehead to Hettie, winked at his employer and slid out of the back door.

Hettie gave her brother-in-law a peck on the cheek and said, 'You're looking very frail, dear. Does the doctor approve of you being out of bed?' At the same time she realized that if he were no longer considered an invalid, a prospective housekeeper would be unable to demand extra money for 'nursing care'.

'Doctor?' Montague looked startled. 'Why bring the doctor into this. I'm not ill. I'm as fit as a fiddle, aren't I, Daisy?'

She realized by his glance that the housemaid had followed her into the kitchen. Turning, she said, 'You can get along now. You must have work to do. I can —' the front doorbell rang – 'oh dear, I wanted to check out the house but Miss Locke is early. Let her in and show her into the sitting room. Tell her I'll be five minutes.' As Daisy hurried to the front door, Hettie said, 'Perhaps you should take a walk in the garden, Montague, while I conduct the interview. I'll send for you when—'

'No, no! I shall join you for the interview.' He smiled at her and she sensed a firmness in his tone. That meddling Daisy! Dismayed, she bit back an angry retort, warning herself to step carefully. The situation may not be as bad as she had anticipated but she would need to consult with Dilys.

When at last Miss Locke, Montague and Hettie were ensconced in the sitting room with the tea tray on a small table, Hettie gradually felt relief seeping through her. The woman reminded her of a hospital matron – heavily built with a large bust and with a loud voice that, Hettie felt, oozed authority. Her original doubts faded and as the three of them talked, Hettie felt that Miss Locke, despite her religious views, would take control of any given situation and run the household with well regimented precision. Miss Locke would certainly not allow Montague and the gardener to lounge about in her kitchen, discussing the government and maligning the prime minister! The salary had been agreed and also the length of the probationary period, and Hettie was on the point of declaring the interview at an end when she remembered that Dilys wanted to be involved. She had promised to discuss it with her sister-in-law and she would have to comply.

She said, 'Well, I shall be in touch with my sister-in-law by telephone later today and I imagine there will be no problem there. She does defer to me on most matters.'

Montague snorted with laughter. 'Don't let her hear you say that, Hettie!'

Hettie had the decency to blush. 'I'm sure she would have no objection,' she replied.

She gave him a warning look but her brother-in-law, who had said very little so far, now decided he had questions of his own.

'I hope you're a dab hand with sausages and mash,' he told Miss Locke. 'I like a few lumps left in the mash. It makes them so much more interesting. Daisy is very good with potatoes. And I like my sausages very dark brown, almost burnt. It makes the skin so crisp.'

Miss Locke's expression was a little frosty, thought Hettie, but who could blame her?

'I'm afraid my mashed potatoes will be smooth and lump free, Mr Pennington,' she said, 'but I dare say I can burn a few sausages if that's how you like them – although they are bad for your digestion.' She turned to Hettie. 'Rest assured I shall see that your brother-in-law is properly fed.'

In an attempt to forestall any further questions from Montague, Hettie stood up and Miss Locke did likewise.

Montague eased himself out of the chair. 'I shall give your application serious consideration,' he told Miss Locke. 'No doubt you will also wish to consider working for me. I can be a funny old cuss – or so I'm told on occasion!'

Hettie broke in quickly with an offer to show Miss Locke round the house but as they left the room she turned back to give her brother-in-law a look that spoke volumes. In a loud voice she said, 'You won't manage the stairs, Montague, so do please leave this part of the interview to me.'

Later, as soon as the front door finally closed behind Miss Locke, Hettie went in search of Montague and demanded to know what he meant by interfering when she was doing her best to help him.

'You have offended Miss Locke by your stupidity and made yourself look foolish and petty-minded!' she snapped.

He adopted an air of innocence as he replied. 'But if you and Dilys are both entitled to a say in who becomes my housekeeper, surely I deserve the same consideration. After all, I am going to have to live with her. You are not. Don't you want to know what *I* think about her?'

'But what do you know about ... about

75

housekeeping?' Hettie stammered, flustered by the unexpected attack.

'Not very much, but I do know the sort of person I want in my home, and Miss Locke may not be the one. I don't think I care for her manner. Rather like living with a sergeant major.' He stood to attention and saluted.

Hettie glared at him furiously. 'She came with two very good references. She specializes in invalid food. She has a certificate in household management. She even agreed the terms and she did not demand a separate bathroom. She—'

'You're right, my dear Hettie. Miss Locke was perfect – but not for me. I didn't take to her.'

'Dilys will be livid!'

He shrugged. 'Should you keep the taxi waiting any longer?'

'Oh Montague! You are quite impossible! Your mother always said you were stubborn. You'll be stamping your foot in a minute!'

Snatching up her purse Hettie stormed out of the room and let herself out. She sat in the taxi for a full minute, fuming with impotent rage, saying nothing. A whole day wasted. She could hardly wait to reach home and telephone Dilys. And Albert would be none too pleased to hear that Montague had out-witted them.

At last she said, 'Take me back to Macauley Buildings, driver.'

Slumped dejectedly against the back seat, she told herself that they should fight Montague for his own good. Surely she and Dilys could outmanoeuvre Montague, she thought desperately. As they pulled up outside her home she sat up a little straighter, forced down her shoulders, and lifted her chin.

'Whatever happens,' she promised herself, 'we'll have a damned good try!'

Hettie found Albert pacing up and down on the front lawn with a large whisky in his hand. When he saw her paying off the taxi, he hurried towards her, his expression anxious.

He cried, 'I'm glad you're back, dear. I've had the strangest encounter. This odd-looking man...'

She held up her hand. 'Please, Albert, at least allow me to enter the house first and sit down with a pot of tea! I have had a very disturbing time myself with your wretched brother.'

He waited unhappily until they sat on either side of the fire in the sitting room, and then launched into his account.

'I was in the garden, minding my own business and watching the goldfish when a man appeared. He gave me quite a fright as a matter of fact.' He took another mouthful of his whisky. 'He was not exactly ragged but ... very unkempt.'

'A tramp? Is that what you mean?'

'Not exactly. He didn't ask for money. Tall, possibly about thirty. Grim expression ... and he just stood there, watching me without speaking.'

'Dumb, do you think – or did he speak?'

'He did eventually but at first he just stared at me.'

He took another drink and Hettie said, 'Go steady on that, Albert. You know it doesn't suit you.'

'It suits me today! It suits me very well today!'

He emptied the glass and Hettie sighed. Whisky made him truculent but, curious to know more about the unwanted visitor, she let the matter drop and said, 'Please get on with it, Albert. I have problems of my own and I have to telephone Dilys.'

It appeared that the man had walked slowly towards Albert with a 'menacing look' on his face.

'To be honest, Hettie, he scared me. I thought he might mean me some harm. I thought he might attack me ... or push me into the fish pond. It was very disconcerting.'

'And who was this man?'

'Lord knows! I don't. I asked him what he

78

wanted and he said it was complicated.'

'Complicated? In what way?' Despite her irritation, Hettie was becoming rather alarmed. 'He must have given you some clue.'

'That's just it. He did not volunteer any information. I said he was trespassing and asked him to leave but he just laughed.'

'Do you think ... Is it possible he was deranged? Should we report this to the police, Albert?' Forgetting her irritation she leaned closer to him. 'He may have escaped from somewhere!'

'The police will call it a simple case of trespass. What can they do? The fellow didn't actually *threaten* me and he didn't lay a finger on me – thank God.'

They sat in silence for a moment and then Hettie said, 'Could you give them a description because he may have done the same thing elsewhere and they might already be looking for him?'

'Thirtyish, a scrappy beard, poorly dressed, dirty, odd ... and tall. Not much to go on, is it?'

An idea came to her. 'He may have called on other people in this street. You could ask the neighbours.'

'You could ask them, Hettie. You're better at—'

'Don't be such a weasel, Albert!' she cried,

exasperated. 'It happened to you, not me. You have all the details. Anyway I have to talk to Dilys. After all my efforts to find Montague another housekeeper – and she was entirely suitable – I'm almost certain he is going to turn her down. Didn't take to her because she was "too forceful"! Really, Albert! Your brother can be very aggravating and that's putting it mildly. And he was up and fully dressed – and throwing his weight about!'

'Up and *dressed*?' He stared at his wife in disbelief.

'Yes. That was *my* strange encounter. My brother-in-law up and dressed and behaving in a very high-handed way.'

Hettie gave him a brief resume of the interview and its aftermath, taking some pleasure at her husband's astonishment.

Another silence fell while they both stared disconsolately into the fire. When Albert got up to add a few knobs of coal, Hettie said, 'Actually, Albert, this tea is doing nothing for me. I think I'd like a small sherry.'

FOUR

The offices of Desmond & Marsh, Solicitors, were situated on The Corridor. The premises consisted of a large office which doubled as a reception, two smaller interview rooms, (made even smaller by the large cupboards along each wall), a smaller 'kitchen' and a cloakroom of sorts. The staff consisted of Mr Marsh, a stolid middle-aged man; elderly Mr Desmond whose health was failing and who was often absent; young Steven Anders who was studying for his first-year examinations, and a secretary who worked for the other three.

Steven Anders had only been with the firm for four months and was very junior indeed although he liked to refer to himself as a trainee solicitor. At twenty-four he was a pleasant young man, slim, with sandy hair and cheerful manner – the sort of man that made the unmarried secretary wish she were not ten years older than him.

Today Steven was being prepared to see a Miss Daisy Letts on behalf of a Montague

Pennington. Mr Marsh gave Steven a little background to the client.

'Wealthy old man, Montague Pennington. Wife also had private money. She is now deceased but her file is still operational ... Haven't set eyes on the old man for years now – bit of an invalid, apparently.' He scratched his thinning hair absent-mindedly and sighed. 'Lives somewhere overlooking Alexandra Park. Nice area. Had to visit him once or twice. Forget why, actually.'

'Mm! Very classy area!' Steven raised his eyebrows.

Mr Marsh was searching one of the cupboards for the correct file, found it and opened it. 'Let's see ... Oh! Wrong "Pennington". This is the wife's file.' He replaced it and took out another one.'

Steven said, 'So the wife has her own file!'

'Yes. There are outstanding matters that ... well, no need to bother you with that. Here's the husband's file.' He riffled through it. 'Ah yes. The housekeeper is authorized to collect the money each week – household bills and so on – on behalf of her employer. A Miss Dutton.'

'I thought I was seeing a Miss Letts.'

'Ye–es. Wonder why that is? Still, you'll find out. Any problems, give me a shout.'

He tossed the folder and Steven caught it and sat down to await his client. This, in his opinion, was the best part of the job. Face to face with the clients. The rest consisted of studying for his next exam, occasionally answering the telephone and writing reports on the interviews he had been allowed to conduct. Very occasionally he was asked to 'run errands' which reminded him how junior he was to the two partners.

His phone rang. 'There's a Miss Letts here for you, Mr Anders.'

He straightened his shoulders. 'Send her in, please.'

Miss Letts seemed eager to begin, settling herself on the chair before being invited to do so, and leaning forward confidentially. 'I suppose you've heard. Miss Dutton left in a hurry and I'm standing in for her until we find another housekeeper.' She grinned. 'I'm the housemaid but at the moment I'm doing everything. Cooking, cleaning, looking after poor old – I mean, Mr Pennington. Not that he's a problem but he is old and I don't let him sit in a draught and I can cook ... a bit.'

'I see,' said Steven, somewhat taken aback by her directness but pleased by her humble position which meant, he hoped, that she would be impressed by a young, up-and-coming 'solicitor'.

She sat up a little straighter. 'I've brought a letter from Mr Pennington about you letting me collect the money each week. That is to say, I'm trustworthy and everything. Which I am.'

'Right. Yes, of course. May I see this letter, please.' He wondered if housemaids were supposed to be so confident. He tried to imagine her in a cap and apron and thought she would look the part. And such lovely red hair...

He read the letter twice to delay her departure. 'Hmm. That seems to be in order,' he told her. Then, for something else to say, he added, 'I'm sorry to hear about Mrs Pennington's death.'

'Mrs Pennington? Oh ... yes. But I never knew her. She was already dead when I took the job ... but she is mentioned sometimes. I think she was very nice. And beautiful. There's a photograph of her with Mr Pennington on their wedding day. Did you ever meet her?'

'Afraid not. I've only recently taken this position.'

'But you are a solicitor?'

He hesitated. 'I will be. There are examinations to pass.' He waved his hand airily as if they were of no significance.

'Really? Examinations. I don't envy you – but if you ever want a reference, come to me.' She smiled. 'I'll say you're very thorough.'

He laughed. 'I'll bear that in mind, Miss Letts. But now ... back to business. I'll keep this letter in Mr Pennington's file and I'll cancel Miss Dutton's permission to accept the money. What happened to her to make her leave? She wasn't sacked, I hope.'

Daisy explained about Miss Dutton's mother and he nodded. 'We all hate the idea of hospitals,' he said. He unlocked the top drawer of his desk and drew out a cash box. Then he referred again to his client's letter of authorization. 'I see he has changed the amount,' he said. 'It's less than before.'

She frowned. 'That may be because he only has to pay me as well as the housekeeping, instead of me and a housekeeper *and* the housekeeping. Does that make sense to you? I'm only getting an extra ninepence a day and that's for staying overnight. He's very afraid of being alone in the house when it's dark.'

'And you aren't afraid?'

'No. I like the dark. It's peaceful. And I'm sleeping in what used to be Miss Dutton's room so that if Monty needs anything in the night he just rings his bell and I rush along.'

Now Steven began to envy the old man. 'You seem very young for all the responsibility, Miss Letts – if you don't mind me saying so.'

'I don't mind. It's not for long and I'm not nearly as good as Miss Dutton. I admit the meals aren't so good although I'm learning, and the place is getting a bit dusty and, you know, untidy round the edges but I can't do everything. And he is very grateful, Mr Pennington that is. We get along. To tell you the truth, I'd rather the two of us just muddled along than have a horrible bossy housekeeper that neither of us likes.'

'I can understand that. But forgive me if I'm a little curious. How did you get the job?'

She frowned, giving the question some serious thought. 'It came about through my father, I suppose. He works on a farm on the outskirts of the town, and Mr Pennington buys eggs, cream and butter from them and my father heard there was a job going there for a young girl. Ma said it was about time I earned a few bob.' She shrugged. 'I'd already left school and I was bored at home and so I said "yes" and here I am!'

And looking very well on it, Steven thought. He said, 'I noticed from the file that the whole family lives around Bath. At least, I assume so. We have clients called Albert Pennington – I think he lives on Widcombe Hill – and a Mrs Maynard who used to be a Pennington. I don't know where they live.'

'I don't either. I only know their telephone numbers. I can use the telephone,' she said proudly. 'It's not as bad as people think although the operators always sound rather stuffy.'

'Er yes. Maybe they do. I think they have to be like that otherwise they would get into conversations and waste time.'

She nodded. 'And it's Dilys who was married to John Maynard but now he's dead, and Albert is now married to Hettie. They're both still alive.'

He smiled. 'Thank goodness. I was beginning to think the family was jinxed!'

They laughed together at the idea.

Daisy said, 'I want Monty – that's what we call Mr Pennington – to live a long time. I like working for him. The only snag is his sister-in-law – we call her Horrible Hettie – because when she comes to visit, which isn't often, she will insist on interfering. And I'm not sure yet about Dilys.'

'Some people can be difficult,' he agreed eagerly. 'A lot of work that we do as solicitors is a result of family disagreements which have often started in childhood and lingered through the years. Sometimes the disagreements are never settled and last for generations and then I suppose they become family feuds!'

'Well, I needn't worry because I'm an only child so I'll have no one to disagree with!'

'Whereas I have two brothers and a sister – all younger than me and a mixed blessing!'

Minutes later, when Daisy had departed

with the money, Steven hoped he had not been indiscreet. He had been rather overwhelmed by the young woman and now thought he may have overstepped the mark. He was glad that Mr Marsh had not been privy to the conversation but decided, if he ever had a few moments to spare, he would investigate the Pennington family, out of interest. Their files would no doubt offer insights and if Miss Letts came in again, he would be more knowledgeable about her employers. He hoped she would come in again and wondered if he could think of a reason to telephone the Penningtons. If he did, presumably Miss Letts would answer the telephone...

Without Miss Letts' presence, he found the office less bright and thought the sun had gone in but when he looked out of the window it was still shining.

Once a month Hettie and Dilys met in the Pump Room to take a medicinal glass of the Spa's well-known spring water. This was more an opportunity to be seen in the town's famous venue rather than a chance to converse but this same morning they each had something to share with the other – and none of it good.

Once ensconced, having each accepted a glass of the famous water, Dilys told her sister-in-law about the man in the soup kitchen queue and Hettie listened silently but in growing horror.

'He sounds very like the man who frightened Albert!' she exclaimed, her eyes wide with alarm and proceeded to tell Dilys her own story. 'So in the end, just to set my mind at ease that we weren't the only ones he pestered, I *did* call on several of the neighbours, as Albert suggested, but only one had had a similar visit and the fellow was not frightening but only asked for a drink of water and only stayed a moment or two.' Out of breath, she paused and went on. 'So why did he upset Albert? You don't think it was the same man who upset you, do you?'

Dilys sipped the water thoughtfully, trying to retain her poise in case any of the other people 'taking the cure' would think her anxious. The elegant Pump Room with its beautiful chandeliers, was a room for quiet contemplation or discreet whisperings.

'If it was just you and Albert,' Dilys hazarded, 'then why hasn't he contacted Montague? I mean, Hettie, if it's a family thing...'

'A family thing? Why should it be? As you said yourself, he hasn't approached Montague.'

Dilys caught the eye of a passing acquaintance and forced a smile. 'Mrs Forster! How nice to see you. Are you and your daughter well?'

'As well as can be expected, thank you. And you, Mrs Maynard?'

'In good health, thank you.'

As Mrs Forster drifted past, the smile vanished and Dilys continued in a low voice. 'But how do we know that he hasn't been to call on them? Maybe he did call and they haven't thought to tell us about it. Perhaps they thought it unimportant or maybe they were out at the time. If he called at Park View and that slip of a girl dealt with him she might not have the sense to tell Montague about it.' They stared at each other in dismay.

Hettie said, 'Maybe we should go over there and find out. He may be harmless and we might be worrying about nothing but...' She shrugged.

After some whispered discussion it was finally decided that as soon as they found another housekeeper they would use that as an excuse to visit Montague and they would then inquire, in a casual way, about the mystery man.

'Which brings me to another matter,' Dilys announced. 'We really cannot expect that young woman to do all the housework and the cooking. I suspect the house will be neglected, simply because there are not enough hours in a day for Daisy to do the work even if she wanted to.'

'Well, if we find a suitable housekeeper the problem will be solved.'

'But what if Montague doesn't like any of them? He's paying the wages, remember. We can't insist. He can be very awkward when he chooses.'

Hettie drained her glass. 'Do you think this water really does you any good?'

'I have no idea. I don't suppose it does any harm and it's supposed to have all sorts of vitamins and things.' She frowned. 'Perhaps, until we find a replacement for Miss Dutton we could find her a woman to do the heavy work. Scrub the floors, wash and mangle and dry the washing. The work my Mrs Gray does.' She looked thoughtful. 'Maybe she would do it for Montague. She only works for me part-time.'

'Just put in two or three hours a week?' Hettie asked. 'Is that what you mean?'

'Exactly.'

Hettie hid her surprise. Her sister-in-law was being very cooperative. She had frequently boasted that Mrs Gray was 'a veritable workhorse'! On an impulse, before the cooperative mood faded, she brought up the question of Montague's financial situation. 'We must reassure ourselves that he is capable of handling what must be a fair income. Possibly he has investments, bonds or shares. If he's as forgetful as I think he is, he could let things slide. I wonder whether we should talk about this problem with the solicitor.' She looked at Dilys. 'It wouldn't be fair if we allow him to flounder if it means losing money. Family money, in effect.' She hesitated. 'It's our money in a way, because if he dies first it will come to us.'

Dilys pursed her lips. 'I'm not sure that Desmond &Marsh would deal with us without written permission from Montague – and we won't get that unless he's declared unfit, in some way.'

'Maybe one of us could talk to his doctor.'

'It would have to be me. I'm his sister. You're only a Pennington by marriage.'

Hettie bridled. 'What difference does that make? I'm part of the family and if you did not exist I would be a perfectly acceptable person – and it was my idea. *I* shall go.'

The room was filling up and as they had finished drinking they felt it only fair to surrender the table so they gathered up gloves and purses and left the Pump Room and stood outside, still talking.

Hettie said, 'I wonder how much of Cressida's money has gone.'

'Presumably she left it all to Montague. She had no one else to leave it to.'

'But why should he need it?' Hettie demanded. 'Montague's comfortably well off and he rarely seems to spend any of it so he'll hardly be using Cressida's money. I wish he *would* spend some on the house. It's beginning to look dilapidated, don't you think?'

Dilys sighed. 'A little shabby, perhaps. I'll find another possible housekeeper and we'll both go over there and see what can be done to improve matters. I don't like that girl being alone with him. If he were to take a tumble ... or have a fit of some kind, she'd probably panic.'

And on this gloomy note they once more agreed and then went their separate ways.

Two days later, which was Wednesday, Hettie sat in the doctor's waiting room as arranged, waiting for the afternoon surgery to begin, and trying to avoid the other patients who were sharing the large space with her. It was an airy, high-ceilinged room with chairs against three walls and a table in the centre on which piles of magazines had been arranged. Hettie was pretending to read 'Country Homes', having already flipped through 'The Literary Scene' without finding anything to interest her. She wondered how many copies of these magazines were sold each month and how many were actually read while they languished on private coffee tables, or in doctors' and dentists' waiting rooms.

Suddenly she became aware that the receptionist was trying to catch her attention. Abandoning her magazine she hurried to the desk.

'Mrs Pennington, we don't seem to have any notes for you. I'm a little confused.'

'I thought I had explained,' Hettie told her irritably, aware that the other patients were listening to the exchange. 'I'm here on behalf of my brother-in-law Montague, who is unable to attend. He is elderly and rather frail and I want to speak to his doctor on his behalf.' She hoped it sounded reasonable.

'Certainly, Mrs Pennington. Then I shall send in his notes. The doctor will need them.'

After another five-minute wait Hettie was called in to the doctor's consulting room and found herself shaking hands with an elderly man whom she took to be in his mid-sixties. He had greying hair and a tired smile. In fact there was a general weariness about him which Hettie hoped might prove to her advantage. A younger, more alert doctor might see through her little plan.

He was reading a thin file which she presumed had been provided by the receptionist.

'And what exactly is the matter with your brother-in-law?' he asked after a very brief final glance at the notes. 'He has no history of serious illness.'

'No, that's right,' she agreed. 'We are, on the whole, a very healthy family but I fear that the last time we visited him – that is my sister-in-law and I – we found him rather vague and forgetful ... that is, compared with the last visit which was about two months ago.'

'You are saying that this deterioration has not been gradual but rather sudden?'

'That's it exactly, doctor. We don't visit very often – he values his privacy, you see, and this noticeable vagueness took us by surprise.'

'Does he live alone?'

'No. He did have a devoted housekeeper but she has left very abruptly and we are trying to replace her. In the meantime there is a young housemaid caring for him as well as she can.'

'Are you connected to your brother-in-law by telephone?'

'Yes.' Hettie was become uneasy. This conversation was not going quite the way she had intended. The doctor was showing little concern for his patient.

After a moment's thought he said, 'I suspect you are worrying unnecessarily, Mrs Pennington. With no previous history of anything serious, I do not see his present condition as particularly worrying. We all become a little confused if we live long enough but it is not a sign of disease. Simply a result of growing old. Is your brother unhappy in any way?'

Hettie tried to think of some way he might be, but failed. 'I think not, doctor, but...'

'Then I can put your mind at ease, Mrs Pennington. I would suggest that your brother is in no danger. The maid can reach you if anything worrying happens.' He adjusted his spectacles and smiled. 'The telephone is a wonderful thing, is it not?'

'But suppose he has a fall?'

'Suppose I have a fall. Suppose you do. It can be dealt with. When the new house-keeper takes up her position she will no doubt report to you if there is a problem.'

'Ye–es. Naturally the telephone makes things easier but...' Hettie knew that she had insisted on dealing with this discussion herself and felt that there was no way she could return to Dilys without a satisfactory outcome. She decided on the truth and lean-ed forward confidingly. 'The truth is, doctor, that my brother is a wealthy man but has no idea of how to cope with it ... in the future, that is. My sister and I are fearful that he is already becoming a little senile and may be being exploited by his staff.' Did that sound reasonable? She hoped so.

'Ah! Now we have it.' He smiled in what Hettie considered a somewhat patronizing manner. 'The family money. Yes. It can be a problem. What you want to know from me is whether or not your vague, forgetful brother might be persuaded by unscrupulous people, to spend his money unwisely. I cannot answer that except by saying that I would have to visit him and make an assessment on his mental state and, if necessary, call for a second opinion from a psychiatrist qualified to determine the extent of your brother's deterioration.'

'So this is not a simple matter, doctor.'

'Oh no! It occurs quite frequently but–' he held up his hand, smiling – 'I'm happy to say that in most cases the deterioration is not sufficient to warrant such interference. Sometimes–' he leaned forward and lowered his voice – 'sometimes we realize that it is simply a ploy by the relatives.' He rubbed a finger and thumb together. 'Money! They are hoping to gain control!' He sat back, his expression enigmatic.

'Good gracious!' she said weakly.

'In an *extreme* case we would then recommend a power of attorney which means that someone else would be appointed to look after his interests and deal with any problems, financial or otherwise.'

At last! Hettie tried to hide her relief. 'Let us hope this is never necessary,' she said quickly, 'but at least I now understand the way the process works.'

He nodded. 'So, Mrs Pennington, are you asking me now to visit your brother?'

'Oh no! Not yet, thank goodness! And it may never be necessary.'

'Let us hope not.' He stood as a sign that the interview was at an end and Hettie withdrew. She walked out of the surgery with a spring in her step. It had been a rather uncomfortable interview but despite a few awkward moments, she thought she had dealt with it reasonably well and they were that much nearer to achieving her plan – the plan she would share with Dilys when the time was right.

While Hettie was with the doctor, Daisy was sitting in the kitchen with Monty. Each of them held a mug of hot milk which was intended to be relaxing.

Daisy said, 'So, according to Hettie, this other woman is coming at twelve o'clock? What's her name?'

'That's a good question.' He frowned, then said, 'Is it Bilson?'

'It's no good asking me, sir. It was you who answered the telephone. You spoke to your sister-in-law, not me.'

'Well, you were nowhere to be found! Just disappeared!'

'I was hanging up the clothes!' Daisy protested. 'I did a bit of washing – just essential smalls. How was I to know the telephone would ring?'

'How was I to know that you were outside?' he retaliated crossly.

'Well, you think it's a Miss Bilson and she's coming today at twelve.' She looked round the kitchen and tutted. 'I'll never get tidied in time but they'll be sure to go round the whole house. What else did she tell you – about this woman?'

He screwed up his face in concentration. 'Something about her age ... fifty-five, I think. Yes, fifty-five. And she's never married. Yes, that was it. Never married because her fiancé was killed in the war with the Boers. He was a soldier.'

'Well, he would be, wouldn't he!' She grinned. 'Let's hope she's a nice person and you think you will get along with her.'

'But if I don't like her – what then? My sister-in-law can be very forceful. I sometimes feel sorry for poor old Albert.'

And suppose *I* don't like her, Daisy wondered. I shall have to work with her ... unless I give in my notice or get sacked. She said, 'If you don't like her give me a wink when they're not looking and I'll try and think of something to put her off. Miss Bilson, I mean, not Hettie.'

He looked dubious. 'What could you do?'

'We–ell ... I could be rude to her and then when Hettie tries to sack me for impertinence you could say that you're my employer and you want to keep me!'

They thought about it for a moment or two but then the telephone rang and Daisy trotted off to answer it.

'Daisy, this is Hettie Pennington. Did my brother-in-law pass on the message about the woman who is applying for the...'

'Miss Bilson? Yes, he did.'

'Bilson? No, no. It's a Miss Willis. He must have misheard. We're coming over tomorrow afternoon...'

'Tomorrow? We thought it was today at...'

'No, Daisy. Do please pay attention. I shall meet Miss Willis there at three thirty but I shall come early to inspect the house and I hope to find it in better shape than last time. Dust under the beds, dead flowers on the landing window sill ... You must make a real effort, Daisy.'

Daisy said nothing. She was wondering how Monty had managed to forget so many details. She said cautiously, 'So her fiancé was killed in the war. How terribly sad.'

There was a silence. Then Hettie said, 'What are you talking about?'

'Miss Willis's fiancé.'

'Her fiancé died a year *after* the war – of meningitis. Did Montague tell you all this nonsense? Tut. He really is becoming very forgetful, poor man – or else he has a lurid imagination.'

Daisy struggled to make sense of what was being said. 'He doesn't usually make things up,' she stammered. 'That is, I've never noticed that he is getting muddled. Mind you, my grandmother had a terrible memory all her life – even when she was younger. So Ma said. She reckoned she'd forget her own name one day.'

'I'm not interested in your grandmother, Daisy. Just put Montague right about the visit...'

'So it's definitely not today?'

'Of course not. I've just told you – it's tomorrow. Probably Dilys will come too. I shall ring her now that I've spoken to you.'

The call ended abruptly and now it was Daisy who felt confused. Slowly and thoughtfully she returned to the kitchen. 'It's tomorrow,' she said. 'That gives me more time to tidy the house. I'll beat the carpets outside while it's dry and—'

'Tomorrow?'

'Yes. And it's Willis, not Bilson. So I must get started.' She gave him a reassuring smile. 'Why don't you ask Len to cut a few flowers

– I'm sure he can find some late roses – and then settle yourself in the summer house and think about what you want to wear tomorrow.' Making such decisions for himself, she had decided, would help him to feel less dependent.

'What about the waistcoat with the brass buttons?'

'That's nice. Whatever you'll feel comfortable in.'

He nodded. 'What's for tea?'

'Egg and cress sandwiches and some of Ma's rock cakes.'

His face brightened. 'I'll go and find Len.'

Daisy watched him go with a feeling of unease. Then, with an effort, she pushed the worrying thoughts from her mind, and hurried inside to find the carpet beater.

The man watched them from behind the shrubs. He was bent over to reduce his height and aid his concealment. He saw the old man talking with the gardener as the two men wandered through the small but neat area behind the house – a small terrace, a strip of lawn, a flower bed with roses and a few shrubs. The old man was very unsteady on his feet and once or twice he clutched his companion's arm to steady himself. Occasionally they stopped to cut flowers although it was October and most of them were finished and would offer no decent blooms until the following summer.

The watching man muttered under his breath about the gardener's laziness – taking his time and thus wasting his employer's money. 'You wouldn't get away with it if I was your master!' Mind you, some people had no idea what real work was like, he argued silently. If the gardener had been through what *he* had experienced, he'd understand the meaning of hard labour.

Growing stiff from his bent position, the man shuffled sideways to hide himself behind the trunk of a large chestnut tree and the gardener caught the sound and turned towards him.

Damn! He ducked down, holding his breath. If they spotted him, he'd run.

'Thought I 'eard something,' the gardener told his companion and took a few steps forward, peering into the foliage half-heartedly.

The old man said, 'You can't be too careful these days, Len. My brother was startled by an intruder a few days ago. Not in the house, but trespassing in the garden, bold as brass.' He tapped his head. 'Bit strange, apparently.'

'Soldier back from the wars, maybe,' said the gardener, abandoning his suspicion. 'Some of the poor blighters come 'ome with their wits 'alf gone. No good to anyone. My aunt's stepson was like that. Drowned 'isself in the end. Best thing he could 'ave done, she said. Wore 'er down with 'is antics.'

The watching man studied the house, nodding as vague memories surfaced. One window was the bathroom ... the rest bedrooms. It all seemed a long time ago – which it was. There was a pretty little maid then. He must have been about sixteen and he had designs on her. Ivy. That was her name. He grinned at the memories. She was willing, too, until he went too far and then the stupid little thing betrayed him. Ran screaming to his uncle who told Father who tried to give him a bit of a thrashing ... His mouth tightened. 'Big mistake!' he muttered. Father got more than he bargained for including a black eye. After that, there was a family decision and the son was packed off abroad as violent and unmanageable.

'Bastards!' he whispered.

The two men were now making their way back to the house. Time to go, he told himself – but he'd be back.

FIVE

At half past ten the next morning Mrs Gray arrived. Daisy looked at her with astonishment. The woman reminded her of a wrestler – a wrestler wearing an apron over a coarse dress. She had huge muscular arms, a large body and fat face, scrawny hair straggling loose over her shoulders – and a pair of men's boots which peeped from beneath her skirt!

'Mrs Gray. Heavy work!' she announced without preamble. 'Mrs Maynard sent me. I'm to help you get ready for someone's visit – a new housekeeper, I believe – and then you might give me a job for a few hours each week. Please yourself.'

She swept past Daisy and said, 'Where's the kitchen?' but set off unerringly towards it without waiting for directions. 'Best start with the kitchen floor.' She stood, arms akimbo, looking at the tiled floor with disapproval. 'Any laundry to do? I'm told you're all at sixes and sevens here!'

Daisy stammered, 'There are a few pillow

cases and some towels and maybe—'

'Get the fire going under the copper.' She looked round the kitchen. 'Where is it? In the outhouse?'

Daisy nodded.

'Right then, put the laundry in to soak. I'll deal with it later. Mangle outside, is it?'

'In the yard.' Wrong-footed, Daisy trailed behind her. She said 'Er ... I think...' and then ran out of words.

Already the woman was rummaging under the sink where she immediately found a bucket and scrubbing brush.

'Er ... just sheets and towels, Mrs er ... .I did some hand-washing...'

The woman nodded.

Daisy stammered, 'I've forgotten your name. I'm sorry...'

'Gray but call me anything you like. Now who's this cluttering up the kitchen?' She glanced up at Monty and began to fill the bucket with hot water from the kettle.

Monty hesitated in the doorway, his waistcoat held up for inspection. 'There's a loose button,' he told Daisy, eyeing Mrs Gray nervously.

Before Daisy could reply the new arrival said, 'I bet you could sew it on better than any woman.' She gave him a stern look. 'My old man was a dab hand with a needle and cotton. Learned it in the army.'

106

'Did he now?' Monty glanced at Daisy for help. 'The fact is...'

In the silence that followed, Mrs Gray began to grate hard soap into the water in the bucket then rolled up her sleeves. 'Out!' she ordered, addressing them both. 'Come back in fifteen minutes and it'll be dry enough to walk on. First thing a housekeeper will look at is the kitchen floor. Second thing is a line full of fresh washing – even if it is Thursday.'

She was already down on her knees, making a start on the neglected tiles of the floor. Daisy led the retreat, taking Monty with her.

'Your sister Dilys sent her,' she explained. 'Might as well humour her. She's also going to do some washing for us.'

'Bit of a bruiser, isn't she?'

Daisy grinned. 'I wouldn't like to meet her in a dark alley, would you?'

He shook his head.

'I'll find you the sewing box, sir,' said Daisy, hiding a grin. 'And you can make a stab at that button while I tidy your bedroom and stow a few odds and ends in the spare room cupboard.'

The house became a hive of activity as Mrs Gray organized the mini spring clean. Daisy gave in gracefully and allowed her to take over. Two and a half hours later a pleasant smell of soap and polish permeated the house, the kitchen floor almost sparkled and the washing fluttered on the line, blown by the wind which had recently replaced the rain.

Daisy was exhausted but Mrs Gray was not even puffing with the effort, and had to be persuaded from starting to explore the attic quarters which she suggested probably needed a 'doing over'. She turned down the offer of a cup of tea and hurried away, after explaining that Mrs Maynard had already paid her for her work.

Monty sank into a chair in the sitting room and sipped his tea.

'A bit of a battleaxe!' He grinned.

'But a good worker.'

'She said I made a good job of that button.'

'Did she? Praise indeed!' Daisy sat thoughtfully for a moment.

He said, 'Did you like her?'

'I'd like her energy!'

'It would only be for, say, three hours a week. Daisy, I've been wondering if we could do without a housekeeper. I know my sister and Dilys seem set on finding a replacement for Miss Dutton but...' He regarded her anxiously. 'Without a housekeeper it might be too much for you, Daisy. What do you think?'

'I think they will think it rather improper for me to permanently stay overnight. And my father would—'

'But you'd be safe with me!'

'It might not look right. You know how people gossip.'

He looked outraged at the suggestion. 'Nobody gossiped about me and Miss Dutton.'

'You may think so but Pa heard things in The Pig and Whistle.'

'Really?' Shocked, he thought about it and then smiled. 'Me and Miss Dutton! At my age?'

'Anyone would think you were on your last legs, sir!'

'I'm sixty eight, Albert is sixty and Dilys is fifty-six. We used to call her the baby. She hated that when she was a little girl. Now she boasts of being younger than "the boys" as we were always called. She adored me then but always has found Albert difficult. He teased her a lot. He was a moody child. Very jealous of me. Always was ... and I dare say he still is.'

Daisy listened, fascinated. As an only child she found it hard to imagine how it was to share the parents' affection and attention. If she had had an older brother, would she have been jealous of him, she wondered. 'So there were eight years between you and your brother,' she said.

'There was another boy. He died when he was three. A freak accident. Nobody was to blame. He fell off the rocking horse and hit his head on the edge of the coal scuttle. There was blood everywhere. I've never forgotten it.' He stared sightlessly over the rim of his teacup, revisiting the drama in his imagination. 'My mother went into hysterics, sobbing and screaming and it was left to Nanny to send for the doctor.' He frowned. 'He never regained consciousness, poor little lad.'

'How terrible to lose your brother!'

'You get over it eventually.' He sighed.

'I've got nobody except my parents.'

He raised his eyebrows. 'You must have a young man. An admirer.'

She shrugged then brightened. 'I think the young man in the solicitor's took a fancy to me!'

'I'd be surprised if he didn't. Men can't resist hair like yours.'

'But it's so frizzy!'

'It's the colour, Daisy. Burnished gold.'

'Ma calls it ginger.'

'She doesn't want you to grow up vain! Believe me, it's very attractive.' He put his head on one side, listening. 'I think the girls are arriving. Better let them in, I suppose.'

By 'girls' he meant his sister and sister-in-law, and he was right. Dilys entered first and nodded to Daisy and stared at her brother as he waited at the bottom of the stairs to greet them.

She said, 'I never thought to see you up and about again, Montague. Hettie told me about the transformation!'

'Well, hardly that!' he protested as she kissed his cheek.

Hettie was already studying the floor of the hall and nodding with satisfaction. 'Your Mrs Gray is certainly a treasure,' she told Dilys.

Daisy said, 'You should see the kitchen floor – and she did some of the laundry wash.'

Monty laughed. 'She swept in like a small tornado!'

Pleased by the praise, Dilys allowed herself a smile. 'But don't think you can poach her, Hettie. I found her, remember. She's been with me for some time. She was simply on loan to Montague. But now let's inspect the house before the new woman turns up.'

Miss Willis was personable, middle-aged and quietly spoken and Daisy could see no reason why she would not be offered the post. While Hettie showed her round the garden, Dilys discussed her with Monty.

'Hettie and I are agreed that she would be quite suitable,' she told him. 'We had a very nice reference from her last employer who said—'

'And why, Dilys, is she leaving that position?'

'Why? I don't know why. It hardly matters.'

'Doesn't it?' He wagged a finger. 'Remember what Mother used to say about servants? That it's not what the reference says but what it leaves out that matters.'

Dilys frowned. 'What are you talking about? She said no such thing.'

'Not in your hearing, perhaps. I heard it more than once. Is she healthy?' he asked. 'She might have a disease. She might be consumptive.'

'Oh? Does she *look* consumptive?'

'No but I'm just saying we should not take her at face value. I'd like to read the references.'

'But there's no need. Hettie and I have read them.'

'But she's applying to be *my* housekeeper! I shall be paying her wages. Suppose she drinks? Some of them do, you know. Secretly, that is. Does she smell of spirits?'

'I – I don't think so.' Thrown by the question, Dilys frowned. 'Why do you ask? Did you notice something on her breath?'

At that moment Daisy entered the room and Montague asked her the same question.

Daisy shook her head. 'No. But she does smell of peppermints.'

Monty nodded. 'Ah! That's a giveaway,

that is. It's to cover up the smell of the gin or the whisky!'

Daisy regarded them innocently. 'But the peppermint might be for medicinal purposes. Maybe she has a bad digestion.'

Monty shrugged. 'I just don't want to fritter family money on a drunk, that's all I'm saying. Is she cheap, this woman?'

Dilys swallowed hard. 'Not particularly.'

Daisy laughed. 'My aunt had bad digestion. She ate peppermints all the time to stop her from burping.'

Monty frowned. 'Burping! How unpleasant!'

Dilys was wavering. The mention of family money had reminded her of the talks she had had with her sister on the subject.

'Maybe we should think it over,' she suggested. 'Talk about it later.'

Daisy nodded. 'Miss Dutton told me that where she was working before she came here, when she was only a parlour maid, the housekeeper used to steal from the house-keeping money and they never did find out. The employers, I mean. The staff all knew but they thought it a bit of a lark.'

Dilys rose to the bait. 'But how did she get away with it? I'd know if my housekeeper was trying to cheat me!'

'The housekeeper was in cahoots with the butcher. He used to overcharge for the meat

and the two of them would split the difference!'

Dismayed, Dilys sat down. 'Well really! I've
never heard such a dreadful thing!'

Daisy looked at Dilys. 'Well, I don't mind
carrying on as I am for a few more weeks
until you find someone you feel satisfied
with. If you could spare your Mrs Gray from
time to time it would be a help.'

Dilys said, 'That's kind of you, Daisy. I'll
talk to Hettie...'

'Talk to *me*,' said Monty. '*I* shall be em-
ploying her. I'm already a bit dubious about
this woman. I think we'll wait a little longer
until someone else comes along with whom
I can feel really comfortable.'

As Dilys hurried into the garden in search
of her sister, Monty turned to Daisy and
winked. 'I think we managed that very well,'
he whispered.

That night Dilys undressed slowly, her mind
on the day's event at Montague's home.
They had promised to let Miss Willis know
within two days, pretending that they had
another applicant to interview. In effect,
however, they had decided against her but
Dilys still felt uneasy about her own feelings.
Had she allowed herself to be swayed by
Daisy's revelations, she wondered.

She creamed her face and then carefully

wiped most of it off again. Staring at her reflection she sighed, wondering why she bothered. She had no husband to admire her – or even to notice her existence ... but she had her friends and her charity work, she reminded herself, and it was important to maintain standards.

She brushed her hair with a hundred strokes and covered it with a muslin cap in the hope that it would not tangle during the night. In times past, her hair had been considered one of her best features only outshone by Cressida's hair. Beautiful, adorable Cressida. So good! So perfect! Saint Cressida! Dilys gritted her teeth. She herself had been quite overshadowed by Montague's wife. The only thing Montague's wife had failed at had been motherhood. No son or daughter for poor Montague. That must have rankled, she thought, with a grim smile. Not that she, Dilys, had produced a child either – but then no one had ever considered Dilys perfect. Casting aside ungenerous thoughts she was soon in bed and drifting into sleep.

When she awoke it was to a feeling of alarm for which she could see no explanation. She stared round the darkened room then sat up with a shiver of apprehension.

'What is it?' she demanded of the empty room.

Listening she heard nothing but some instinct urged her to slide from the bed and make her way cautiously to the landing from where she looked down into the hall. Nothing unusual there. Vaguely reassured she returned to the bedroom, lit the bedside candle, pulled on her dressing gown and returned to the top of the stairs. Flickering shadows filled the space around her ... and then she heard a sound from the sitting room below.

'My God!' she whispered, her heart thumping wildly. Someone or some *thing* was down there. Should she, dare she, go downstairs? Instead she called out. 'Who's there?' but the sound of her own voice, weak and trembling, frightened her almost as much as the sounds she was now sure were being made by an intruder. Her first thought was to call the police but the telephone was in the hall close to the sitting room and that meant...

She heard something drop and it was followed by a muffled curse. Terrified, Dilys rushed back into the bedroom and slammed the door. Maybe the noise would alarm whoever it was, she thought desperately. There was no key in the door so she was unable to lock it so she sat on the floor with her back to it.

Her imagination was working overtime.

Suppose whoever it was came up after her ... sought her out and murdered her! 'Oh please God!' she whispered. Within minutes she could be lying dead on the floor and nobody would know.

With an effort she tried to calm her fear, aware that to panic would be a serious mistake. She must stay alert. She must find a way to protect herself. 'I'd be safer in the bathroom,' she told herself. There she could lock the door – but that meant abandoning her bedroom to run the length of the landing and he might already be on his way upstairs.

'Oh please God!' she begged again, straining for sounds of the intruder's whereabouts.

Minutes passed. When would it be safe to venture out from the bedroom? Maybe never! It seemed that she sat there for at least an hour while her heart beat increased and she found it hard to breathe. At last she heard sounds from the kitchen and assumed the thief was making his way out. The back door slammed and she scrambled to her feet and ran to the window from where she saw a man making his way towards the gate at the rear of the house.

So she had not imagined it! The proof made her shudder with delayed shock and she stumbled to the bed and threw herself on to it, face down. Immediately she recalled the man in the queue at the soup kitchen. 'It was him!' she told herself. She recalled the look of him, the intense expression and his muttered word 'Dilys'. Yes! She had been right all along and they had all been wrong to try and persuade her otherwise.

But why had he chosen her – and why draw attention to himself? Why should he make his intentions so obvious?

'The police!' she muttered. Now she would contact them and tell them her suspicions and they would go after him. Still shaking from the ordeal, Dilys made her way downstairs and called them.

A young constable arrived ten minutes later on a bicycle and the two of them sat at the kitchen table, each with a mug of cocoa which he assured her would help soothe her nerves.

Dilys had dressed herself during the wait for his arrival and had also had time to discover the loss of various items.

'A small carriage clock from the sitting room,' she told him, 'and a silver backed hair brush and mirror which my husband gave me for a wedding present.'

'Any of it worth anything?' He paused in his note-taking.

'Worth anything?' she repeated angrily. 'Most certainly they were worth something. They were silver backed! A considerable amount, in fact, constable, not to mention the sentimental value!'

He wrote again and turned the page. 'Roughly how much, would you say – for the clock?'

'I would have to consult my insurer. Everything of worth has been listed ... and my diamond and garnet ring has gone!' It had gone from the dressing table, she reflected with a shiver of realization. 'That man was upstairs, in my bedroom, *while I was sleeping! I might have been murdered in my bed!*' She watched for his reaction. Surely he would be as horrified as she was.

He said, 'Good job he didn't then, or this would be a murder scene! Think yourself lucky, Mrs Manning.'

Dilys felt like slapping him. 'It's Maynard,' she reminded him and spelled it for him. 'And for your information, I don't feel at all lucky!' He seemed impervious to shock and outrage. Perhaps stolidity was one of the requirements for young police cadets. She felt totally violated but he was treating it as a routine burglary.

'Maynard,' he repeated and gave her a sudden smile. 'I knew a man called Maynard once. Long time ago. He was a teacher at my school. Terrible wild hair, he had. Mangy Maynard we called him, the way you do at school. A nickname, you see. Mangy like a lion has a mangy mane.'

Dilys stared into his young blue eyes and prayed that he would never be given a promotion.

He finished his cocoa and picked up his pencil. 'Now can you describe this man you think you saw in the...'

'I didn't *think* I saw him, I *did* see him!'

'But it was dark, you said.'

'I saw his shape – tall and thin with an intense stare and a...'

'It was dark and in the garden but you could see his intense stare?'

'Only because I've seen him before.' She explained the incident in the soup kitchen. 'It's him. I'm sure of it.'

'Knows ... the ... perpetrator...' he wrote then glanced up.

'You make it sound as though he's an acquaintance,' Dilys protested. 'I didn't say that.'

'What is he then – a friend, a neighbour, what exactly?'

'A *friend*?' She almost groaned. 'A friend would hardly break into my house and steal from me!'

'But you said you know the man.'

'I don't *know* him. I recognized him from that earlier incident at the soup kitchen. I don't know who he is but at the time I had a distinct feeling that he meant me harm.'

120

'And you can't imagine anyone carrying a grudge for something in the past? Could he be someone you or your husband sacked? A lazy gardener? Someone like that?'

'I can't think of anyone.' She looked at him helplessly.

'A jilted lover from your past?'

'For heaven's sake!' she snapped. 'Now you're being ridiculous!'

'Just asking,' he said, unperturbed, and added a few more words to his report. 'You never know.'

'I'm a perfectly respectable widow. Put that in your notebook!'

After a pause, he said, 'Maybe he assumes that all the people involved in the soup kitchen must be filthy rich so are worth robbing!'

'I suppose we are, in their eyes.' Dilys was thinking hard. 'Has there been a similar break-in at the homes of any of the others who help at the soup kitchen?' Her enthusiasm for the theory was growing. 'If there have been similar incidents then it's a pattern. You could cross-check any similar burglaries and—'

'Are you telling me how to do my job, Mrs Maynard?' He spoke mildly and he seemed quite taken with her idea. 'I dare say that if you are poor enough you must almost *hate* rich people. They've got nothing and, by comparison, the "do-gooders" have everything.' He wrote briefly.

Dilys gasped, finding the remarks offensive. He seemed to suggest that if you had money you were a legitimate target for those who had none. Abruptly her patience deserted her and she raised her voice. 'You are not taking this seriously! I can see that quite clearly. I'm going to report you to your superiors! I'm giving you plenty of useful information – *vital* information – and you are hardly writing anything!'

He gave her a pitying look. 'You're upset, Mrs Maynard. A bit hysterical. You've had a bit of a shock, that's all.'

'A bit of a shock? That's what you think, is it? That shows a lack of experience, constable! I'm shocked to the core and I don't know how I shall get through the rest of the night until daylight. Suppose he comes back.'

'He won't. They never do. Rest easy on that account.' Unperturbed, he closed the notebook. 'This will do for now. You go back to bed and get some sleep. I may be back in the morning unless we've caught him by then.' He stood up and held up a hand. 'I'll see myself out.'

Wordlessly she watched him heave himself from the chair. He said, 'Did we establish how he gained entry?'

She pointed to the broken window behind him. 'He must have smashed the window, put his hand in and unlocked it then pushed up the lower half.'

He nodded. 'May have cut himself,' he said hopefully. 'Serve the blighter right if he has!'

'And the back door was open so...'

'So that's how he left the premises.' He made a few last jottings in his notebook. 'We'll see what we find in the morning. It'll be light then. Might be lucky and find footprints.'

When he'd gone Dilys started to laugh, and then she cried. Eventually she went to the telephone to waken Albert and Hettie but had second thoughts. It could wait until the morning when she was more in control. She didn't want their pity. Hettie might even gloat over her misfortune – she had often derided Dilys's attempts to help the poor and needy. Dilys could imagine her sister-in-law saying, 'That's the thanks you get for your "do-gooding".'

Slowly she made her way upstairs, leaving all the lights on behind her. The thought of the broken window made her even more nervous so she had locked the kitchen door which led into the hallway. If he did come back he would be unable to get further than the kitchen.

Upstairs she walked into her bedroom and

stared around her. The man, whoever he was, had been here, watching her sleep. Suppose she had roused from her dreams and surprised him ... how would he have reacted? Would he have fled downstairs in a panic or ... or stayed to *'hurt'* her?

She swallowed hard while her insides trembled. She had never been so near to violence in her life, she reflected; had never been so vulnerable to attack – and the thought terrified her. Unable to stay in the bedroom a moment longer, she pulled the eiderdown from the bed and carried it downstairs. In the sitting room she curled up on the sofa and covered herself with the eiderdown. Too late she thought about a pillow but nothing would induce her to go back upstairs so she reached for a cushion instead and settled herself for the healing sleep which unfortunately did not come. Instead she spent the hours until dawn reliving the whole ghastly experience and wondering how to protect herself from further unlawful visits.

While Dilys was suffering a traumatic experience, Daisy lay in bed smiling up into the darkness. In the next bedroom she could hear Monty snoring and the occasional creak of the bed springs. She was thinking about Steven Anders at the solicitors' office and wondering how to arrange another meeting. Either she could go to the office on some pretext (she would have to invent a reason) or she would have to think of a reason for him to make a call at the house. She *could* ask Monty to invite him to the house to discuss something ... or she could go in to the office on some excuse without telling her employer. He would probably never find out.

'Mr Steven Anders,' she said. 'And Mrs Steven Anders ... and their three children!' It sounded wonderful, she thought wistfully.

Daisy tried to recall what he looked like. Not plump, grey eyes and a nice smile. He'd been wearing the usual clothes for a man in his position – dark suit with a bit of handkerchief showing in the top pocket ... and a starched collar. Probably well-polished shoes.

She was pretending that he was a bachelor. Surely he wasn't a married man? That would be too awful to think about. Instead she imagined a doting mother cooking his breakfast of bacon and eggs and waving him off at the front door as he left for the office.

She wondered if the secretary was in love with him. Daisy had no real experience of secretaries but it seemed like the sort of thing they might do. 'Marrying the boss'. It had a chillingly familiar ring to it.

More than an hour later Daisy fell asleep in

the middle of planning what she would wear when she and Steven Anders next met. She knew she looked quite fetching in her maid's outfit but she would hope to look more mature dressed to visit the offices of Desmond & Marsh.

She was woken by the sound of the telephone and scrambled from the bed, only half awake. She ran down the stairs and snatched up the receiver.

'Yes?' she said breathlessly.

It was Hettie. 'Listen carefully, Daisy, and don't interrupt. There has been an unpleasant occurrence. I've had Dilys on the telephone in a state of near hysteria. The house was burgled in the middle of the night and she saw the wretch escaping through the back garden. She thinks—'

'Oh! Poor Mrs Maynard!'

'I asked you not to interrupt, Daisy. Please pay attention.'

'But is she all right?'

'Of course she is. Very frightened but unhurt. The fact is she refuses to stay there alone and wanted to come here for a few days but that is quite out of the question. I have suggested she stays with Montague so I'd like to speak to him a little later. Please ask him to telephone me around ten o'clock.'

'Has she told the police? They should be told. They—'

'You're doing it again, Daisy! Let me do the talking, please.'

Daisy stifled a groan. They had got rid of Miss Willis but now Mrs Maynard was going to move in! She could imagine what poor old Monty would say – and she herself was none too pleased. No more cosy chats. She would have to be a dutiful maid again.

'So, Daisy, you had better prepare one of the spare bedrooms. Put a hot water bottle in to air the bed and open the windows. A little polish wouldn't come amiss or a few flowers. And be prepared for histrionics. My sister—'

'Histrionics?'

'Rather hysterical behaviour. My sister-in-law is very highly strung and this episode has upset her. I shall ask her doctor to call on her before she comes to you. He can give her something soothing. I think that's everything. Remember, around ten o'clock. Tell Montague what has happened. I must rush. The chimney sweep is due any moment.'

Daisy replaced the receiver with a sigh. Dilys was coming to stay. She must prepare Monty. There was no way to soften the blow. He would not be pleased.

SIX

At half past ten on the following day Dilys arrived and Daisy saw at once what Hettie had meant. The effect of the night's terrors was clearly marked on her face. She was very pale and a little dishevelled as though she had not been able to take the usual care with her appearance. She was dressed in warm but unfashionable clothes, as though she needed the comfort of her familiar tweeds, and her ankles revealed thick lisle stockings inside sturdy lace-up shoes. She sat with Monty in the sitting room with a tray of tea and told Daisy to sit down with them. Nothing loath, Daisy settled herself and prepared to be shocked.

'I want you both to hear what has happened,' Dilys told them. 'It will help you to be on the lookout for this dreadful man. Even here I don't feel safe – no offence, Montague – because I'm convinced he has a grudge against the family. We are all potential victims!'

Daisy felt a tremor of something akin to

fear as she watched Dilys's expression as she relived her nightmare. 'I think you're very brave, Mrs Maynard,' she told her. 'It must be terrible even to talk about it.'

Dilys smiled wanly. 'I'm sure the man is the one who trespassed at Hettie and Albert's home and behaved very oddly. Not threatening exactly but strange behaviour. You, Montague, might be next!'

'Good Lord!' he said. 'I hope you're wrong about that, Dilys.'

Daisy said, 'We haven't seen anybody lurking about here, have we, sir?'

He shook his head uncertainly without answering.

Dilys stirred her tea. 'That doesn't mean he won't appear or do something unpleasant. I spent an hour with the police this morning and they don't seem to take it very seriously although they will be checking the pawnbrokers and second-hand shops with the list I gave them of what was stolen from the house as well as the old bicycle he stole from Mr Trew's garden shed.'

Daisy said, 'It's nothing short of wicked! Frightening people and taking their jewels.'

Dilys shrugged. 'The world is no longer a safe place for the innocent. That's what this is telling us.'

Monty frowned thoughtfully. 'Were you able to give them a description of this wretch? They can draw a picture, you know, just a pencil sketch, and sometimes it can be a very good likeness.'

Dilys shook her head. 'He was outside in the dark ... To think that a complete stranger was standing beside me while I slept – completely unaware of the danger! Anything could have happened! I could be dead!' Her mouth trembled.

Monty said, 'Now hold on there, Dilys. Nothing did happen. Cling to that thought. If he intended to harm you, you wouldn't be sitting here now. Take comfort from—'

'I can't take comfort from anything!' she cried. 'Don't you see where this is leading? What is it about us?' She turned to Daisy. 'I will do the rounds with you every night to make sure the windows and doors are bolted – not that it prevented the break-in back home. He simply smashed the window.'

Daisy said, 'We could get a dog.'

They considered the idea but Dilys pointed out that a puppy would take months to train by which time it might be too late.

'But it would be useful later,' Monty argued. 'And a cat would be nice.'

'But you don't like animals. You never did as a child. Dogs scared you.' She looked at him reproachfully. 'I wanted a puppy but because of you Mother said no.'

'I was only nervous of the noisy, yappy

dogs. Like ... like terriers and those with the squashed up noses. We could get a quiet one.'

Daisy pointed out that a quiet, un-yappy dog would probably not frighten away a burglar and added, 'Anyway, some burglars poison the dog! They give it a piece of meat with—'

Dilys cried, 'Do stop, Daisy! Forget about the dogs.'

Her brother turned to her. 'Why didn't you stay with Albert and Hettie? You might have been safer there. Albert plays golf. He could set about a burglar with one of his clubs. Put the fear of God into the blighter!'

Her face fell. 'Hettie said it was out of the question. I expect she's busy.'

She drank her tea but Daisy noticed that her hands were still shaking.

'Would you feel better about going back home some time if there was someone else in the house?' she asked.

Monty brightened. 'Maybe the gardener.'

'Mr Trew?' His sister gave him a withering look. 'And get myself talked about? Really, Montague, that is not very helpful.'

'I suppose not,' he said, suitably chastened.

'And what would Mr Trew's wife think about it?'

They fell silent for several minutes while the teacups were refreshed.

'What about a woman?'Daisy suggested. 'Your Mrs Gray, for instance. That woman would frighten any burglar and people couldn't gossip about you being alone with a woman.'

Dilys considered the idea. 'It's a possibility, Daisy. I could ask her – but she has an invalid brother she looks after. She probably wouldn't leave him alone at night.'

The conversation finally faltered, Daisy suggested taking Mrs Maynard upstairs to see if the spare bedroom held everything she would need for a short stay, and the two women left Monty to his unsettling thoughts.

That afternoon the secretary at Marsh & Desmond took a telephone call and hurried into Steven Anders' office.

'It's a call from a Mrs Pennington,' she told him. 'She wants to talk to Mr Desmond.'

'He's at the dentist. An extraction.'

'I know. That's why I'm telling you – in case you want to deal with it in his absence. Poor Mr Desmond's having an extraction and he won't feel like returning to the office. He's sure to go straight home afterwards.'

'Can't you give her an appointment for tomorrow?'

'Mrs Pennington says it's urgent and Mr Marsh already has a client booked for eleven.'

Steven's mind worked fast. He would have time to read through the notes before she arrived and this was the family that Miss Letts worked for. It would be interesting to know what was happening in the family and just might lead to a visit from the young housemaid.

He smiled. 'Right you are then, I'll take it,' he said with a ring of false confidence, crossing his fingers that he would be able to understand the problem and offer something constructive.

Before she arrived he tidied his desk and arranged a variety of documents on it to suggest a workload in progress. He tidied his hair and straightened his tie and rubbed each shoe against the neighbouring trouser leg to improve the polish. Inspecting his hands and nails, he wished, not for the first time, that he wore a heavy gold ring of some kind. On his partners' hands he felt they added an air of experience and sophistication which his own lacked.

Steven was practising a businesslike smile when Hettie Pennington strode into the office and Steven realized immediately that she was someone to be reckoned with. His heart sank a little as he realized that the forthcoming exchange might not go according to his expectations but he assumed a cheerful expression and leaned across the desk to shake her hand. She was dressed in an expensive suit in a dark grey wool and the felt hat, which revealed a severe bun at the nape of her neck, was held to her head with a large hatpin. A string of blue beads completed the ensemble and she carried a large leather purse.

She sat down at once and regarded him severely. 'You must understand, Mr Anders, that this conversation must remain confidential. I want you to know that I am acting in the best interests of my brother Montague. I see you have a folder on the desk in front of you. Is that ours?'

Steven, ruffled, felt that she had somehow taken charge of the consultation. Pointedly, he said, 'Good morning, Mrs Pennington. I'm sorry Mr Desmond cannot see you but rest assured I shall pass on all relevant details to him when he is next in the office. Now how can I help you?'

Slightly taken aback she quickly rallied. 'The folder in front of you – is that ours?'

'Yes.' He patted it. 'This is for Mr and Mrs Albert Pennington.'

'Ah! Just what I feared. We actually need my brother's file and not ours. The matter is somewhat delicate but I am here to speak about my brother.'

Steven hid his dismay. All his prior reading had been a waste of time. 'Your brother –

that is Mr Montague Pennington.'

'Exactly. That is what I have come to consult you about.'

'But we have a confidentiality clause, Mrs Pennington. I could only produce that file if you have a letter from him giving you permission. You must understand that our clients are naturally very sensitive to matters of privacy.'

Hettie sighed, making her frustration obvious. 'Mr Anders, you must understand that such a letter is not possible in these circumstances.'

'And these circumstances are...?' He waited. The woman was definitely nervous, he thought curiously.

'I have my brother-in-law's best interests at heart – that is we do, my husband and I – and, you see, this is very difficult ... painful in fact, for me.' She sighed. 'The money in our family has always been passed down to the eldest son which in this case is Montague and so far this has never been a problem. However, he is showing signs of increasing senility lately and my husband and widowed sister-in-law...'

She paused for air and Steven saw a faint blush rising in her neck. Now he was beginning to suspect her purpose.

'Oh dear!' Mrs Pennington smiled thinly. 'This is so very difficult for me.'

She laid a hand on her heart and took a deep breath and Steven could not tell if she was acting or not. He said, 'Take your time, Mrs Pennington. My time is yours.' He felt rather pleased with the last sentence and hoped his client was impressed.

With her head bent, she put a hand across her eyes.

He said, 'Perhaps it would be better for you if your husband dealt with the problem.'

Her head snapped up at once. 'Oh no! My husband is very upset by this – this *development* and cannot bring himself to accept the deterioration which *I* recognize in Montague. Albert has always looked up to his older brother in a way – not that they like each other very much. Sibling rivalry, I suppose.' She fiddled with the blue beads, staring into the past. 'Each one trying to take whatever the other had. Jealousy, plain and simple, Mr Anders, and within a family it can be very corrosive.' She hesitated then continued. 'Monica Tatchet was supposed to wed Montague but Albert coveted her. Albert *stole* her from his brother. You can imagine!'

Steven said, 'How ... how unfortunate!'

She rolled her eyes expressively. 'Unfortunate is definitely an understatement, Mr Anders! It was nothing less than disastrous. They had a son but then Monica died and meanwhile Albert met Cressida.' She smiled mirthlessly. 'You can guess what happened.'

Steven blinked. 'You don't mean ... that Montague stole her from Albert?'

'Exactly! Can you credit it? They say revenge is sweet! You might say the family was torn apart. No doubt the whole of Bath was discussing the Penningtons. The family is very well known in the area.' Shaking her head, she was obviously reliving the experience. Her shoulders had slumped and her lips were pressed together tightly as if to prevent further disclosures.

Steven waited, trying to hide his interest. How much of this story could he pass on to Daisy, he wondered. Trying to maintain an impassive expression he gently rearranged his pen and pencil on either side of the blotter and allowed his client time with her thoughts.

Eventually she straightened her shoulders and looked at him sharply. 'But that was all before I joined the family by marrying Albert. I like to think we have resolved the friction and are reasonably united these days. Water under the bridge.' She gave him a stern look. 'I don't expect you to repeat a word of what I have told you, Mr Anders. If you do I shall ensure your instant dismissal.'

'Not a word, Mrs Pennington!' he assured her with a rush of anxiety and guilt – because he did not doubt that this formidable woman would carry out her threat.

'What was I saying?' she demanded.

'Er ... about your husband not wanting to—'

'Oh yes. Albert finds this very distressing. Poor Montague is becoming somewhat disorientated in the way older people do, and shows no interest in finance and I am afraid he will allow matters to slide – if that's the right way to put it. I am hoping that one of us – preferably my husband – will come round to facing the truth before it is too late. The truth that Montague needs our help. There is such a thing as...' She hesitated.

'Power of attorney? I believe that means going through the courts.'

'Yes. Unless Montague agrees to sign such a form before he becomes too ... too confused to understand the meaning of it, we may well find ourselves in difficulties. I am looking for advice, Mr Anders, as I am rather in the dark, so to speak. If this particular problem is not part of your brief then I shall make another appointment and speak to Mr Desmond. He has always dealt with the Pennington affairs.'

Although Steven felt completely out of his depth, he was not prepared to admit it. 'I find it quite straightforward,' he replied with what he hoped was a confident smile. 'I assume you have spoken to other members of the family as well as your husband. Are they in agreement with your assessment of Montague Pennington's state of mind?'

Mrs Pennington explained that she had spoken to Dilys Maynard who agreed with her, and to Albert who was reluctant to discuss the problem. 'The responsibility seems to rest on my slim shoulders,' she told him.

Steven nodded. 'How does your brother manage on his own? Does he have staff who could also corroborate your diagnosis? A housekeeper or ... a housemaid?' He wanted to hear mention of young Miss Letts.

'A housekeeper? Strange you should ask that. Until recently my brother-in-law had a housekeeper, a Miss Dutton, who seemed to be a little too friendly, if you take my meaning, Mr Anders. He relied on her too much, in my opinion, and she tended to discourage us from visiting him. I never did quite trust her.'

'Hmm. A difficult situation.'

'It has been known for an elderly man to become ... *ensnared* by his housekeeper.' She clutched her beads. 'To *marry* them, even. They become so dependent on them they imagine...' She threw up her hands in a gesture of helplessness.

'These things do happen, of course.' Did they? He was surprised.

'Fortunately Miss Dutton left abruptly and

now we have to find a replacement but in the meantime there's a young housemaid by the name of Daisy. She will recently have found him confused, I know. That is,' she corrected herself hastily, 'I don't *know*, but I'm sure she will have noticed his general deterioration. By all means ask her, Mr Anders. I spoke to my brother recently on the telephone and he passed on the most amazingly garbled message to the housemaid. Almost every detail was wrong! Goodness knows what she thought.'

'Could that be just his memory? Elderly people can get forgetful without being senile.'

'Who can tell?'

Steven decided that he now had an excuse to get in contact with Daisy Letts. Mrs Pennington had given her permission, *in so many words*. If she ever queried it, he would explain that he obviously misunderstood her. Maybe he and Daisy could meet in a nearby tea shop during his midday break. His excitement grew as he considered the possibilities. He could tell her he needed confirmation of Mrs Pennington's suspicions. But the nagging question was – did she already have a young man? That would be a fly in the ointment and no mistake.

To give himself a chance to think, he pretended to write in the folder although in fact he had placed a separate sheet in the folder for rough notes and would write a better report later.

'Are you listening to me, Mr Anders?'

He glanced up guiltily and nodded.

'I am telling you about the advice I was given by his doctor,' she insisted. 'He seemed very perturbed when I explained the situation. Without professional advice I really do not know how to proceed. Should I insist that the doctor attends, maybe with a colleague? Where does one start in a case like this?'

'Hmm. It's difficult, I agree.'

'I simply want to do what is best for him. I'm not asking that he be committed or anything drastic, but nor do I want him to mismanage large sums of family money. I have no wish to look back in a year's time and see that I could have helped prevent a financial catastrophe. You can surely understand my very natural concerns.'

Steven wrote again then laid down the pen. 'I suggest that I present my notes to Mr Desmond and he in turn will take the matter further. Be assured we will be in touch again.' He paused and then smiled giving his client a chance to recognize that, in his opinion, the meeting was at an end. Mrs Pennington rose to her feet with some reluctance.

At the door she hesitated. 'And these notes you have made will remain confidential, Mr Anders.'

'Certainly they will – except for Mr Desmond who obviously will see them on his return.'

The secretary saw her out and Steven was left with a broad smile on his face. It did rather feel as though a kind fate was acting on his behalf. 'Everything comes to those who wait!' he whispered as he returned to the desk to study his notes.

On Saturday, with some trepidation, Daisy served the midday meal, certain that Dilys would find fault with it. She had reheated some stew from the previous day and added dumplings to make it enough for three. The cabbage was a little soggy and the potatoes slightly underdone but to Daisy's surprise and relief, Dilys ate hers without complaint. Monty gave her a wink and she felt she had survived the first hurdle.

'There is no pudding, I'm afraid,' she said apologetically but Dilys brushed aside the apology.

'Tomorrow I shall cook for us,' she announced. 'I like cooking but it is soul destroying for one. I shall cook fish pie so I will tell you, Daisy, what to order from the fish man and you can telephone it through later.

My mother used to adore fish pie. Do you remember, Montague? I always cooked it when she came to visit. The only problem is the bones and I always took the time to remove them.' She smiled at Daisy. 'I'll teach you how to make it. Add it to your repertoire.'

'Thank you, Mrs Pennington.' Daisy was genuinely pleased. If Dilys taught her a few more recipes, she, Daisy, could soon become a reasonable cook which would help her career.

No one had so far mentioned the previous night which passed without incident. Dilys had slept with her door ajar, insisting that Daisy did the same so that in case of an intruder, they could each contact the other by shouting and ringing the bedside bells. By agreement, Daisy and Monty had agreed not to talk about the dangers that Dilys feared.

Now, however, Dilys raised the matter herself. 'I shall go down to the police station,' she told them, 'to see what progress they have made but first I shall speak to Hettie and satisfy myself that they have suffered no harm from this wretched man – and tell her that we have survived the night here.'

'The police may have caught him already,' Daisy suggested hopefully. 'He may already be locked up.'

'Most unlikely. I don't think they are

treating the matter seriously. To them it is just another burglary.'

'But they were going to investigate and maybe they found a footprint. It's amazing what they can learn from the sole of a shoe.'

'But dozens of men would be wearing the same shoes, Daisy. Maybe hundreds. I'm afraid I'm not impressed by their claims or the suggestion that the theft was random. I know better. I understand that our family is being marked out for attention by this dreadful man, for reasons that escape me. He knew my name!' Querulously her voice rose a little. 'He called me Dilys! No one seems to believe me but I heard it quite clearly in the soup kitchen. Not missus, but Dilys. Certainly the wretch is not normal. I think this is the beginning of harassment but the police give the idea no credence. They insist the intrusions are random but ... first Albert and Hettie and now me.' She looked at her brother. 'I hope you are not next, Montague. I don't mean to frighten you but we must be on our guard here.'

'Well, safety in numbers, eh?' Monty smiled nervously.

Daisy wished that Dilys would drop the subject – but suppose she was right. Maybe the Penningtons *were* being sought out for some reason.

Dilys sighed. 'We must all be particularly

careful. Admit no one to the house – no stranger, that is. And we must ask Len to keep an eye open in the garden for any trespassers.'

Despite her determination not to be scared, Daisy rose to clear the table with growing trepidation. There was some truth in what Dilys said about the family and it might be that Monty was next on the list for aggravation from this man.

Later in the morning a police sergeant visited them to inform them of the latest developments. The small clock had been recovered from a pawnbroker in the town and they had a description of the man who had brought it in. Tall, thin and shabby. A trawl of neighbours had produced a man who, while walking his dog on three separate occasions, noticed a man who seemed to be watching the house. He also fitted the description, the sergeant told them, and they were keeping a lookout for him.

Monty, Daisy and Dilys received this news with gratitude and the mood in the house lightened considerably.

Meanwhile Constable Cresswell waited patiently in the incident room as his sergeant thought about the break-in at Dilys Maynard's home.

145

'So there were footprints, Cresswell?'

'Yes sir, and they've taken a cast.'

'But that won't help until we have a suspect and can compare shoe soles.'

'No sir.'

'Still it's better than nothing.'

The constable nodded and the sergeant skipped through the thin file for the second time.

At last the sergeant said, 'So now we reckon this chap's got it in for the whole family?'

Constable Cresswell shrugged. 'So they reckon. Because of the trespasser at the brother's place.'

'Namely Albert Pennington.'

'That's about it, sir.'

'And they all claim they have no enemies. No idea who this can be?'

'No sir.'

'It's too much of a coincidence. They must be lying. They're hiding something.'

'Yes sir. But we've asked the neighbours. It's all in my report.'

'Then what do you think we should do next, Cresswell?'

'Widen the search, sir?'

'Exactly. Who else might know something? Maybe something in the long distant past. A long-held grudge. Who has known them for a long time? Anyone?'

'There was a housekeeper, sir, but she left

146

not long ago. A Miss Dutton – or Button. Something like that.'

The sergeant's expression changed. 'Sacked? See, that could be the motive! People have long memories and as long as they get revenge they don't care how long they wait for it.'

The constable scratched his head. 'You're not saying it was the housekeeper, sir?'

'Of course I'm not, you idiot! I'm saying she might remember someone who was sacked and now has a grudge against the family.'

'The housemaid said she left to look after her mother who was very ill. Just upped and left.'

'Pity.'

'Yes sir. But we can find her.'

The sergeant's hopes lifted again. 'If she'd been there for a long time she might know more than the rest are saying! Get after her, Cresswell. Find her and grill her to within an inch of her life!' They both grinned. 'It may be a dead end but at this moment this Miss Dutton is all we've got!'

Dilys and Monty were in the summer house when the telephone rang later that afternoon and Daisy hurried from the kitchen to answer it. She now considered herself an experienced hand with the machine and

147

answered crisply. 'Montague Pennington's house. Who's calling?'

'This is Steven Anders from Marsh & Desmond, the—'

'The solicitors!' Daisy could hardly believe what was happening. That nice Mr Anders was telephoning them! For a moment she could hardly speak.

He said cautiously, 'Is that Miss Letts?'

'It is!'

She assumed he needed to talk to Monty or Dilys but he went on, 'I have a confession to make, Miss Letts. You gave me a sample of your signature but I accidentally spilt tea over it and I don't want to look a fool in front of my partners. I was wondering—'

'If I could call in and give you another one? I could.' She cheered silently. 'It would be no trouble, Mr Anders. None at all. When should I come in? I'll have to ask...'

'Well, the thing is, I'm going past Mr Pennington's house this evening and I could bring the form with me. It would only take a moment.'

This very evening! Daisy's face was one large smile. She was going to see him again. Struggling to maintain some sort of calm she asked what time he was likely to be passing.

'Around six thirty? Would that be acceptable, Miss Letts? Do you need to ask permission from your employer? I don't want

148

you to get into any trouble.'

'I won't. Mr Pennington will understand. I shall be ... that is, I look forward to seeing you.'

'It will be a pleasure, Miss Letts.'

'Oh!' She could hardly breathe. Was he just being polite?

He said, 'A real pleasure.'

Daisy searched for the right reply. If she was misunderstanding any of this, she must not give herself away, but if he was trying to tell her something – that, perhaps, he had taken a fancy to her – then she must encourage him. The silence lengthened as she sought a suitable reply.

'Miss Letts?'

'Yes. I mean ... yes, it will be a pleasure for me, too!' She crossed her fingers in case she had gone too far. He might be laughing at her. Could he be leading her on? Her smile faded.

'Then I'll see you at six thirty, Miss Letts. Goodbye for now.'

'Goodbye.' She replaced the receiver but remained staring vacantly towards the front door. What was she supposed to think now? He might just be making fun of her – raising her hopes only to dash them! Would he even turn up at half past six? If he didn't she thought she might die of disappointment. Briefly she closed her eyes, uttering a prayer that she would survive.

'Trust him, Daisy!' she told herself in a whisper. 'He's a nice man. He wouldn't...' She couldn't even put the thought into words.

Footsteps sounded behind her and a voice startled her. She spun round to discover that Dilys had come in from the garden and was standing a few feet away from her.

'Are you ill, Daisy?'

'No. I was answering the telephone.' She explained about the signature and Dilys frowned.

'I thought it was Mr Desmond who dealt with our family's business. This Mr Anders – who is he exactly?'

'He's only been there a few months so you may not have met him. He was only standing in for Mr Desmond because he'd gone to the dentist. He's awfully nice.' Immediately she wished the last few words unsaid.

As she expected, Dilys pounced. '"*Awfully*" is not the word you want to use there, Daisy. *Very* nice is better. And how would you know how nice he is? I hope you are not getting any foolish ideas, Daisy. Remember your place. You are only a housemaid. Mr Anders—'

'At the moment I'm a trainee housekeeper,' she protested. 'Mr Pennington says...'

'Don't interrupt your betters, Daisy! You'll

never be a housekeeper with manners like that! As I was saying, this Mr Anders is obviously a well-educated man with a career ahead of him and if he *is* showing any interest in you, he will certainly have no *serious* intentions where you are concerned. Apart from which my brother obviously does not wish you to encourage followers. So please do not encourage Mr Anders.'

'I wasn't ... I mean, I won't.' What do I mean, she wondered, thoroughly confused. It had seemed that *he* was encouraging *her*.

'When he calls,' Dilys went on, 'take him into the sitting room to do the signature and I will come in with you. That way he is unlikely to attempt any unseemly flattery or nonsense of that sort.'

'There's no need, ma'am.'

'I feel there is.' She sighed. 'We really must get Montague a new housekeeper.'

'But I can learn and—'

'I'm not blaming you, Daisy. You are doing your best in difficult circumstances. It is a housekeeper's job to keep an eye on the housemaids and there is no one to guide you. Poor Montague is somewhat out of his depth – in more ways than one. My sister-in-law is extremely worried about him. She thinks he needs help with ... certain family matters.'

'I think he's coping very well.'

151

Dilys raised her eyebrows. 'I haven't asked for your opinion, Daisy. Do pay attention to the advice I give you since Miss Dutton is no longer here to supervise you.'

As she swept out of the room Daisy stuck out her tongue and began counting the days until Monty's sister would feel able to return to her own house.

That same afternoon PC Cresswell arrived at Emily Dutton's cottage. It was small and the neat parlour in which they sat was what estate agents liked to call 'compact'. It was also dark because a large oak tree outside hid the sun and it smelled of cats. PC Cresswell forced a smile. He sat uncomfortably in a wing-backed chair that creaked ominously whenever he moved, and to complete his discomfort, the trailing leaves of a tradescantia in a pot on the mantelpiece to his right dangled close to his face, which he found irritating.

The old lady, introduced as Emily Dutton, sat in a rocking chair surrounded by cushions, her nightwear discreetly hidden by a blanket which was well tucked in around her. She was working at something white that the policeman took to be crochet. Probably cuffs, he thought irritably. His grandmother had always been embroidering tablecloths. Why did elderly people always have to pretend they were busy, he wondered, as he pulled a notebook from his pocket and found a clean page for his notes.

Emily Dutton's daughter, whose name was apparently Edie, balanced her comfortable body on a small stool, with her hands clasped in her lap, and the constable was reminded of a childhood illustration of Little Miss Muffet awaiting the arrival of the spider.

'Well,' said Miss Dutton, in answer to the constable's first question, 'I wasn't there when Monty's wife was alive because I suppose *she* ran the house but when she died he advertised for a housekeeper and I got the job.'

Her mother nodded. 'That's right. You can write that down, Mr Cresswell. Edie was just on twenty-three when she went to work for Mr Pennington but she was already a dab hand with pastry. You can take my word for it that nothing but butter goes into her shortcrust.'

The policeman counted to ten as he scribbled the words 'twenty-three', and 'pastry'. 'And as far as you were aware, Miss Dutton, there was no one who might feel a grudge towards the family. No falling out of any kind?'

'No one. Mind you, Monty kept himself to himself meaning he never invited the neigh-

153

bours in or family members except at Christmas and on his birthday. But there were lots of photographs of his wife. Cressida. That was her name. Everyone loved Cressida. That's what he used to say, anyway.'

'What about the rest of the family – were they on good terms with each other? No family feuds?' He looked up hopefully.

'Goodness no!' Miss Dutton snorted at the very idea. 'I shouldn't have cared for that sort of goings on! I would have been out of there like a shot!'

Her mother nodded. 'Like a shot, Mr Cresswell. You can take that as gospel.' She turned to her daughter. 'Maybe our visitor would like a cup of tea, Edie, and a biscuit.' She smiled at him. 'D'you fancy a cuppa tea, Mr Cresswell? I'd offer to make it but it's my leg. I fell and broke it. Snapped right in two, it did – the bone that is. Leastways, that's what I reckon. The doctor said it's a fracture but I know better. What do they know, these doctors? It's still swollen and I can't get my shoe on that foot so I—'

'No!' he said hastily. 'That is, no tea, thank you, Mrs Dutton. I mean, I'm sorry about your accident but I'm a bit pressed for time. Got to catch this blighter and put him behind bars!'

'And serve the chap right. Bothering

154

people and sneaking about like that.' She leaned forward. 'Thing is, Mr Cresswell, I ask myself where will it end. He might be getting worse. Might go on to murder someone.'

Miss Dutton said, 'Mother! The policeman hasn't got all day. This is urgent.' She turned back to him apologetically and was rewarded with a smile.

He said, 'Now, Miss Dutton, can you give me some brief details about the other members of the family – just to corroborate what I know already.' He studied his notes. 'Albert, the younger brother, and Dilys, the sister.'

'Well. Let's see now. Not a lot to say about Dilys,' she informed him. 'She married John Maynard and they had no family. He passed on quite recently ... Albert is married to Hettie and they have a son called George Egbert. No, sorry, that's George *Albert*. He married a French woman but they didn't take to her one bit, and when they went to live in France...'

Her mother rolled her eyes. 'Funny lot, the French!'

'...so I never saw the young couple but Monty did say once that her father owned a farm in Brittany – wherever that is.'

'Did they ever have a falling out, Miss Dutton? The father and the son?'

'Not to my knowledge. Not that Monty ever spoke about him. Just the odd mention, maybe.' She shrugged then leaned forward as if to read his notebook. 'Are you getting all this, constable? Albert and Hettie's son George Albert. I got the impression they'd lost interest in him. Out of sight, out of mind, as the saying goes.'

He wrote carefully. 'I see that they all live around this corner of Bath and yet they don't seem a very close-knit family.'

'I don't reckon they are. Monty was bedridden for years but they hardly ever came to see him.' Realizing suddenly that she had answered his knock at the door while still wearing her pinafore, she hastily pulled it off, folded it and set it on the table beside her. 'Birthdays, of course, and Christmas. Monty didn't seem to care but I felt for him. I mean Christmas can be a lonely time when you're old.'

The old lady said, 'People can be very selfish. 'Specially family. I remember wonderful Christmases when I was a child. Everyone came.'

The constable coughed and turned pointedly towards the daughter. 'You were saying?'

'Albert had been married before and they had a son but I never set eyes on him. Never seen a picture of him and they never men-

156

tioned him in my hearing.'

'And his name is...?'

'I don't even know his name! He was long gone. Packed off to Ceylon to a friend of the family who managed a tea plantation. Leastways that's what the gardener said. Lord knows why but rich people do things like that, don't they?'

Emily said, 'Funny lot, rich people!'

The policeman saw a glimmer of hope. 'So would you think, Miss Dutton, that this first son might have quarrelled with his father and mother? Is that why he was sent off to Ceylon?'

While Edie considered her answer, the old lady said, 'I fancy a cup of tea and a biscuit.'

'Mother! We're trying to concentrate!' She turned back to the constable. 'There *might* have been a quarrel. D'you reckon that's who's doing these awful things, then? Stealing and trespassing and such like? The long lost son?'

He shrugged. 'It has to be a remote possibility if he's still in Ceylon but I shall go to see Albert Pennington next and ask him directly. It just might be, if he's back in England, that this is our first lead.' Head bent, he wrote furiously. It would have been helpful to get a description of this alienated first son but that sounded unlikely. Who, he wondered, might have seen the young man before he was sent into exile. And what had been his crime, if there was one? A quarrel with his father or something worse?

'Keeps me awake at night, this leg does. Throbbing like mad, whichever way I turn. Can't get comfortable.'

PC Cresswell ignored the interruption as he scanned his notes. He still felt vaguely dissatisfied with his enquiries which had provided a very thin possible lead. He racked his brain for anything else that might prove more fruitful. 'And the sister, Dilys, thinks the man was in the free soup queue last week ... Maybe we'll find someone else who can add something to her description; maybe remember something else about him. His voice, perhaps. He might have had an accent.'

The mother said, 'A foreign accent, you mean?'

'Not exactly.'

The daughter said, 'Only Dilys could answer that, Mr Cresswell.'

'Never mind, Miss Dutton. I appreciate your time.' He sighed. 'If he turns up at the soup kitchen again we'll be waiting for him!'

'A dab hand. Oh yes! Rough puff, too. Even pie crust! My daughter once won a prize at the village fête for a game pie! She can turn her hand to anything, my Edie can. She should be married by now instead of waiting hand and foot on a useless old man!' The old lady held her crochet work up to the window and peered at it with obvious dissatisfaction, muttered something then rolled it up and stowed it in her knitting bag.

Then she turned to the police constable and, assuming a determined smile, said, 'If you've finished with your questions, Mr Cresswell, Edie can make us all a nice cup of tea—' she gave her daughter a triumphant smile – 'and you won't say no to a biscuit!'

SEVEN

Almost to the minute Steven Anders arrived on the doorstep and rang the bell. While he waited he stepped back a pace or two and glanced up at the front of the house which had impressed him with its size and location and made him grateful that this was not Miss Letts' home. That would have put her way out of his reach.

The small front garden was neat with a strip of lawn and what was left of the summer's flowers – sparse hollyhocks, marigolds and wallflowers. He had remembered to remove his cycle clips, which now were in the basket of his cycle, and carried a file which he hoped made him look businesslike. As he waited, he glanced at his reflection in the bay window, removed his hat and smoothed his hair carefully. The ring was finally answered and as the door opened he straightened his shoulders and smiled broadly.

'Miss Letts!'

'Mr Anders!'

They smiled at each other.

He said, 'I've come about the signature.'

'Oh yes. Please come in.' She glanced over her shoulder and lowered her voice. 'Mrs Maynard wishes to join us.'

'Ah!' His smile wavered and he pulled a face but stepped inside.

'May I take your hat, sir?'

'Thank you.' He winked.

Trying not laugh, she took the hat and hung it on the hallstand. 'This way, please.'

He followed her into the sitting room which was elegantly furnished and smelled of beeswax polish but there were ashes in the grate and the aspidistra on the broad window ledge looked in need of water. A leather-edged blotter and an inkstand had been placed on the large table which stood in the centre of the room. He had brought a copy of the original sheet and he now produced this from the file with a flourish. In fact there was nothing at all wrong with the original – this had simply been a ploy to meet her again in circumstances other than the office but Mrs Maynard would never know that.

A tall woman joined them, announcing herself as Dilys Maynard and he shook the outstretched hand. Another of the original Penningtons, he thought with interest. She seemed less formidable than her sister-in-law, however, and her slight frown and flustered manner suggested that she was distracted by the interruption of his visit.

With a thin smile she told Steven, 'You will have to be more careful in future!'

For a moment he was at a loss for her meaning but then he remembered. 'Ah yes! The tea I spilled on the original form?' He contrived to look chastened. 'I certainly won't do that again!'

They all laughed politely.

He said, 'Miss Letts has been very kind to allow me to—'

'Truly, it's no trouble, Mr Anders.' Daisy smiled at him briefly.

He swallowed hard then laid the sheet on the blotter.

Daisy signed her name carefully and returned the pen to its place on the stand.

'Thank you so much, Miss Letts.' He was hoping that Mrs Maynard might offer a little refreshment which would prolong his visit but she said nothing.

He said, 'Well, that's a relief. I'll be off home. My trusty steed awaits!'

Mrs Maynard smiled. 'Your bicycle, I presume.'

He nodded.

Miss Letts said, 'I'll show you out, Mr Anders.' And led the way back to the front door. Behind them Mrs Maynard was walking back towards the kitchen. Miss Letts whispered, 'She's going back to the kitchen.'

Recognizing his chance now that it had come, he whispered quickly, 'I don't suppose you could meet me one Saturday. We could have tea together.'

'I might be able to if Mrs Maynard goes back to her own home. How could I let you know?'

He pulled a card from his pocket. 'Ring the office and ask for me.' His throat was dry with excitement and his voice sounded strained. 'Say you are Miss Letts and you need to speak to me. I don't always work all day Saturdays but sometimes I stay later to study for my exam. What about you?'

'At the moment I work every day but if Mrs Maynard goes home I think Monty would give me time off if I ask him nicely.'

He held up crossed fingers. 'I shall hope for the best, Miss Letts.'

'So will I. I'll have to go now. I don't want to rouse her suspicions.'

He held out his hand and she took it. It felt small and warm and he was reluctant to let it go.

She said, 'Thank you for coming ... It was a good lie – about the spilt tea!'

'I am rather proud of it!'

He cycled away with a broad smile on his face and a gleam in his eye. His thoughts were whirling and in his mind's eye he saw the two of them cosily ensconced in Miss

Maude's Teashop and, distracted by this delightful picture, he narrowly missed colliding with a coster's barrow loaded with walnuts.

A day passed and Sunday evening turned into night. The sky was dark but clear with a few stars and the man sitting in the summer house leaned back with his eyes closed, waiting for midnight. He felt at ease, comfortable with his plan of action and certain of its effect. Midnight. That would be the perfect time for his next attack. Let them all get off to sleep, falsely secure in the knowledge that there was safety in numbers and that the windows and doors of the house were securely locked and bolted. He smiled grimly as he watched the pattern of lights in the house change. First one of the bedrooms was lit and curtains closed. Probably Uncle Montague.

In a mocking accent he said, 'Goodnight, Uncle Montague. Sleep well! Don't let thoughts of your nephew disturb your slumbers. Think only of yourself, like all the Penningtons.

'You silly old fool! Doddery old imbecile!' He'd been quick to agree to the idea of sending his nephew away where they need not think about him again ... But slow to realize that he might come back!

Another light went on upstairs – most

likely Aunt Dilys who had taken refuge there. Stupid old bat. She had not spoken a word, either, in his defence.

'Nightie-night, Auntie!'

Nor had John Maynard spoken up for him but then he was not a family member except by marriage so his advice had probably not been sought. Only the sister and brothers had been asked to comment on the idea. 'Get the little blighter out of harm's way,' his father had insisted. 'Give him a dose of real discipline. He can come back when he's learned civilized behaviour.'

Now the kitchen light had gone off which meant that the housemaid had finished for the day and would soon follow the others to bed. It was a shame for her. She was in no way to blame but that was not his fault. In the wrong place at the wrong time. That was her misfortune.

A cat wandered into the summer house and approached him but he clapped his hands and shooed it out, helping it on its way with the toe of his outstretched boot.

He pulled a sandwich from his pocket and unwrapped it. An old woman had given it to him as he sat with his back to a shop window in the town centre earlier, his cap held out for pennies. Said she had no money to spare but returned ten minutes later with a sandwich. So there were some people left in the world with a shred of decency, he thought, biting into it. Cheese and pickle. Not at all bad.

Ceylon was supposed to make a man of him, according to his father. His mother had protested at the distance but gave in weakly when he insisted it was 'for the boy's own good' and 'would make a man of him'. Unfortunately he'd been exploited by his father's so-called friend and, after revenging himself, had been finally betrayed to the authorities who had locked him up after a flawed trial. Eight years hard labour. So had it made a man of him? No. It had turned him into an ill-natured thug. 'And that's what I am and always will be!' he muttered bitterly.

The church clock struck midnight and he stood up, stretching cramped muscles. Moonlight illuminated the three large rocks he had chosen the previous night. One for his uncle's room, one for Dilys and one for the maid. He hesitated. Was it fair? She had done nothing to hurt him ... but she was part of it. Part of the cosy family set-up that he was about to shatter. The set-up he had waited so long to destroy.

He moved forward, picked up the first rock and hurled it with unerring aim through the window of the maid's bedroom. Before the first alarmed cries rang out he sent the second one into the old man's room, and the third into his aunt's room. For a moment he simply stood there, listening to the confusion his assault had provoked then, smiling grimly, he walked slowly round the side of the house and made his way along the pavement. He made no attempt to hide or hurry, just ambled along, head down, his hands thrust into the pockets of his coat.

By the time he had reached the corner and glanced back he saw that behind him neighbours had been roused and a small crowd was gathering outside the house. All the lights were on and he could imagine what was happening inside and it brought a gleam of deep satisfaction to his hard eyes.

'Your turn next, Father!' he whispered.

The sound of the rock smashing its way into the room shocked Daisy into an upright position in the bed, the bed clothes clutched defensively round her. As she listened, there was a second crash and then a third. With a shock she realized that they were being attacked! For a moment she sat there in the darkened room, frozen with fear, then cautiously reached for matches and lit her bedside candle. A rock had shattered the large casement window and rolled across the room. Shards of glass scattered across the floor. She thought of Monty and Dilys, equally shocked and imagined them blundering about.

'Don't move!' she screamed. 'There's glass on the floor. I'm coming!'

Slipping her feet into her shoes, she pulled on her dressing gown then tiptoed carefully past the broken glass and out of the room. Once in the passage she could hear Dilys moaning and Monty calling for help in a wavering voice.

'The windows are broken,' she told them. 'There's glass. Stay where you are!'

She went first to Monty's room and opened the door.

'What's happening?' he cried. 'Do you think it's that man trying to get in?'

'Maybe. Stay in bed for the moment, sir, until I can clear away the glass.'

'Is he out there? Or is he inside the house?' His voice rose querulously.

'I don't know yet but I'll just check on your sister and then I'll go down and find out.'

'Oh no, Daisy! You mustn't go downstairs. He might get you!'

'I have to go down to telephone the police.' She tried to sound calm and reassuring.

In Dilys's room she found Monty's sister sitting on the end of the bed, clutching her left arm. 'That rock!' She pointed. 'It must have landed on my arm before it bounced off on to the floor. I'm afraid my arm may be broken. A good job it wasn't my head! It might have killed me.'

Daisy urged her to stay where she was until she had brought up a bucket and brush to clear up all the glass. 'Then we'll all go downstairs and have a cup of Ovaltine and wait for the police. How bad is your arm? Shall I send for the doctor?'

Dilys thought about it then shook her head. 'I can't feel any bits of broken bone so maybe it will just be a large bruise. I'll see the doctor in the morning surgery to make certain.'

Her voice was shaking but Daisy spent no further time with her. It seemed more sensible to alert the police. The man might be in the house but she doubted it. The bedroom windows were all on the first floor and if he had wanted to get inside, she reasoned, he would have broken in through a ground-floor window. But he might still be wandering the streets and the police might catch him if they were alerted in time.

The telephone conversation took less time than she expected. As she was unable to give a detailed description of who they thought the perpetrator might be, the police understandably had little to go on and, at such a late hour, very few constables were available to 'chase round the streets', as they put it. They would, however, send someone round to take statements and tomorrow, in daylight, they would check out the premises where the assault took place.

Daisy then put her next part of the plan into operation and carefully swept each bedroom before allowing the occupant to walk about. Twenty minutes later they gathered in the kitchen, warmly wrapped, hands clasped around mugs of Ovaltine which, Daisy hoped, would calm their nerves and help them recover from the shocks they had suffered.

Dilys was understandably the worst affected as she had been physically hurt and this was the second time she had been under threat. Ten minutes later she was still shivering intermittently and her face was chalk white. 'He might still be out there!' she whispered. 'He might be planning something else. Something worse!'

'Dilys, dear,' Monty said gently, 'I know you hate to be contradicted but it could hardly be much worse!'

'Of course it could!' She glared at her brother. 'He could be setting a fire! That would be worse!'

'Oh well,' he argued, 'if you look at it that way I dare say he could be rushing in with an axe to chop off our heads!'

Dilys screamed.

'Stop it!' cried Daisy, exasperated. She glared at Monty. 'You sound like two squabbling children! Haven't we got enough to worry about without you two making it worse? The police will be here soon so let's calm down and behave like grown-ups.' If that's possible, she thought. The hint of earlier family quarrels made her think that being an only child might have its compensations.

Abashed, Monty muttered an apology which his sister accepted with a bad grace and they relapsed into silence, sipping their Ovaltine and waiting for the police to arrive.

When a constable finally cycled up to the house nearly an hour later he was not in a very happy frame of mind. He made a whirlwind tour of the house and garden and declared the culprit 'long gone'. He took down a few notes which he promised to pass on to Constable Cresswell or the sergeant who was dealing with the case. 'When they've done looking for clues you can get a glazier to repair the windows.' He gave them a brief smile. 'You've got nothing to worry about now so go back to bed,' he advised as he climbed back on to his bicycle. 'If you *do* have any more alarms, telephone at once and we'll be with you as soon as we can.'

Hardly convincing, thought Daisy as she watched him go. But she did agree that a second visit seemed unlikely. She saw Dilys and Monty back into their respective bedrooms. When she finally fell into her own bed she promised herself time to think about Steven Anders but was, in fact, asleep within minutes.

The next morning found Albert, Hettie and a police sergeant discussing the recent events. Husband and wife sat on the sofa together looking up at the sergeant who sat on an upright chair. Hettie felt intimidated although she tried not to show it. In fact, she was put in mind of being sent to the headmistress while she was at boarding school for cheeking Mr Belling who had taught them geography. She felt that somehow the sergeant wanted to blame the family for what had happened and she resented it although secretly she was slowly coming to the same conclusion.

'So,' the sergeant said, 'you have no idea who might bear your family some kind of grudge – because that is how it looks to me. Too great a coincidence, wouldn't you say?'

Albert shook his head without answering.

'We have been speaking to your late housekeeper,' the sergeant continued, 'and I was given the impression that somewhere in your past there was trouble with a son.'

Hettie stifled a gasp. What on earth had that wretched woman been saying? She glanced at her husband whose mouth had fallen open.

He stammered, 'She had no right to discuss our family. No right at all. There is such a thing as confidentiality. My brother was much too lenient with her.'

'On the contrary,' he replied, 'withholding information where a crime has been committed, can be a punishable offence.'

Hettie felt her insides tremble. This was the past returning to haunt them, she thought fearfully. It was Albert's fault. He should never have married that dreadful woman, and their son was another mistake.

Albert drew a shaky breath and let it out slowly. 'Miss Dutton was right to an extent ... that is, I did have a son, Stanley, by my first wife but he has long been gone from our lives. He now lives and works in Ceylon.'

After a silence Hettie saw that Albert was unable to continue so she leaned forward. 'Stanley was a very wilful child and he grew into a troublesome young man who ... who went off the rails.'

The sergeant was now all attention. 'Go on.'

Albert was staring down at his folded hands. 'His behaviour became bizarre ... and bordering on dangerous. That is to say, we thought him a danger to himself and to others. He was quite wild and Monica, that was my first wife, thought he needed medical attention but she was terrified he would end up in an asylum.'

Hettie was now in shock for the second time that morning. When she married Albert she told him she did not want to hear a word about his son or his first wife. She wanted to start afresh as though nothing had happened before her marriage to Albert. It was the only way she could reconcile herself to what she had been told by others about her husband's stormy first marriage.

The sergeant held up his hand while he caught up with his note-taking. Hettie glanced at Albert and thought him strangely pale. This, she knew, must be very painful for him.

Albert said, 'So we sent him abroad to an old friend of mine – an old school friend in fact. He agreed that the discipline of the hard life out there would almost certainly help the boy.'

'The boy, Mr Pennington? How old was your son at this stage in the story?'

'Just nineteen.' His voice shook. 'Stanley didn't want to go. He begged us ... but we were desperate and Monica was so afraid for him. The mental aspect...'

'So he might have felt you were abandoning him.'

Albert hesitated. 'We were, I suppose ... if you look at it like that.'

'But you did it for the best.'

Albert nodded slowly. 'We never heard from him. He never answered our letters but John, that's my friend, he wrote once or twice but then even he gave up. I hoped Stanley would marry. Sometimes the love of a good woman will settle a young man...' He shrugged.

Hettie said, 'Don't blame yourself, Albert.'

'After he'd gone my wife had a ... a breakdown of some sort. The doctor said it was guilt. She became depressed and ... and was found in the river thirteen months later.'

Hettie put an arm round his shoulder and he glanced up at her in surprise and suddenly it was her turn to feel guilty. Maybe all those years ago she should have allowed her husband to talk to her about it. Perhaps she should have steeled herself to listen while he unburdened himself. The fate of his son and his wife must have weighed on his mind.

The sergeant looked from one to the other. 'Would you be surprised if this son decided to return to England ... and if so, is he capable of these acts of what might be revenge?'

Hettie almost held her breath. If this Stanley was back in England it was possible that he was trying to punish the family for what happened years earlier. She shivered. If he had stolen from Dilys and terrified Montague, what was he planning for his father?

Her stomach churned.

Albert said, 'I dare say he might but ... after all this time we didn't expect to see him again. Do you think we are in any danger, sergeant?'

'Hard to say but best be on the alert. Sensible precautions. You know what I mean.' He glanced through his earlier notes. 'Your sister thinks she may have recognized the man who was in the soup kitchen queue.'

Hettie said, 'She thought he whispered her name. So it could be Stanley. Does that mean you might be able to catch him?'

'If he goes back for more soup we might be lucky. I'll put one of my men on it – in civilian clothes, naturally. A uniform lurking nearby would set alarm bells ringing for him! We'll get your sister-in-law to identify him and Bob's your uncle!'

'She's in a frightful state about all this. I don't think she'll want to be anywhere near him!'

'If she wants him caught and put away she'll make the effort! So – his name's probably Stanley Pennington. Now we're getting somewhere. Thanks for your help. I'll get back to the station.'

When he'd gone Albert and Hettie sat in shocked silence for some time. Albert poured himself a large whisky and sat down with it, waiting for his wife to say something.

At last she said, 'Do you think it was a mistake to ... to send him away?'

'You didn't know him as we did. You would have wanted to get him out of your life. We told ourselves it was for his own good. That it would sort him out.' He took a large gulp of his whisky and closed his eyes. 'Monica was afraid of him. He had moments when he was almost violent and he threatened us on several occasions. It was frightful. We were trying to hide the fact from family and friends because...' He shook his head.

'You were ashamed of him?'

'Partly, but also ashamed of ourselves for not being able to deal with the problem. I made the decision and I was the one who had to tell him. After he'd gone I thought it was all over and we could lead a normal life but...'

Hettie waited but he didn't finish the sentence. 'You told me Monica died. You didn't say she drowned herself.'

'You said you didn't want to know the sordid details, remember?'

'No, I don't remember.'

'Well, take it from me, Hettie, you did say that and I was grateful for that because all I wanted to do was forget about him. It was a nightmare. I wanted to pretend it had never happened! How could I ask you to marry me with such a tragic past?'

They sat for some time in a brooding silence, avoiding eye contact.

Finally Hettie glanced at her husband. 'I wonder why he's come back to England. I wonder what happened to him over the past years.' She looked at him fearfully. 'Do *you* think he's come back looking for revenge?'

He swallowed the rest of his whisky and stared into the empty glass. 'It's beginning to look that way.'

Hettie felt the heat drain from her body as she studied her husband's face. He had not been strong enough to deal with the problem twenty years ago and he was no stronger now. Weaker, in fact. She shuddered as the realization hit her – Albert's worst nightmare was with them again.

Now that Dilys was staying with them, Daisy felt able to take a few hours off and go home to her mother. She sat sipping tea while Martha wrapped up a plum tart she had made for the Penningtons.

Daisy said, 'You'd like Steven, Ma. He speaks very nicely and he always looks clean and neat.'

'Nice fingernails?'

Daisy smothered a laugh. Her mother had a 'thing' about men's fingernails. 'Very nice.'

'Fingernails tell you a lot about a man. If he doesn't take pride in his fingernails then he has a low opinion of himself and you should be warned. I read that in a magazine. Teeth, too.' She laid the tart gently in the basket for Daisy to carry back with her.

Daisy steeled herself to tell her mother about the night's events. 'We had a bit of a scare last night,' she said, trying to sound as casual as possible. If her parents knew exactly what was going on they would insist that she came home at nights so she had decided to play down the event. 'Some idiot threw stones up at the back of the house and broke a window.'

Her mother stared at her. 'Lord love us! Whatever next? Poor old Monty. Must have given him a bit of a fright.'

'It gave us all a bit of a fright but the police came and sorted it out. They reckon it was the same chap that burgled Dilys. They'll catch him in no time.' She held her breath but there was no protest. She rushed on, reverting to the subject of her tea with Steven Anders. 'He said he can't wait for Saturday to come and neither can I. He must be quite clever, mustn't he, to work in a solicitor's office?'

'You'd think so.' She fixed her daughter with a stern look. 'Just remember what I've told you. No larking about. No kissing and cuddling – leastways not yet. You hardly know him and he might have a reputation

179

with the ladies. Good-looking men often do, so just be warned. Don't allow any liberties until you know him better.'

Daisy rolled her eyes. 'I know all that, Ma. You told me when I was going out with Tim from the dairy.'

'I don't care, Dais. You can't hear it too many times ... And remember what happened to young Tim?'

'His pa warned him off me. I didn't do anything. Tim was too young to start courting.'

'Well he was, wasn't he?'

'He's only a year younger than me!'

'But he's a boy and they grow up slower than girls. How old's this Steven fellow?'

'He didn't bother to tell me!' She tossed her head. 'And I didn't bother to ask! It's only tea and cakes at Miss Maude's. It might not last.' She crossed her fingers and hoped it would.

'Well, just be sensible – and if he does ask you out again, you tell him to collect you from here so I can get a look at him.'

'Yes Ma!' said Daisy but she made a note not to mention him again until matters between her and Steven were a little more definite.

While Dilys, Monty and Daisy were enjoying

their plum tart, Hettie and Albert were eating silently without speaking, each one busy with their own thoughts and afraid to air them. Hettie was struggling to swallow each mouthful but unwilling to share her fears with her husband. She was, in fact, terrified of the developing situation for which she held Albert responsible. He had behaved foolishly and his mistakes were coming back to haunt them. She was almost blameless, she told herself bitterly, but now she was embroiled in what promised to be a dangerous exchange between father and son. After what had happened to Dilys and Montague, she had no doubt that she and Albert would be the next victims.

But why, she argued, should she be punished for something Albert had done years before she even met him? It was grossly unfair so why had he so far failed to see this and to find a way to place her in a safer environment? Because, she told herself angrily, he was so selfish and was only thinking of himself.

He glanced up from his plate and she noticed that he was having no difficulty eating.

'Nice piece of cod,' he said.

'Is it?'

'Don't you think so, dear?'

'I haven't given it a thought, Albert. Too

much on my mind, I suppose. Too busy wondering what is going to happen when your wretched son gets round to us!'

He laid down his knife and fork then sighed. 'I was afraid of this – that you would panic, Hettie. Try to understand, dear, that if he tries to reach us, the police will be on to him in a flash. They said they would keep an eye out for him, remember?'

'And you think that is good enough? I don't. I think he will find a way to ... to hurt us. And what have I done to deserve such treatment?' She gave him a challenging look but her insides were tense. 'Why don't you think about me for a change?'

'Think about you in what way exactly?'

Hettie hesitated, seeing a red flush creep into his face. It wouldn't do to push him too far, she thought desperately. He was the right age for a heart attack. 'It doesn't matter. Forget what I said. Forget that I'm afraid. Don't give me another thought!'

She closed her eyes, annoyed with herself for allowing her resentment to be so obvious when he already had so much to regret. Pushing back her chair, she scrambled to her feet and, ignoring his cry of, 'Wait, Hettie!' almost ran from the room.

She locked herself in the bathroom and burst into angry tears but even while she sobbed, she realized that he had made no effort to come after her, and her sympathy for her husband began to evaporate further. He was a weak man. Always had been and always would be. Drawing a deep breath she dried her eyes on a nearby towel and stood up. Staring at her reflection, she said, 'It's up to you, Hettie. He'll do nothing.' But what could she do? What *should* she do?

Minutes later the idea came to her. Safety in numbers. She would ask her sister-in-law to come and stay with her for a few days. Then there would be three of them in the house and if the son tried anything they would outnumber him.

When approached, however, Dilys was not willing to stay with them. Her voice on the telephone was high with indignation. 'Come and stay? Are you mad, Hettie? Haven't I been through enough already – first in my own house and then here with Montague? Why should I put myself through anything else?'

Hettie cursed her stupidity. She had been a fool to ask.

Dilys said, 'Why don't you come to me? That would make more sense, surely. We could go back to my house. I can't face many more days here with Montague and the wretched Daisy. She does her best but...'

'But suppose this man—'

'He's not likely to come back here, is he?

183

You and Albert are the only ones he hasn't upset and you're the ones to blame!'

'I'm not to blame! It was nothing to do with me.'

'You're right, Hettie. I'm sorry. That was unfair of me. Look, come to me and we'll offer Miss Gray money to stay overnight for, say, one week. If we share the cost we can make it worth her while. She can't be that well off, can she? Just nights. Safety in numbers!'

'We–ell.' Hettie thought rapidly. 'If she'll come, I'll come. Let me know as soon as possible.'

Hettie went back into the dining room where Albert was enjoying a large helping of currant duff with custard. My God! she thought. You'd eat at your own funeral, given the chance! Aloud she explained that Dilys had asked her to go and stay.

'And you said "yes", I presume.' His expression was cold but Hettie was past caring. She would stay with Dilys and it would be a sort of holiday and a chance to get to know her better. They had never been close although they had found some common ground in their dislike of the wonderful Cressida-who-could-do-no-wrong!

The knots in her stomach were disappearing and she felt her fear lessening. Assuming that the promise of easy money would persuade Miss Gray to sleep there for a week, Hettie felt much better and went into her dressing room and began to pack.

EIGHT

Three days passed and the day of the Saturday soup kitchen arrived. A highly nervous Dilys waited in the Drill Hall for the distribution of food to begin. She was accompanied by a plain-clothes policeman who now stood with her, just out of sight of the window. They were discussing what she must do if she saw the man they suspected.

'This Stanley Pennington,' he asked. 'Run through the description again, please.'

'Tall, thin, unkempt-looking with intense eyes.' Dilys searched her memory for some more helpful details. Thin and unkempt could apply to many of the men. 'He'll be carrying his own bowl ... and he was wearing a very long coat. Shabby with no buttons...'

'Hair colour?'

'I thought I'd told you that already. It's thick and brown ... mid-brown you could call it. He had a sort of beard...'

'He might have shaved it off.'

'Possibly.' Dilys shrugged. 'And if I see him approaching me in the queue I must put down the ladle and tidy my hair – that's the signal – and you'll come out and I'll point to him...'

'That's right. You finger him and I'll have him in handcuffs before you can blink! No time for him to scarper. I don't want you to worry yourself, Mrs Maynard. It'll all be over in a minute or two. Then we'll have him behind bars and you can all sleep easy again.' He gave her a 'thumbs up' sign and grinned cheerfully.

Dilys gave him a weak smile. She had no real confidence in the plan and feared that if Stanley guessed what was about to happen he would certainly struggle and might make a run for it and might easily outrun the policeman. If he escaped capture he would know that she had 'fingered him', as the policeman so crudely put it. She would then be even more vulnerable. It was essential that he was caught and immediately put behind bars.

Miss Gray had agreed to sleep in the house for a few days but it was costing money that Dilys would have resented as outrageous in any other circumstances. Still, she could hardly complain if the woman would be sharing the risks with her and Hettie. Miss Gray's invalid brother had been extremely reluctant to let her do it and increasing the payment had been the only way to earn his approval.

Marguerite glanced at the large clock on the wall and said, 'Well now, ladies, we must make a start.'

They took up their positions and someone opened the door. Within seconds those first in the queue were jostling for position and demanding to know what was on offer. An old man with one sleeve pinned up looked enquiringly at Dilys.

'What ith it, mithuth?' he asked through several broken teeth.

She forced a bright smile. 'Potato and onion,' she told him, 'with some bits of ham thrown in for good measure. Very tasty. The alternative–' she indicated someone further along the tables – 'is beef gruel.'

He made his choice known by holding out his bowl and she emptied the ladle into it. 'Don't forget the bread,' she urged from habit although no one had ever done such a thing. She snatched a glance along the queue in search of Stanley but there was no sign of him. If he was present he must have changed his appearance and she did not know whether to be pleased or sorry. If he did put in an appearance, apprehending him would cause a scene which would no doubt find its way into the local paper which would be embarrassing. If he didn't come it meant he was still free to wreak havoc on their lives.

Marguerite whispered, 'Any sign of him?'

'Not so far but I don't—'

She was interrupted by the next person in the queue. 'What you got today then?'

Dilys recognized the deaf woman and described the soup in a loud clear voice. 'It's very nice, Mrs Carter,' she urged.

'I'll 'ave some,' she replied. 'I 'ope it's nice and 'ot. Warms the cockles of your 'eart, soup does, but not when it's lukewarm. I can't abide tepid soup.'

Dilys sneaked another glance at the door and for a moment her heart almost stopped beating. A tall thin man had come into the hall and, contrary to instructions, she stared at him. But he wore a hat jammed down over his hair, the wide brim hiding his face ... and he carried nothing in his hands. Did the absence of a bowl mean it was not him?

Seeing her reaction Marguerite looked at him. 'Is that the one?' she whispered.

'I don't know. I don't think so ... and yet it could be...' Gripped by indecision she watched as the queue shuffled past and the man drew nearer until he stood in front of her. Suddenly she recognized the very long buttonless coat and her throat dried. It was him! For a moment she was frozen with fear but then recalled the policeman's instruc-

tions and put down the ladle. As her hands
went up to tidy her hair the policeman leap-
ed forward, rushed towards him and grabbed hold of his arm.

'Got you!' he cried. He jerked him from
the queue and pushed him roughly against
the wall. There was an immediate outcry as
people scattered in alarm and then tried to
reclaim their places in the queue.

Marguerite said, 'They've caught him!'
and gave Dilys's shoulder a congratulatory
pat.

Dilys, unable to believe it was all over,
drew a long shuddering breath. The man was
now in handcuffs and the policeman beckoned her over. Abandoning her post at the
table, Dilys crossed the room and arrived
just in time to see the policeman remove the
man's hat. Stepping back hurriedly, she
gasped, 'Oh no!' because the man's head was
covered with short ginger hair. 'It's not him!'

He began to laugh.

Confused, Dilys turned to the policeman.
'But he's wearing the coat! The long coat
without buttons!'

'Claims his name is Sammy Coots.' The
policeman gave the man a shake. 'Where did
you get that coat?' he demanded.

'Swapped it, didn't I?'

'Who with?'

'That'd be telling, that would!'

Dilys longed to lay heavy hands on the wretch. She saw at once that Stanley had set this up to make fools of them; to prove how easily he could manipulate them all. Just one slap, she thought furiously, on that sly, grinning face!

Behind them people were sniggering behind their hands and she felt the colour rush back into her face.

The policeman gave him another shake. 'If you don't tell me before I count five I'll run you in for wasting police time!'

In a low voice, Dilys said, 'It's not him. You'll have to let him go.'

'That's for me to decide!' he snapped and Dilys realized that he, too, had been made to look foolish.

The policeman pulled him away from the wall then slammed him back against it.

Deciding the joke had gone far enough, the man cried, 'Hang on! I've not done nothing wrong! It's not a crime to swap me coat, is it?'

Dilys stammered, 'I'm sorry. It's not a crime but you have—'

The police glared at her. 'Let me do the talking, if you don't mind, Mrs Maynard. It is my job, after—'

The man interrupted. 'OK. I'll tell you. It was a tall chap. Staring sort of eyes. I don't know his name, I swear it. He come up to me and said, "A tanner for you if you swap coats with me," but I wasn't 'aving any of that old malarkey! I said, "What? Only sixpence?" So I got him up to a bob and *then* we swapped coats.' He sighed. 'Mine was older and thinner, see, but it still 'ad a bit of red silk lining *and* all the buttons bar one. *And* a little furry bit of collar. Pretty, it was, that red lining.' He peered down at his coat.

'This is better, though. Thicker, see. All I need is a bit of string to tie it round the middle.' He stuck his hands in the pockets and turned to and fro.

Like a woman showing off a new dress, thought Dilys, astonished by a sudden pang of compassion that swept through her.

Reluctantly the policeman took off the handcuffs and said 'Get to the end of the queue. You've lost your place and it serves you right. My advice to you is – don't mess with the police in future or you'll live to regret it!'

Sammy Coots sprang to attention and gave him a mock salute which earned him a heavy cuff round the ear but undeterred, he regained his balance and sauntered off to rejoin the queue to the accompaniment of a small round of applause.

Sick at heart, Dilys watched him go but the policeman shook his head as a look of keen disappointment replaced his earlier excitement.

'See what we have to put up with?' he asked. 'The scum of the earth!'

'I feel that it was all my fault,' Dilys offered with genuine regret. She felt guilty about the harsh treatment meted out to an innocent man. 'I should have waited a little longer to be sure.

'Not your fault, Mrs Maynard. You did your best. But a pity, nonetheless.'

'Stanley must be laughing at us, knowing how upset we must be.'

'Don't worry. We'll get Pennington eventually and then he'll laugh on the other side of his face! Don't give up hope. I'll get back to the station and write up my report.' He drew a long breath and let it out. 'Stanley Pennington is a sight too smart for his own good. He might have wrong-footed us this time but we'll get him. And I'll be keeping an eye on the other one. The ginger nut. Sammy Coots.' He nodded. 'I'll be breathing down his scrawny neck if he so much as sneezes on my beat!'

Dilys was deeply embarrassed by the mistake and when the ginger-haired man reached her she felt obliged to apologize. In a low voice she said, 'I'm sorry about all that. Please take this–' she slipped him a florin – 'and buy yourself a nice belt to go round the coat.'

He looked at her as though she was quite mad and said nothing but he took the money and slipped it into his pocket. When he'd passed along, Marguerite whispered, 'He'll probably steal a belt and spend all the money on drink!'

'I don't care!' Dilys felt her face redden. 'I need to feel better about it, that's all.' And just because he's homeless, she thought, it doesn't follow that he's a thief.

Later that evening when Dilys recounted the fiasco to Hettie over the telephone, she heard her sister-in-law laugh.

'It wasn't funny!' Dilys snapped. 'Just wait until it's your turn to be harassed.'

'I'm sorry, Dilys. It was the way you told it.'

'Well, the police don't find it funny, I can assure you of that.'

She wondered for a few moments, if she really did want Hettie to come and stay with her but, on reflection, thought she would go ahead with their plan. She said, 'Miss Gray starts tomorrow. She'll do the heavy work as usual but stay every night for a week, so come along any time after lunch and you can settle in.' Another thought struck her. 'I hope Albert didn't object to the idea.'

'He doesn't know yet,' Hettie told her. 'I know he'll raise all sorts of objections but it won't make me change my mind. This is his mess – his and Monica's – and I don't intend to be dragged into it.'

'Poor Monica,' Dilys said thoughtfully. 'You never met her and you shouldn't judge her too harshly. It's not really her fault that Stanley was sent away. It's a long time ago now, but I do recall that Albert had had enough of him and his wild ways and—'

'When you say "wild ways"...'

'He was wild in the sense of unpredictable and quarrelsome. Getting into mischief and being destructive. He had a terrible temper. John and I gave up visiting them.' She hesitated. 'This will sound terrible, Hettie, but one day they found their cat dead and Albert immediately blamed Stanley.'

'And was it him?'

'We never knew, for certain. Cats don't live forever. Monica confided one day that Stanley didn't seem able to accept that he had done anything wrong. Not ever. She felt that "the difference between right and wrong eluded him". Yet some days he was very pleasant ... but it never lasted. She wanted him to see a psychiatrist but Albert wouldn't hear of it. He was ashamed to think there might be anything wrong with the boy. Men are like that about their sons. If they are not perfect and reflect well on the parents...' She broke off, troubled by the unwelcome memories.

'So he chose to get rid of him?'

'That sounds very harsh but I dare say you're right. When Monica protested about the idea to send him to Ceylon, Albert told her it was either that or he would have him committed. Monica couldn't bear the idea of him being locked up and we had a family conference to decide what to do ... and it seemed kinder to give him another chance in a new country. We all just hoped for the best.'

Dilys heard Hettie's heartfelt sigh.

'And now, it seems, Dilys, that the pigeons are coming home to roost – with a vengeance!'

'Oh Hettie! I'm so sorry ... but what can be done now?'

'Nothing. There's no way to put things right. We just have to hope and pray that the police catch him before he kills the pair of us!'

Daisy decided it would look too eager to be on time so arrived five minutes early and waited on the other side of the street until it was five past. When she went in, however, Steven Anders was already seated at a table in the window and he had been watching her through the net curtains.

'Oh, you weren't!' Daisy cried, mortified.

195

'I was worried, Miss Letts,' he admitted. 'I thought you were changing your mind and I willed you to cross the road and come in – and you did!'

Daisy settled in her chair, patted her hair and treated him to a beaming smile. 'Suppose I had suddenly run off? What would you have done?'

'Run after you! What else could I do? The waiting has been forever!'

How wonderfully honest, she thought, surprised. 'I began to think there were more than twenty-four hours in each day!' she confessed.

The waitress arrived, notebook and pencil at the ready and looked from one to the other. 'Made up your minds?' she asked, 'or shall I come back in a couple of minutes.'

'That would be helpful. Thank you,' said Steven, picking up the menu and opening it. 'Let's see, they do a variety of sandwiches or scones with jam and cream. Or you can have something more substantial such as a poached or scrambled egg on toast.'

Or I could just sit here with you and not bother with the food, Daisy thought to herself but she said, 'I fancy the poached egg if that's not being too greedy.'

'Then we'll both have that,' he agreed quickly, 'and a pot of tea and a plateful of fancy cakes to follow. How does that sound,

Miss Letts?'

'Wonderful. This really is awfully kind of you ... Mr Anders.'

'I'd like us to use Christian names if you're willing. Miss Letts sounds so formal.'

'I am willing, Mr ... that is, Steven!' *More* than willing, she thought. I'd be utterly wretched if he hadn't suggested it.

He caught the waitress's gaze and she hurried back to take the order.

As soon as she had left them Steven thrust a hand into his jacket pocket and pulled out a small parcel wrapped in tissue paper. Startled, Daisy stared at him.

'You must forgive me,' he said. 'It's just a little gift – of no real value, but as soon as I saw it I thought you would like it.' He looked at her anxiously.

'I do forgive you,' she told him, reaching out for it. She opened it excitedly and found a small pink velvet pincushion in the shape of a mouse. The eyes were two small buttons and the tail was narrow pink ribbon. 'Oh, how sweet!' she cried, utterly entranced. 'I love it! I shall throw away my old one and use this one instead – although it will be difficult to stick pins into such a nice mouse!' She looked at him with shining eyes. 'Thank you so much ... Steven.'

'I'm glad you like it. I found it in the market yesterday on a stall for raising money.

197

Everything on the stall was handmade by the Ladies Group. They raise money to help fund the soup kitchen.'

Daisy's eyes widened. 'I know one of those ladies,' she told him and explained that Dilys Maynard was a member of the group, and that snippet of information led to an account of the trouble the Pennington family was having.

Steven's expression changed as he listened to her account of Dilys's robbery and Monty's broken windows.

'I wish you weren't working for them, Daisy,' he confessed. 'It sounds as though you've been lucky that no one has been hurt. Mr Pennington had no right you ask you to stay overnight in that house after what had happened.'

'But it hadn't happened then. He asked me because the housekeeper had left suddenly and he was afraid to be alone. The burglary happened later.'

'Even so, I wouldn't like anything to happen to you, Daisy. Looking after him is quite a responsibility and you're rather young ... at least, you look young.' He flushed. 'That is—'

'I'm nearly eighteen,' she told him, touched by his concern for her welfare. 'It's a rather big house and I didn't like to think of him all alone at night and frightened because at the time he'd been a semi-invalid for years and—'

'Isn't he now?'

'No.' She regarded him proudly. 'I discovered that he wasn't ill or anything so I persuaded him to get up and about and now he quite likes it – being mobile again, I mean, and not stuck in his room with no one to talk to.'

'You really are an amazing girl, Miss – I mean Daisy.' After a moment's deliberation Steven said, 'I could take a quick look at some of the family documents, if you like. It's strictly against the rules but...'

Daisy was immediately torn. Part of her was thrilled with the idea of learning more about Monty's family but she understood the risks he would be taking.

'I don't want you to get into any trouble on my account,' she told him. 'Perhaps you'd better not.'

'I'll be careful, Daisy, but I won't do it if you don't want me to.'

Daisy hesitated. 'I must admit I'd be interested to know more,' she confessed.

He smiled. 'I won't promise anything but I'll see what I can do. It will be our secret.'

'I promise I won't tell a soul!'

The waitress returned with the poached eggs and saw the mouse pincushion.

'That's so pretty,' she said as she set down

the plates.

'It's a present,' Daisy said proudly, with a glance at Steven.

The eggs were just how Daisy liked them, without the uncooked white that always spoiled eggs for her. By the time they had finished off the cakes and had a second pot of tea, they reluctantly parted. Steven made no attempt to kiss her but he did hold her hand for a long time and Daisy parted from him with the promise of another meeting ringing in her ears and the precious velvet pincushion clutched tightly in her hand.

Daisy went straight home to tell her mother all about her time with Steven Anders and her mother listened eagerly without interruption but followed her self-imposed silence with a string of questions. How old was this Steven? Was Daisy sure he was single and not already walking out with another young woman? Were his intentions honourable? When was she going to bring him home so that they could meet him and hopefully approve the friendship?

Daisy did *not* tell her mother anything about Steven's promise to see what he could learn about the Pennington family. That seemed a step too far. But she remained intensely curious and looked forward to learning more about the family with which she was so closely involved.

'So the two of you are meeting up again?' her mother asked.

'Yes. That is he said so ... and I believe him.'

'I shall feel a lot happier when we've met him, Daisy. You must let him know that. Young men these days sometimes feel it's their right to take liberties with a young woman and you are very young.'

'Nearly eighteen, Ma!' Daisy reminded her. 'You married Dad when you were nineteen.'

'Things were different then, Dais. Things were simpler ... more straightforward.' She took a deep breath. 'Look Daisy, there's something we need to talk about. You do know, Dais, that your pa and me ... Well, we've always done our best by you.'

Daisy nodded. She was only half listening and her eyes were on the velvet mouse. She would treasure it all her life, she vowed silently, and she would never, *never* stick pins in it! It was a token of Steven's love for her. Well, maybe not *love*. Not yet. But a token of something ... maybe of his interest in her...

'Daisy! Are you listening? This is important.'

'I'm listening, Ma!' Daisy insisted untruthfully.

'The thing is that we love you, Daisy, as

any real mother and father love their children.' She looked at Daisy earnestly, her face slightly flushed. 'To us you truly are our daughter. Nothing will ever change that, you see. Nothing can ever change the way we feel about you so you mustn't think that anything we tell you will alter that.' She waited for a reaction but when none came she said, 'Do you understand, Dais?'

'Yes, Ma. I do.' Daisy pressed the mouse to her lips. I know he loves me! I *know* he does! she thought. She closed her eyes, wrapped up in her new found joy.

Her mother laid a shaking hand on Daisy's shoulder and searched for the right words. 'Sometimes, Dais, a woman finds it hard to have a child and ... and *cannot* have one so she, I mean they – her pa and ma have to ... to find a child to love and your father and I ... Are you listening, Daisy?'

'Yes, Ma!' Daisy glanced at the clock and jumped to her feet. She threw her arms round her mother and said, 'Say "love to Pa" for me. Tell him he'll like Steven! You both will.' But not as much as I do! she thought. 'I'm going to be late back at work. 'Bye for now.' She kissed her mother and almost ran from the cottage. Maybe this time next year she would be living with Steven as a married woman! With her face aglow at this wonderful prospect, she hurried back along the lane to see what, if anything, had happened during her absence.

Behind her in the cottage, her mother rested her arms on the table, laid her head on her arms and began to cry.

When Tom came home later that day, Martha told him about the new young man in Daisy's life and spoke about the Penningtons.

'I don't understand why they are being pestered by this wretched man,' she told him. 'I wonder if we ought to take Daisy away from there until the police catch him. Then she could go back.' She looked at him anxiously as she stirred the stew. 'She might be in danger.'

Tom frowned in concentration. 'We can't make her, Martha, and you know how determined she can be.'

'Determined? Stubborn, you mean!'

'Well ... yes. She does dig her heels in sometimes.' He sighed. It had been a long day and they had got very little work done. The bay had gone lame and they needed both horses to pull the harrow.

A day wasted meant a day's money lost and the boss wasn't too pleased about it although he couldn't blame Tom. A horse was a finicky creature and could go lame at the drop of a hat!

He became aware that his wife was looking at him, waiting for an answer to something she had said that he had missed. 'What's that again?' he asked.

She was ladling stew on to his plate. 'I said we should never have agreed to let her stay there overnight with old Pennington, they're a funny lot. But the money's useful and they're not too far away and she seems to like it there.'

He stared hard at her, for the first time noticing her reddened eyes. 'You been crying? You have! What's going on, love?'

'It was nothing really but...' She swallowed hard.

'It must be something.'

'It was just ... I suddenly felt like Daisy was going to leave us before long and I ... I tried to tell her about the adoption and she wasn't even listening! All she could talk about was this young man ... and he'd given her a pincushion like a mouse ... velvet with a ribbon for a tail. You'd think it was a diamond ring!' She swallowed. 'And I thought I was trying so hard and telling it rather well so as it wouldn't come as a shock–' suddenly her eyes filled with tears again – 'and all she could think about was the stupid mouse!'

Tom hid a smile.

'I'm telling you, Tom, she wasn't even listening to me! It was so important but she didn't take a word in and next minute she'd gone dancing off, back to the Penningtons without a care in the world!'

Tom searched for the right words. 'Maybe it was for the best.'

As he feared she seized on them. 'How for the best exactly?'

'That she didn't take it all in. I mean she was so happy perhaps it was the wrong time to give her a shock. To bring her down to earth, like.'

Brushing away her tears, she stared at him. 'Do you think so, Tom? Really?'

'I reckon so.' He held his breath.

'Perhaps you're right,' she said hopefully. 'Better to tell her when she's a bit calmer, eh?'

'I reckon so.' Tom handed her a none-too-clean handkerchief. 'Eat your dinner, love. It's getting cold.' He pushed a mouthful of potato into his mouth, watching her warily. One thing he hated was women's tears. He never knew what to say and whatever he said seemed to come out wrong. If he tried to cheer her up, she needed sympathy. If he offered sympathy it seemed that all she wanted was to be cheered up. Now he decided to take a chance. 'Cheer up, lass!' he advised. 'You can talk to her some other time. Any rate, most likely some of the words sunk in without her noticing.'

'It's not an easy thing to talk about, Tom,' she told him earnestly, pushing food on to her fork. 'You try. See just how hard it is. It's so important to get the words right so she isn't upset. She thinks I'm her ma and I'm not. She thinks you're her pa—'

'You are her mother, Martha!' He stopped eating. 'And so am I – her father, I mean! We're all she ever had, all her life. She'll understand. She's bright, is Dais. She'll see how lucky she was to come to us who really wanted her. Her real mother didn't or couldn't. Who knows or cares? Dais came to us and we've loved her every minute and done the best we could for her. She might have gone to an orphanage and been one of dozens of children!'

'But Tom—'

'Eat your dinner!' The words came out harder than he expected but he knew he was in a strange land where he rarely put a foot right. Like walking across a rain-sodden moor, he thought, and putting your foot in a boggy hole and being sucked under.

The silence grew and Tom felt the food beginning to stick in his throat but at least she was eating again and he felt hopeful that maybe she was over the worst.

At last she said, 'I have a feeling about this Steven Anders fellow. It might be serious between them.'

He didn't answer. A 'Steven Anders fellow'. Was that good or bad, he wondered. To change the subject he said, 'Those Penningtons – it's not an uncommon name round here. There was a woman used to come to the farm especially to see the horses and we'd exchange a few words.' She was listening so he rushed on. 'Nice woman. A bit highfalutin' but nice enough. She came every Saturday for eggs and cream and honey. So she said. But always came to see the horses and ask after the family. She knew we had a daughter and she was interested. Christina – that was her name.' He frowned. 'No. It wasn't … but summat like that like that. Cassandra! That was it. Or was it? Anyway, she brought a few carrots for the horses. But she was always pleasant. Always asked after Daisy.'

'Doesn't she still come?'

He shook his head. 'No. It was years ago. Died in an accident … Had a fall – summat of the sort.' He could see he had distracted her and felt rather pleased with himself.

Martha said, 'Asked after Daisy? You never told me.'

'Nothing to tell, really.'

Martha sighed then frowned. 'Come to think of it there's another Pennington on the far side of Bath – a vicar. Or maybe not.' She sighed, pushing her unfinished food away.

'Anyway, if Dais mentions this Steven you'll know who he is. Be nice about him, Tom.' She smiled. 'I know you. Don't ask too many questions. Let her tell you in her own way.'

'Anything you say, Martha.' He leaned over and kissed her. 'And don't worry about anything. Things'll work out. They always do.'

She managed a smile. 'Let's hope you're right.'

Hettie took a deep breath and looked her husband squarely in the eyes. 'Why am I packing? Because I'm going to stay with Dilys for a few days, Albert. She's moving back to her own house.'

He glared from the doorway. 'And when were you going to tell me? Or was I supposed to guess?'

'I started to tell you earlier but you said you were reading and asked if whatever it was could wait! Snapped my head off, if you remember!' She picked out a pair of black leather shoes and slipped them into a shoe bag. 'And before you ask me not to go I'll tell you I'm determined. I can't let Dilys down now. She's expecting me.' Had she packed enough, she wondered. A nightdress, underwear, a dressing gown and slippers. She turned to the dressing table for her hair brush and mirror. Maybe a warm cardigan?

'And when are you coming back?' He advanced into the bedroom and stood with his arms folded.

'When they catch Stanley and not a moment sooner. I did suggest that we went away for a few days ... to a hotel or somewhere. That way when he comes for us we would be absent but oh no! You wouldn't even consider it.' She straightened up and pushed back a lock of hair. 'You may not mind being a sitting duck but I'm weaker than you, Albert. The idea of staying here, just waiting for a stone through the window or worse ... I can't do it. So I'm going to stay with Dilys until the police have him behind bars.'

Albert frowned unhappily. He did not care for the idea of a son in prison even though it might be better than a son who was roaming the streets, intent on mischief. Why, he wondered, were women always wanting children? He could not subscribe to the theory that children kept a family together. It certainly didn't apply in his own case. They were disruptive, expensive – at least Stanley was. The least said about Stanley the better! George was not so bad but Albert could not put his hand on his heart and say he had enjoyed him as a child either although Hettie had been close to the boy. He shook his head ruefully. Stanley had caused a rift between him and Monica ... With a start he returned to the present.

'You and Dilys will be at each other's throat in no time,' he warned. 'You have never really liked her.'

'Only because she didn't like me. Cressida was much nicer to me than Dilys was.'

'Cressida was nice to everyone!'

'She was certainly nice to you! And you lapped it up. We all noticed it. Dilys certainly did. She said on one occasion that you were practically *ogling* her!'

Albert's heart gave a small lurch at the memories. 'If I did she didn't seem to object!' he snapped. 'And Montague was such a dull old stick! Why she ever married him is a mystery to me.' He walked past her and stared down into the street, trying to hide his discomfort because he *had* thought no one had noticed his philandering ways. He had had a way with women in those days and had always enjoyed the thrill of the chase. 'Anyway, that was years ago,' he said. 'Water under the bridge.'

She gave him a poisonous look. 'If you say so, Albert.' Riffling through the wardrobe she selected a warm tweed skirt and jacket. 'Your son is here in Bath to make trouble, Albert, so be on your guard. Lord knows what he means to do but he is here to get some sort of revenge. I had nothing to do with sending him away so I don't see why I should stay here and be terrified. He might kill you! Have you thought of that. If I stay he might kill us both!'

Turning, he faced her, leaning back against the window. 'He's hardly going to kill anyone, Hettie. He's not a murderer – just very disturbed. Always has been. Really, Hettie, you do love to exaggerate. Always have.' He crossed to the door, trying to appear nonchalant. 'Well, you must do as you wish. I'm not going to try and stop you even if you hope I will.'

'You couldn't stop me, Albert! Ten minutes and I'll be gone. I've ordered a taxi.' She surveyed the contents of her case and, satisfied, closed the lid. 'You could carry this down to the front door for me if you wish.'

'I don't wish to. Carry it yourself!'

He made his exit and Hettie listened to his muffled footsteps on the carpet as he made his way along the passage. She had a sudden moment of doubt as she pulled on her coat but she forced it back and reached for the case which was heavier than expected. She dragged it to the top of the stairs and dropped it down, one step at a time, and was at the front step and waiting when the taxi arrived.

NINE

The taxi picked up Hettie and then made a detour to Alexander Park to collect Dilys, and the two women drove away together looking vaguely triumphant. Daisy watched them go from the front step and then returned to the kitchen where Monty was busy at the big table, applying polish to his best shoes. The polish, brushes and cloths were neatly arranged on a sheet of *The Times* and the rest of his shoes waited in a basket at his feet for their turn for attention. Daisy had discovered that keeping Monty happily occupied prevented him from becoming bored and tetchy.

He glanced up and, referring to Hettie and Dilys, said 'Good luck to them! I'll give those two three days and then they'll be squabbling like school children. They've always maintained what I saw as a well-mannered truce but they've never lived in the same house before.'

'Why should they squabble?'

He shrugged. 'Women are funny creatures!'

'Not half as funny as men!' Daisy picked up a finished shoe and nodded. 'Quite a nice shine!'

'Thank you, ma'am!' He grinned. 'Maybe I could get a job as a shoeshine boy!'

'A job? You don't need a job!'

'How do you know what I need, Daisy? Just because I live in a biggish house it doesn't mean I'm rich. As a matter of fact I shall have to send for Mr Desmond soon and have a chat with him about the family money. It might just see me out but the house needs some maintenance which I can't put off forever.'

'You could send for Steven Anders!'

'I'm afraid he's too young and probably inexperienced. You said he's only been with the firm for a few months. No, it will have to be Mr Desmond or his partner.' He tutted as he reached into the box at his feet and found a sturdy pair of muddy boots. 'It's a mistake, Daisy, to live too long.'

'I'll try and remember that!' She watched him reach for the brown polish. 'You can't put polish over mud!' she scolded. 'You'll have to wipe off the mud and then let them dry before you polish them.' Seeing his look of dismay she said, 'Give them to me. I'll do it.'

He surrendered them willingly. 'I can tell that Hettie is becoming impatient. She pass-

ed comment several times when she last telephoned, hinting about finances and hinting
at Cressida's money but I told her – Cressida's money is not family money. Cressida
brought money into the family and she
managed it herself. I didn't need it and later
she insisted that she had plans for it.'

'What sort of plans?' Daisy asked, intrigued.

'She wouldn't tell me but she left a will
that was to be read at the end of 1902. It's
always been a bit of a mystery.'

Daisy stared at him. 'But that's quite soon!
It's 1902 and almost November.'

'Is it? Are you sure?'

'I tell you it is!' She darted to the calendar
which hung from a hook on the dresser.
'There! This is the last week of October – the
twenty-fifth, in fact. Only a few more days
and it will be November and then Decem-
ber.' Her face fell. 'Will I still be here then?
Suppose the new housekeeper doesn't like
me or ... or says she can manage without
me?'

'I'll tell whoever it is that you go with the
job!'

'Thank you!'

'So don't think about marrying that young
man – at least not yet!'

'*Marrying* him? Good heavens! It never
entered my head. I hardly know him.' In case

214

her expression betrayed her, Daisy fussed over the boots and then handed them back to their owner. 'You see? Now you must let them dry.'

She turned away, reached for a wiping-up cloth and started to wipe the clean washing up which was stacked on the draining board.

Monty looked at her thoughtfully. 'Cressida used to say that women were harder to understand than men and prone to making rash decisions. The heart ruling the head. That sort of thing. She was a deep thinker. Took life very seriously.' He sighed.

'What happened to her?'

Monty settled the boots in his lap. 'It was an accident – some time after she came back from Switzerland. She'd been staying with an aunt over there, an aunt who had no one and was in rather desperate straits. Very depressed. A clinical depression – that's what Cressida called it. She was there for ages – four or five months ... I missed her terribly.'

'It was very kind of her, wasn't it.' Daisy tried to imagine herself as a selfless heroine. 'She must have been a very caring sort of person to go all that way, and live in a cold place surrounded by all those mountains and things. Very different from Bath I should think. Mountain goats and pine trees and all that snow!'

Monty nodded. 'When she came home I

could see a change in her. She was very quiet and withdrawn. I suppose that's the best word for her mood. Living with a depressed aunt would be awful for her. She was naturally a sunny soul.' He smiled at the memory.

'Had the aunt recovered, then?'

'No but she was going into a clinic and didn't need Cressida.' He frowned. 'My poor wife was badly affected by that stay. I should never have allowed her to go but she insisted. She wouldn't talk about it when she returned. Said it preyed on her mind and she would rather not think about it. I thought she would eventually get over it but she didn't. It changed her somehow. One day while I was out she must have tripped at the top of the stairs and banged her head on the way down. That's what the doctor thought had happened.'

'Was she still conscious? I mean, did she know you?'

'No. That was the dreadful part of it. She was already dead so we had no time to say our "goodbyes" the way you can if you know the end is near. Poor Cressida.'

'It must have been awful for you.'

He nodded, saying nothing, then began to polish one of the boots.

Daisy said earnestly, 'But you have to tell yourself that she had a happy life and a happy marriage to you. You were everything to her, Monty. I'm sure you were and that must be comforting.'

'I see that now but at the time there seemed no way to gain any comfort. Our whole life together ended – just like that!'

He was becoming saddened by the memories, thought Daisy and searched for a more cheerful subject without being too obvious. 'At least you had your family to support you.'

After a moment he said, 'They weren't as supportive as I would have expected, to tell you the truth. Hettie had always been jealous of Cressida because she was so beautiful and had such a sweet nature. Her hair was her crowning glory – deep auburn waves. Of course she wore it up most of the time but when she was ready for bed, in a white night-dress, with her hair down over her shoulders ... she always reminded me of an angel.'

'An angel? Goodness!' Daisy was impressed but she, too, was aware of a twinge of jealousy and wished that her own ginger hair was instead a deep auburn, and that the bouncy curls were gentle waves. No one could accuse her of looking angelic, Daisy reflected. She was also beginning to see that the wonderful Cressida had not entirely endeared herself to her sisters-in-law ... but through no fault of her own.

Monty said, 'Hettie came to the funeral

dressed to kill! She had obviously spent a fortune on new clothes and had had her hair newly styled. Everyone was looking at her. She looked quite ... Well, almost smug.'

'Hettie did? Oh how awful!'

'Yes, smug. That's the word exactly. I think she felt that with Cressida lying in her coffin, Hettie could finally shine.' His tone was bitter. 'She seemed to flaunt herself, even Albert could see what she was doing. He was embarrassed. I've never forgiven her ... You could say it was Cressida's day but Hettie stole it.'

Daisy hid her sense of shock. 'What a pity you had no children,' she said desperately. 'They would have supported you.'

'But then when Cressida died they would have lost their mother and that would have made the tragedy even worse!'

'I suppose so. I hadn't thought of that.'

After a long silence he made an effort to lighten the atmosphere. 'Well now, Daisy, I've finished the shoes. If you have no other little tasks for me I think I'll finish my newspaper. I'll be in the sitting room.'

'And you'll want a pot of tea.'

'Yes please.'

She watched him go, thinking about the long-dead Cressida and the abrupt end to their marriage. There was no way she could undo the past but perhaps she could cheer him up. She took the biscuit tin from the cupboard and picked out a selection of his favourite biscuits – two garibaldis, one chocolate wafer and one with pink icing. She then weakened, popped the pink one into her own mouth and replaced it with a custard cream.

Albert awoke the next morning to the sound of rain pounding the roof of the garden shed. 'Sunday,' he muttered. 'A day of rest!' He laughed bitterly then was immediately seized with a feeling of panic. Hettie was gone to stay with Dilys and he was alone in the house. Somehow he must force himself to get out of bed and go downstairs and see if Stanley had visited him during the night. To see what if anything was missing or damaged. And if it were so, what would he do? Alert the police? At least he had not been murdered during the hours of darkness – or even attacked. He had heard no windows being smashed ... but he was a sound sleeper and anything might have happened of which he was unaware.

'If nothing's happened, Hettie will look such a fool!' he muttered as he pushed his feet into his slippers and reached for his dressing gown. He would take it carefully, he told himself, just in case Stanley had found a way in and was waiting for him – lurking round a corner or hiding in the shadows. He picked up the poker on his way to the bedroom door and stepped out on to the landing. His throat was dry as he waited for a sound that might indicate the presence of someone else.

'Who's there?' he called, in what was meant to be a strong voice but which came out with a tell-tale tremor.

There was no answer which was a relief – except that it meant if Stanley *were* to be present, he must be hiding. Albert moved slowly towards the top of the stairs, throwing open each bedroom door as he passed it, and casting a quick, anxious glance inside. No sign of anyone.

With several cautious glances behind him, Albert moved down the stairs. He might be in the sitting room, he thought and imagined his son relaxed in an armchair, his intentions hidden behind a smile. What should he do, Albert wondered, if he *did* find his son on the premises? He could rush from the house, screaming for the police – but how stupid that would look to an outsider! The neighbours would think he was mad to be afraid of his own son.

The sitting-room door creaked as he pushed it open but a quick survey of the room disclosed no occupant. He uttered up a silent prayer and began to feel a little more hopeful. Another positive sign was that there seemed to be no signs of disruption and no hint that anyone had been in the house. Furniture, cushions, pot plants – all seemed to be exactly as they had been when he went to bed the previous night.

At the very moment that Albert decided he had been spared an unwelcome visit he felt the first flutter of pain near his heart. It came and went. He closed his eyes thankfully and made his way into the kitchen. The pain came again but briefly and he instinctively put a hand to his heart. The sun was streaming through the large kitchen window as he sank gratefully on to a stool.

'Fright!' he said aloud. 'Panic. Nothing more.' He wondered whether to make a pot of tea or to go back to the sitting room and pour himself a whisky. He had just decided that alcohol would be the best stimulant when he caught his breath in alarm. A letter lay on the kitchen table. For a moment he froze. *Stanley had come and gone!*

He said, 'Oh God!' but dared not touch the letter. He read the word scribbled on the envelope.

FATHER. The letters were heavy and uneven and written in black ink.

He sank down on to a chair, his heart pounding in earnest now and the pain returning. 'Damn you!' he muttered. 'Damn you to Hell!' He looked round the kitchen wondering how Stanley had gained access to the house. And what had he done while he was in the house and Albert was asleep? Had he stared down at him as he lay defenceless? Had he toured the house, maybe taking small items, the way he had done with Dilys?

With shaking fingers he opened the envelope and drew out a single sheet of expensive cream paper which matched the envelope. *The bastard has used my own note-paper!* He swore under his breath and then repeated the word aloud. There were five words on the sheet, written in the same fierce, unsteady hand:

THERE WILL BE A RECKONING!

'What have I done to deserve this?' he whispered. But he knew the answer. He had buckled under the pressure of his wild, un-manageable son and had sent him as far away as possible. 'Hoping never to set eyes on you again!' he told his absent son. He had sent him away against the wishes of his wife, having persuaded her that he was trying to give Stanley a fresh start in life.

The truth was he had craved a fresh start in his own life, without the overwhelming pressure of failed attempts at discipline, breakdowns of communications, screams of recriminations and regular outbursts of furious, sometimes frightening temper – his own and his son's.

'You had to go!' he whispered. The boy had been a threat to his marriage and there had been no one to advise them. No one to turn to. Montague had found their rare visits unsettling and quickly realized that they could offer no help. Dilys had been frightened of her nephew and kept her distance. The last straw had been a manic outburst on the boy's part in public and the police had been called. Stanley should have been up before the magistrate on charges of 'wounding with intent' but, 'to protect him', Albert had had Stanley shipped abroad.

'There will be a reckoning!' There was no sense of shock. Albert had felt for years that his betrayal of his son would one day come back to haunt him. That day was dangerously close.

Stanley sat outside Sally Lunn's Refreshment House listening to the church bells and watching the people hurrying past on their way to church. He sat with his back to the wall and patted the dog he had borrowed from another homeless man for the price of a sixpence. It was well known that, for a beggar, the addition of a sad-eyed dog would soften the hearts of passers-by and open the purses of kind-hearted matrons busy about their shopping, or younger women on their way to meet friends and chat over tea and cakes in the Pump Room.

Stanley was hungry but he felt relaxed and almost cheerful as he considered his recent adventures. He had put the fear of God into his family and had now sent a chilling warning to his father. He had no doubt that, alone in the house, Albert Pennington would be frightened by the note he had left the previous night. Now the problem was to decide what to do about it. He rather drew the line at murder although he had once killed a man but it had been an accident – a drunken fight soon after he reached the plantation and started the job which was meant to be the making of him! Instead it had undone him totally. Ironic, that.

'Eleven years for manslaughter!' he muttered and his face crumpled into a twisted smile. 'Did you ever know that, Father?' Of course you didn't. Because you didn't make contact. Because you didn't want to know what happened to me. I was nineteen years old, Father, and sick in my mind. 'Only nineteen.' He glanced at the dog – a rough-haired mongrel – and it cocked his head on one side as though it was listening. 'He didn't try to find out what was happening to me once I had been spirited away out of sight.' No doubt he breathed a sigh of relief, thought Stanley, and carried on happily with his own life while I languished in prison doing hard labour and fighting my corner day after day, week after week, for what seemed an eternity!

A well-dressed woman stopped and eyed him sympathetically. 'Are you ill?' she demanded. 'You look ill.' She was very overweight, her ankles swollen over her shoes, her powdered face plain.

'Ill?' he replied. 'I'm dying, ma'am. Slowly but surely.' That was true. Everyone on the planet was heading towards their death.

'Dying? Oh dear! What is your ailment exactly?'

'It's a foreign disease. I've been working abroad in Ceylon.'

'Working abroad' sounded respectable, he thought, and it was the truth. Working in a prison gang would certainly classify as work by anyone's standard.

Their conversation was attracting attention and a middle-aged man carrying a silver-topped cane also paused to examine him through narrowed eyes.

Stanley picked up his tin mug and rattled it hopefully but the man ignored it and asked suspiciously, 'What sort of foreign disease would that be?'

'Something like malaria – only much

worse. Gets into the bones and then you're done for! You can never get rid of it.' Stanley prayed silently that the man was not a doctor.

The man said, 'Being ill doesn't mean you can't get your hair cut and have a wash, does it. You look disgusting. A disgrace to the town of Bath!'

The woman bridled. 'The poor man obviously doesn't have any money! How can he afford a barber? He may not even have a home!'

'He can afford a dog!'

Stanley said, 'I'm looking after it for a friend.'

The man sniffed to indicate his disbelief in Stanley's story, rolled his eyes then walked on, swinging his cane.

Stanley muttered 'Stupid old fart!' but only the dog heard his words. He barked in reply and Stanley grinned and patted him.

The woman hesitated, not wanting to admit that she had been affected by the man's hostile attitude. After a moment's thought she went into Sally Lunn's bakery and came out with a paper bag. Opening it she offered one of the two teacakes to Stanley and then began to feed the second bun to the dog!

She was feeding the damned dog! Stupid, ugly, fat old woman! With difficulty Stanley resisted the sudden familiar urge to scream the words aloud and hurl further abuse at her. He wanted to wipe the silly smile from her fat face and force the bun down her throat until she choked. Clenching his fists he closed his eyes as his head began to throb with the familiar pain as his anger sparked and flickered and a bitter resentment deepened, hurtling into hate. He was overcome with panic as his rage surfaced but a small voice within him warned that he dare not give way to his instincts – and certainly not here in the town, where his behaviour would be observed and reported to the authorities. *Hold back!* the small voice urged. If he laid so much as a finger on the wicked old crow he would almost certainly be arrested and then his long awaited chance for confrontation with his father would be gone.

Wrestling inwardly with his ungovernable temper, Stanley watched through half-closed eyes until the woman walked away then breathed deeply until she disappeared into the jostling crowd of passers-by, and he was able slowly but surely to control his emotions and to force his thoughts back to his father.

He could threaten to somehow reveal his father's callous behaviour ... or blackmail him for a large sum of money ... or insist on moving back into their home. A thin smile touched his gaunt face. That would put the frighteners on Hettie but would that be quite fair since she had not been around when it happened and his mother was long gone and cold in her grave.

'Mother did try to help me,' Stanley whispered, clutching for a small grain of comfort. She had tried to persuade his father to seek medical help for their difficult son – to no avail. 'But she wanted to help me.'

Swallowing hard, he brushed tears from his eyes. The dog was licking up the last of the crumbs as his real owner ambled up to collect the animal, elbowing his way through the narrow street, whistling aimlessly.

Maybe, thought Stanley, he would give his father another thrashing and leave it at that...

Daisy was delighted that she and Monty were alone again and she sensed that he, too, was relieved that his sister had moved out after a brief stay. He sat on a chair by the window of his bedroom while Daisy stripped the sheets from the bed and eased the pillow cases from the pillows.

She said, 'Wash day again. I've always hated Mondays. The smell of the soap and the steam and everything.'

Monty was in a world of his own and made no answer but finally he said, 'Dilys is a decent sort although I loathed her when we were children. Come to that I hated Albert, too. It's not easy being the first child in a family. The others come along and steal the limelight.'

'You're lucky to have a family,' Daisy retorted, pulling the linen into a bundle to be taken downstairs and soaked. 'It's not easy to be the only child, I can tell you. Because you're so important to your ma and pa and they've no one else to think about. If anything, you get too much attention.'

'But the first child gets used to the undivided attention and then along comes the second and he suddenly takes centre stage! I couldn't understand all the fuss about Albert – he was a baby and I was seven nearly eight and all he did was cry and wave his arms and legs about. Quite useless, I thought.'

Daisy grinned. 'I suppose at that age you didn't understand that you'd done exactly that when *you* were a baby.' She tossed the bundle of bedding out on to the landing and reached for two clean pillowslips. 'Aren't you going to offer to help?' she prompted.

He moved slowly to the bed and began clumsily to pull the second pillowslip into place over the pillow. 'And by the time I was adjusting to Albert being around along came Dilys and then my nose was definitely put out of joint because she was the little princess everyone could admire and she knew it. The trouble was that as she grew up she adored me and followed me around.'

Daisy giggled as she imagined it. 'Lucky you! No one adored me – except my parents. They were very down-to-earth about me but I think deep down they adored me.'

'What about your grandparents?'

'They didn't seem to take much interest. It didn't strike me as odd at the time but now I look back...' She shrugged. 'I asked my grandmother once if I took after her side of the family and she said, 'Hardly likely, Daisy.'

Tossing the under sheet on to the mattress she and Monty pulled it into place and tucked the sides and ends under the mattress.

He frowned. 'Hardly likely? Strange thing to say. You must have looked like one side or the other.'

'I thought so but Pa was always making jokes about the milkman which I didn't understand.' She shrugged as she shook out the top sheet. 'I like Dilys better than Hettie.'

'So do I,' Monty admitted. 'Hettie is a bit sharper. Maybe more self-centred. But I make allowances for her. When she married Albert he told her very little about his first marriage and I feel that is always a mistake. She was shocked when she found out about

Stanley.'

'But she had a son of her own.'

He shrugged. 'George Albert. Mm. A rather dull child, I'm afraid. I suspect the truth is that he and Hettie weren't particularly fond of children. *Any* children. Some people aren't. They can't help it.'

Together they finished making the bed and Daisy gathered up the bedding. 'I'll put these to soak in the copper.'

He nodded. 'I'll open the window a little wider to let the sun in and then I'll make us both a cup of tea.'

Daisy grinned. 'Wonders will never cease ... but thank you. I'd love one.'

Monday morning loomed large and, as always, Steven wondered where the weekend had gone. It was always the same. Mondays to Fridays dragged but Saturday and Sunday sped past so quickly that he barely had time to adjust to his weekend existence and never seemed to have made the most of his leisure time but didn't know who to blame.

As he stepped into the office, Steven glanced at the clock on the wall and reminded himself that as soon as he could afford it, he would buy himself a watch and chain for his waistcoat. Earlier he had planned for a heavy gold ring but since then he had raised his sights. Both Mr Marsh and Mr Desmond had watches – both gold and both frequently produced and glanced at in order to impress or hurry their clients. Steven felt at a distinct disadvantage without one.

Miss Field glanced up from her typing and said, 'Mr Desmond won't be in today. He has an infection caused by that tooth he had extracted. His wife says he is very poorly.' Miss Field was in her thirties and still unmarried. Steven considered her only mildly attractive but she had been hired for her typing and shorthand speeds and was excellent in those areas.

He said, 'Mr Marsh isn't here yet. What's his excuse.'

She shrugged then grinned. 'The morning after the night before!' she suggested.

They both laughed because Mr Marsh was a sidesman in his local church and allegedly strictly teetotal, but she had once seen a bottle of sherry in his desk drawer and had shared the discovery with Steven. Mr Marsh had once insisted the alcohol was for his favoured clients and not for himself. 'A small courtesy expected by some of my more important clients,' he had explained.

The telephone rang and was answered. When Miss Field hung up the receiver she said, 'Well! Mr Marsh isn't coming in either so it's just you and me!'

'What's *his* excuse?'

'He's got gout!'

'Gout! That's priceless!'

She gave him a reproving look. 'Gout is not at all funny. It's very painful. Agonizing. My uncle gets it and when he does, he can hardly walk!'

'I hope it's not catching!' he said flippantly and glanced round the office. 'So I'm in charge!' he remarked. 'You'll have to watch your Ps and Qs.'

Her eyes widened. 'You? Why should you be in charge? I've been here much longer than you have.'

'Maybe, but you're a secretary and I'm going to be a solicitor in due course.'

'But I've been here much longer than you, Mr Anders, and I've picked up lots of information along the way ... and I know where to find everything. I understand the business.'

'So when will you be taking your exams, Miss Field?'

'Never – but when will you be passing yours, Mr Anders?'

'I certainly expect to!' Steven was reluctantly impressed by her quick thinking and smiled. 'The thing is, I don't think the clients will be impressed if the office has been left in the charge of a secretary. It really has to be me, but if I get stuck I'll come to you for help. How's that?'

She nodded. 'Fair enough.'

Intrigued by the novelty of the situation Steven thought rapidly. This was his chance to impress the two partners with his capabilities. He said, 'If there are any telephone calls put them through to me at once. I'll be in Mr Desmond's office, checking his diary and also Mr Marsh's. I obviously cannot deal with everything but I'll let you know which appointments I shall have to rebook and you can notify them.'

Steven hoped he had surprised her by this display of efficiency and he walked out of the reception area with his head high – and his fingers crossed.

He was halfway through checking the day's appointments, deciding to deal with some of the easier ones and rescheduling others, when the idea came to him. This was an ideal opportunity to delve a little deeper into the Pennington family background – information which he knew would intrigue Daisy when they next met. Learning more background might also enable him to take over the Pennington family matters when one of the partners eventually retired.

Firstly, however, he talked with a man who had been left some Australian shares but was unsure how to claim them and convert them into cash. Steven did not know, either, but he promised he would take down the details, consult with whichever partner returned to the office first and then send written instructions.

After that there was a Mrs Burrows, recently widowed, who had had some repairs done to the roof of her cottage. Two days later it was leaking again and she was withholding the final payment. The builder was threatening to sue her and she needed advice on what to do next. Steven, feeling very professional, offered to write to the builder on her behalf, asking for details in writing of what had actually been done by way of a repair. She agreed with alacrity and he realized he was beginning to enjoy himself.

It was almost twelve when he at last found time to settle down and read through the first of the Pennington files. This dealt with Montague Pennington and appeared to be satisfactory with no surprises. The grandfather had been reluctant, on his death, to split the family money because this would mean diluting the impact of the inheritance. He had passed it on to his elder son, who had duly passed it on to his elder son, Montague, with the strict instructions that on Montague's death the money and the house would pass to his son (if there was one) or to his brother Albert.

'Hm. Interesting,' said Steven, wondering whether Albert had taken kindly to the news. He imagined that he would not have done so. 'I wouldn't be in his shoes!' he muttered.

He then set the files aside and went to lunch which consisted of a ham sandwich and a glass of ale at the 'Queen and Garter'.

He returned five minutes later than he should have done, to find Miss Field busy at work. With a reproachful look, she informed him that he was late and that a Miss Letts had telephoned and would call back later.

Steven still had half an hour to kill before the next client – a Mr Stubbs. He was a farmer who had rented a tractor for three days from a neighbouring farmer, by the name of Lennard. The plan was for Stubbs to see how he got along with the tractor, before he approached the bank about a loan to purchase one for himself. The tractor owner was now demanding more money because he claimed that Mr Stubbs had kept the tractor for ten days.

After some thought, Steven telephoned Mr Stubbs to hear his side of the story and having heard it, offered to make a telephone call to the tractor's owner asking him to come into the office instead and give *his* version of events. If necessary, he would then set up a meeting between the two parties at a later date and this Mr Stubbs agreed.

Feeling rather pleased with himself, Steven then returned to the Pennington files and delved deeper but was about to close them when he noticed a file for Cressida Pennington, the wife of Montague. He flipped it open and began to read and his eyes widened in astonishment. Headed 'Strictly Confidential' there were several documents concerning a child that had been born to her in Switzerland while she was staying with an aunt – a child who had subsequently been brought back to Britain and put up for private adoption.

Steven sat back in his chair and whistled. Daisy had told him that her employer was childless. Did this mean that the child was illegitimate? Or was there some other reason why Cressida Pennington had wanted to hide the child's birth from her husband and the family? Did Montague Pennington know about the existence of the child? In which case he must have agreed to the adoption...

Intrigued, Steven reread the details – at least those that were readily accessible but there was an envelope sealed with red wax that was to be opened when the child reached eighteen years. He puzzled over the possible contents but felt that he had probably gone as far as he could with that particular mystery. No doubt he would learn more before the end of the year when the envelope was opened. The gender of the child was not mentioned but if it were a boy he would then presumably be in line for the family money and Albert would have waited in vain to inherit.

He jumped when the telephone rang.

'Mr Lennard is here,' Miss Field told him.

'Please send him in.'

Steven closed Cressida Pennington's file and put it back with the rest of them in the cupboard. He would have some very interesting news to tell Daisy when they next met.

That evening, in the public bar of the 'Queen and Garter', nothing out of the ordinary was happening. The gas lights flared and spluttered; two mongrels eyed each other, lusting for a fight; a very old woman smoked a clay pipe and mumbled to herself, and Pete Lunnings sat in a corner with his legs sprawled out in front of him, eyeing the squat man who sat opposite.

'So what is it?' Lunnings asked, while his shifty eyes darted to and fro, alert for any sign of a policeman. This bar was his place of business and always had been and he knew all the regulars by sight. A stranger entering would be enough to make him take off through the back door into the alley and beyond. In his youth Pete Lunnings had been a cat burglar, aided by his slim, wiry frame which rendered most windows accessible from the outside. Later he had progressed and was now a fence, buying and selling from other thieves. The shady nature of the business of some of the 'Queen and Garter's' customers was well-known to the police but the odd raid was considered one of life's hazards by the customers and rarely made a dent in the amount of illicit trading that went on there.

The squat man squinted at Lunnings from beneath a thatch of dirty hair and whispered, 'Bracelet. Nice.'

'I'll be the judge of that. Let's see it then?' Lunnings's eyes narrowed. He had a face like a ferret and could have been any age from thirty to fifty.

The man took a small package from his coat pocket and slid it across the table. 'Good bit of stuff. Nice and weighty!' he insisted, throwing nervous glances in all directions.

'Hot, is it?' Be just like this fat little tyke, he thought, to offer him something the police were actively looking for. If they had put out a description he'd never sell it on. He'd been caught like that before.

'No, it's not hot! I'll bet they don't even know it's gone. I was in and out like a shot and—'

'Like a shot? You? Never. Look at the size of you! In and out in a pig's eye? Don't tell me! I don't need to know.' Lunnings lifted his glass and took a mouthful of ale before unwrapping the bracelet. It was a series of red stones set in gold filigree and Lunnings saw at once that it was indeed a 'good bit of stuff' and he knew he could sell it to a shady jeweller in the next town for eight or nine shillings. He wrapped it up and pushed it back across the table. 'It'd be difficult to shift,' he said dismissively. 'You keep it.'

'I don't want it!'

'Give it to the missus!'

'Silly cow's bunked off. Just give me a price.'

Studying the sawdust scattered generously over the floor, Lunnings made a pretence of thinking about it. 'Two bob!'

'Give over!' The squat man's mouth tightened.

''Alf a crown, then.' Lunnings shrugged. 'You're going to get lumbered with it, else.' He drank deeply, pretending disinterest.

'Three bob and it's yourn! That's a fair price, that is. You know it is. That's your last chance. Three bob or I take it away with me and someone with a bit more up 'ere–' he tapped his forehead – 'will make a nice little profit on—'

'Right you are.' Lunnings gave in abruptly for he had caught sight of the man he was really waiting for and it was no longer worthwhile to haggle any further over a bracelet.

'Three bob!' He fished three shillings from his pocket and handed them over. He scraped up the parcel with the bracelet in it and said, 'Now 'op it! Go on! Get out of 'ere.'

The man moved with surprising speed and headed for the door, and with a toss of his head Lunnings beckoned the newcomer over. The man was wearing a loosely knotted red tie that had seen better days and that was the sign they had agreed. They nodded by way of a greeting.

The stranger sat down. 'So have you got something for me?'

'I 'ave.'

'Without identification marks?'

'Yep. Just like you wanted.' He lowered his voice even further. 'Filed it off, like you said. Wasn't easy.'

'No one suggested it would be. So what are you asking for it?'

'Not 'ere! Well talk outside, down the alley.' As he led the way out of the bar Lunnings considered. Selling on a gun was always risky because it meant a serious crime would be committed and the pistol, if found, might be traced to him. Not that he would be foolish enough to admit to anything but the police would love to get their hands on him.

The two men stood together in the dark alley while the stranger studied the gun by

241

the light of a small torch. He finally took the pistol from Lunnings' hands and aimed it at a nearby dustbin.

He said, 'If it doesn't work I'll find you and strangle you with my bare hands – and enjoy it!'

'Course it works!' Lunnings glanced up and down the alley, wondering if it had been a mistake to bring this man into an alley and hand him a pistol.

'Have you tried it?' the man asked.

'Course I haven't tried it? Fire a pistol? What d'you take me for?'

'Is it loaded?'

'I dunno. Can't you tell?'

Fumbling with the pistol, the man discovered two bullets. 'It's loaded,' he grunted. 'So how much is it? And don't pull any fancy tricks with me or you'll get the first bullet.'

'I gave 'im twenty shillings and I want thirty for it.'

'Twenty-five. Take it or leave it.'

Lunnings cursed inwardly. 'Thirty,' he repeated nervously. 'Think of the risk I'm taking and I filed off the number...' His voice rose to a squeak as the man grabbed his throat with one hand and squeezed.

'You deaf? I said twenty-five shillings!'

'Done!' he gasped hoarsely.

The man released him. He counted out five shillings, added a pound note and handed them over. Then without another word he pocketed the pistol and walked quickly away.

Lunnings fingered his throat which was still painful. 'Murdering bastard!' he muttered hoarsely and walked off in the opposite direction, wondering who the man was going to shoot.

TEN

Daisy and Steven strolled together along the bank of the river, the sun shone but the wind was sharp and they were each warmly wrapped. Steven had promised on the telephone that he had some interesting news to tell her but Daisy, with something of her own to disclose, took the initiative.

'My father wants to meet you,' she announced breathlessly, 'and so does my mother. Pa says I'm very young and he doesn't want me walking out with someone he has never met.' She turned to him. 'Could you do that, do you think? He's not a bullying sort of man and would be most polite and ... and not critical at all.' She paused for breath. 'He just feels it would be more proper.'

To her alarm, Steven stopped walking and turned to look at her. She felt her face flush. 'It doesn't mean anything, Steven. That is, it doesn't mean he thinks we're ... walking out or anything. Not properly because I know we're not. I mean, we don't even know each other very well.'

After a long pause he said, 'I might be persuaded to come and meet your parents.'

'Oh! Good.' She regarded him doubtfully.

'Naturally I would want something in return.'

'Oh?'

'I'd want to walk along this river bank now hand in hand.' He smiled. 'What do you think, Daisy?'

She laughed with relief. 'I think it's a fair exchange!'

He held his hand out and she slipped her hand into his with a small shiver of pleasure.

Equally delighted, they walked in silence until Daisy remembered her request. 'They thought you might come to Sunday dinner next week – come at twelve and stay until four.' She glanced at him. 'Does that sound too formal? It will only be a roast hen and potatoes and carrots and one of Ma's fruit pies. Ma mashes the carrots with a knob of butter and some pepper.'

'It sounds perfect, Miss Letts. I accept with alacrity in case they change their minds! But please don't allow your mother to become anxious. Dry bread and cheese would be sufficient for Sunday dinner if you were there.'

Overwhelmed by the compliment, Daisy opened her mouth but nothing came out.

'That's settled then,' he told her. 'Please thank them for the invitation and say I accept.'

As they began to walk on he said, 'And now for my news. It's about the Pennington family but I'm telling you in strictest confidence and you must promise never to tell a soul that I told you.'

'The Penningtons?' She frowned. 'What is there to tell about them? I probably know more about them than you do! I *live* with them – and work for them. They're a difficult family in some ways but...' She shrugged.

'So–o, what exactly do you know about them?'

'Let me think ... Hettie is a busybody, Albert I hardly ever see, Dilys is a widow and rather nicer than Hettie – but then Hettie is only a Pennington by marriage. Monty is Monty and he's rather nice, I think. A ... a *mild* man.'

'And what do you know about Monty's wife? Anything?'

'Only that she died years ago ... and everyone loved her. She was very kind...'

'And she was childless?'

'Yes. That must have been disappointing but...'

'Suppose I told you – and remember this is in strictest confidence – if anyone in the office finds out I've told you, I could lose my job.' He stopped and looked at her.

Immediately nervous, Daisy said, 'Then

246

maybe you'd better not.'

'But I trust you to keep a secret, Daisy. You would, wouldn't you?'

'Most certainly I would. Cross my heart and hope to die!' She looked at him earnestly. 'Is it very dreadful? It's not a ... a murder or anything?

'No! It's nothing like that.' He smiled. 'Don't look so worried.'

'But I am worried.'

Steven took a deep breath. 'Mrs Pennington, that is Cressida Pennington, went to Switzerland, had a child and brought it back to England for adoption.'

Daisy stopped in her tracks. After a long moment she said, 'I don't believe you! Is this supposed to be a joke or something?'

'It's not a joke, Daisy. It's the truth. Cross my heart and—'

'Stop it, Steven! Cressida didn't have any children. I told you ... and if she had, why would they have the baby adopted? It does not make sense. You've got it all wrong.'

'I've seen it written down in black and white!'

'Then it's lies!'

They walked on in an uncomfortable silence.

Steven squeezed her hand. 'You don't have to defend them, Daisy. They must have had their reasons. The child may have been ... ill in some way and they might have had it adopted by a nurse who could look after it properly.'

'Then why keep it a secret?'

He shrugged. 'Maybe that's not the reason. It might have been ... Well, how can I put it? Montague Pennington might not be the father.'

Daisy gasped. 'Not the father? Steven, how could you say such a thing!'

'I'm only guessing. But you can't deny the facts. There are documents to prove that there was a child born in a clinic in Switzerland – and Cressida Pennington is named as the mother.'

'And the father?' They reached a seat and Daisy brushed off a few leaves and sat down. For a few moments they gazed in silence across the river while a few hopeful ducks paddled towards them.

'It was "Father Unknown".' He hesitated, sitting down beside her. 'Sometimes that means that the mother doesn't want the father to be named.'

Daisy felt confused and totally stricken. She had assumed that she knew the family reasonably well and now she was having doubts. Cressida had always been a well-loved but tragic figure, ministering to her unfortunate aunt but now it appeared that she was somewhat devious and had had a child by a man who was not her husband. It was shocking but, if she was honest, almost thrilling in parts ... and she could not share her new-found knowledge with anyone.

After a moment she said, 'Was it a boy or a girl?'

'A girl named Dorothea.'

'That name was on the birth certificate?'

He nodded.

'Does it say who adopted her?'

Steven shook his head. 'I suppose the adoption papers would say who they were but we don't have a copy. But there is one more envelope that cannot be opened until sometime next month. Very hush-hush!' He patted her arm. 'Don't take it to heart. It's hardly the end of the world.'

'But it's so sad ... and poor Cressida! And poor Dorothea!'

By this time Steven was regretting his decision to pass on the information. He stood up. 'Well, that was my news,' he said briskly. 'No more to be said. Time to retrace our steps and pop in somewhere for a nice pot of tea and a cake.'

Daisy rose slowly to her feet. 'I won't tell a soul,' she promised, as they turned back the way they had come.

'So you're not upset?'

'Upset? No, why should I be?'

'And not a word to anyone.'

'Cross my heart!'

'It's just a nice little mystery.' He grinned at her. 'I thought you'd like it.'

'I do like it,' she admitted with a rush of honesty. 'I don't think I should but – I do!'

Hettie's letter to her brother-in-law arrived by the first post the next day and while he read it, his face grew red and his porridge grew cold.

Daisy watched him, puzzled. Who could this letter be from, she wondered anxiously, and why was it upsetting him? 'Do eat your porridge,' she suggested, hoping he would be prompted by her interruption, to share the contents with her. It worked.

Slowly he looked up, pushing the letter aside. 'It's from Hettie and Dilys.'

'Oh no! Has something else happened there?'

'Nothing to do with the harassments but–' he paused to eat a spoonful of porridge – 'read it for yourself, Daisy. You'll need to know what's going on. It has hurt me very deeply and you will see what I mean when you've read it.'

Daisy, thoroughly alarmed by this, reached for it with some hesitation.

She read aloud. *'Dear Montague, Dilys and I are sure this letter will come as a relief to you and we want to assure you that we are both most concerned for your happiness and peace of mind over the coming years. That is in the forefront of our minds.'*

'Forefront of their minds! Poppycock!' he muttered.

'I think they mean well,' Daisy said dubiously.

'Well I don't!'

She went on. *'You, will, I'm sure, admit (if only to yourself) that you are becoming rather vague and no doubt find daily life more arduous than of late when you were a few years younger. The management of the family money must weigh heavily on your shoulders and this is a burden Dilys and I are willing to share with you. In fact, if the doctor feels that the strain is too much for you, we will undertake to deal with it in its entirety on your behalf...'*

Daisy glanced up at him. 'Becoming rather vague? What does she mean exactly?'

'That I'm a silly old duffer in my dotage and no longer fit to handle the family finances!' He added more sugar to his chilled porridge, tasted it and frowned. Putting down the spoon he said, 'They've ruined my appetite! Beastly interfering old women!'

'You're not at all vague!' Daisy regarded him with concern. 'You're perfectly fit and able. Elderly, yes, but vague, no! And what is this hint about a doctor? Are you ill?'

'Certainly not! I'm as fit as a fiddle. A

darned sight fitter than I was a year ago when I was tucked up in bed all day! I know Miss Dutton meant well but she was wrong to coddle me.' He added milk to his porridge and stirred it angrily. 'Read the rest of it.'

'If a visit to the doctor results in a confirmation of your limitations, Albert and I would be prepared to apply for an order of power of attorney which means that you need no longer worry about the state of the family finances.

Do please give this idea serious consideration, Montague. You know you can trust us to do whatever is best for you (and for the family) and that your welfare will always be our first concern.

Your devoted sister-in-law, Henrietta.'

Daisy raised her eyebrows. 'Henrietta? Is that her real name?'

'For her sins.' He fell silent, brooding but then snatched back the letter and tore it in half. 'Devoted sister-in-law? Who does she think she is fooling with this nonsense. Firstly, I do not need help with financial matters and secondly, if I ever do, I shall certainly not turn to Hettie or Albert – or even Dilys although I'm sure my sister has been dragged into this plan against her better judgement.' He tried the porridge half-heartedly and said, 'You always make it too sweet!'

Wisely, Daisy ignored the comment. 'What will you do about the letter?'

'Nothing ... at least, nothing that Hettie

252

will ever know about.' He smiled slowly. 'I shall make an appointment to see my doctor and explain the position I am in. He will doubtless give me a clean bill of health.' He narrowed his eyes. 'And I shall ask for a written statement, dated and signed, of his professional medical opinion. If the matter is ever raised again, I shall send them a copy and that will pull the rug from under their feet!' His smile broadened. 'And they will fall on their *derrieres*, my dear, and I shall be there to applaud their fall!'

'But you won't answer the letter?' She rather hoped he would. Then there would be fireworks. A bit of excitement!

'Certainly not! I would not lower myself to take any heed of it. I may decide to ignore it completely. That will infuriate them.'

'Suppose they ask me if you received the letter?'

He thought about it. 'Then you will say I did receive a letter but I laughed, tore it up and tossed the pieces into the fire! When you asked me about it, say that I replied that "it was of no consequence".' He frowned. 'Or I could compose a stinging letter in reply ... or telephone her and tell her what I think of the letter. If they want to follow this up, they will have to approach me face to face and I doubt they would dare.'

Later, thinking about the letter and

Monty's choice of reply, Daisy felt a flash of anger towards Hettie and Dilys because she was not fooled by the old man's show of bravado. Their suggestion of his incompetence had hurt his pride and she would not forgive them for that unkindness.

Soon after two o'clock Daisy returned from her trip to the butcher with a triumphant smile on her face. She had been dispatched to his shop with a letter of complaint from her employer and now waxed lyrical about the confrontation. 'He read it,' she told him, 'but then a customer came in for some liver and then after that he read it again and he didn't know what to say. The boy was bustling around, boning a leg of lamb for one of the customers and he kept looking at me – the boy, I mean – and then he winked.' She smiled at the memory.

'I didn't send you down there to make eyes at the butcher's boy!' Monty grumbled. 'What did he say about my complaint.'

'He was very sorry and didn't know how it happened. He'd never charged anyone twice for the same bill. He said Miss Dutton would vouch for that!'

'Well, of course she would,' Monty told her. 'He didn't dare try it on with her. She had too much experience to be caught like that! He was trying it on because you're new and inexperienced. So did he return the money you'd given him?'

'Yes.' She grinned. '*And* he sent half a pound of bacon rashers "by way of an apology and a sign of good faith"! That's how he put it. I put them in the larder.'

'Half a pound of bacon, eh? That was good of him. Also makes me think he was guilty as charged but we'll give him the benefit of the doubt, Daisy, but watch him in future.'

'Like a hawk!'

He frowned. 'I need you now to run another errand for me, Daisy. I'll send you over in a taxi – to Albert's, that is, because it worries me that he's all alone there now that Hettie has hightailed it to Dilys's place. I don't like to think that he might be in any danger from Stanley.'

Taxi rides were few and far between in Daisy's life and she immediately agreed to the idea.

'I don't want him to think I'm fussing,' Monty explained, 'so I shall pretend I want to invite him to lunch tomorrow – what are we having? Will there be enough for three of us if he accepts?'

'I could make a bacon roll – we've still got some suet – and a rice pudding? Would that do?'

'Certainly it would although I doubt he'll accept the invitation. He's a lazy devil and likes his home comforts.'

'He might wonder why you didn't just telephone him.'

'Say ours has been out of order for the last twenty-four hours. I just want to know that he's dealing with everything.'

The taxi arrived promptly and Daisy soon found herself at Macauley Buildings on Widcome Hill. She told the taxi driver to wait for her then rang the bell. Waiting on the step, she peered through the window on either side of the steps but saw no sign of life. Thinking that maybe he was a little deaf, she used the knocker – three loud knocks. Still no reply. She crouched down to look through the letterbox. All was quiet.

'So either he isn't there,' she reasoned aloud, 'or he is unable to come to the door.' At once she felt a flutter of apprehension. Putting her mouth close to the letterbox she shouted, 'Mr Pennington! It's me, Daisy, from your brother's house!'

The uneasy silence continued. Was he ill in bed? Or worse, had he been attacked by his son? Stepping back she stared up at what she assumed was a bedroom window.

The taxi driver called, 'Out of luck, ducks?'

'I'm not sure.' On a whim, she began to search for a key and found one almost immediately, hidden under a flower pot containing a dead shrub. She held it up to the taxi driver and said, 'I'll just check. I won't be long.'

Letting herself into the house was an uncomfortable feeling and as she closed the front door behind her, she was aware of a growing alarm, not only for Albert Pennington but also for herself. Stanley might be around, hiding somewhere.

'Mr Pennington! Are you there?' her voice echoed as she looked around the passage with its red tiled floor and an ornate mahogany coat stand which also catered for umbrellas. Receiving no answer she began to inspect the rooms, fearing to discover the worst.

Five minutes later, having satisfied herself that there was no intruder hiding on the ground floor, she was halfway up the stairs, still shouting for Mr Pennington and announcing her own presence, when a door creaked at the far end of the landing.

'Who's there?'

Above her, on the landing, Albert had suddenly appeared wearing a dressing gown over his nightshirt. He looked dishevelled and anxious, darting nervous glances around him.

'It's me. Daisy. Your brother sent me. I didn't mean to frighten you.' He stared at her as if at a ghost. Worried, she asked gently,

'Are you ill?'

'No ... that is, yes. I mean I have felt unwell and thought it best to rest.'

'Should I call the doctor?'

'No, no! I'm quite recovered. I'll come down and we'll have a cup of tea together – or maybe a glass of sherry!' He forced a timid smile.

Daisy found her way around his kitchen which was in something of a muddle. Soon they were sitting at the kitchen table nursing cups of tea and Daisy was explaining her mission when there was a knock at the front door.

Albert jumped in alarm. 'I'm not here!' he cried loudly. 'Whoever it is I'm ... I'm away for a few days.'

Daisy stared at him. 'If you're not here you can't be shouting at him.'

'Oh! No. I see that.' He sank back on to his chair. 'Don't answer it.'

'But there's a taxi outside the door. The driver knows I'm in here.'

Albert's face grew pale and his lips quivered. 'What shall we do? It's him! It's Stanley!'

'It might be the taxi driver.'

He was too frightened to understand her. 'What's that you say?'

'I said, 'It might be the taxi driver. I'll go and see.'

'Be careful, Daisy!'

258

She hurried down the passage and stood hesitating by the door her hand on the catch. 'Who is it? Is it the taxi driver?'

'Yes.'

With a sigh of relief she opened the door but her greeting died on her lips as the door was immediately pushed back, knocking her over as a man shouldered his way in. Before Daisy could get back on her feet he had closed the door behind him and Daisy knew instinctively that this was Stanley. He was unshaven, shabbily dressed and smelled appalling. Worse still, he was carrying a pistol.

'Who the hell are you?' he growled. 'Where's the old man?'

Reaching out he grabbed her arm and jerked her to her feet.

Daisy said nothing. The shock of his arrival had affected her mind and all she could do was stammer incoherently. Fortunately Albert appeared in the doorway of the kitchen, in a pathetic attempt to go to Daisy's aid.

'Leave the girl alone!' he said shakily. 'She's nobody. Nothing to do with me. My brother's housemaid.'

Affronted, Daisy found her voice. 'I'm a trainee housekeeper!'

Pushing Daisy in front of him, Stanley made his way into the kitchen where he pushed her on to a chair and stood over

259

them both, the pistol at the ready.

He said, 'Don't either of you try anything!'

His father looked on the point of collapse and shook his head.

'Nothing to say to me then, after all these years?' Stanley thrust his face closer to his father. He looked around. 'Where's the new Mrs Pennington? I gather there is one.'

Albert said, 'She's away, staying with friends. You have no quarrel with my wife.'

'What's the taxi for?'

Daisy said, 'It's to take me back.' She was thinking rapidly, now that the shock had faded. 'I've brought a message from Mr Montague Pennington.' It crossed her mind that all the time she was here she was a witness, and hopefully Stanley was unlikely to shoot his father. She was willing to remain ... but for how long?

Albert was trying to rally himself. He said,' What are you doing here, Stanley?'

'I live here, don't I? I mean, this is my parents' home. It was my home once – before I was banished to the other side of the world. I thought I might be welcome here. The simple truth is, I don't *feel* very welcome.'

Daisy said indignantly, 'How can you think you would be welcome if you bring a gun with you?'

He turned towards her. 'Ah! But is it a real

gun? Or is it a toy. Or a copy? Or a real gun that no longer works? Would I be stupid enough to arrive home flourishing a loaded gun that works? It's probably illegal to carry a loaded pistol.'

There was a short silence while both Daisy and Albert weighed up the possibilities.

Daisy said, 'Suppose we ask you to leave. Will you go?' She was annoyed to notice a tell-tale tremor in her voice. 'Your father has been unwell and you are upsetting him. He has ... he has a weak heart. Do you mean to frighten him to death?'

Albert said 'He doesn't frighten me!' but he sounded very frightened indeed.

They were interrupted by the front door bell which was followed by the clatter of the letter box.

'Are you alright in there, Miss?'

'It's the taxi driver,' said Daisy. She looked at Albert. 'I could ask him to fetch the police.'

Stanley pointed the pistol in the direction of the front door. 'Be a shame to get the taxi driver shot,' he remarked.

Albert said, 'You said it was not a real gun.'

'Maybe I lied.'

Before either of them could guess what he would do next, Stanley turned and backed away towards the back door. He opened it, fired a shot into the kitchen ceiling and stepped outside into the garden, pulling the door to behind him. They heard his heavy footsteps as he ran down the path towards the back fence.

Albert cried, 'Let him go, Daisy!' and sat back exhausted by the ordeal.

Daisy ran to the front door, opened it and told the taxi driver that an armed intruder had threatened them.

Startled, he said, 'You'd best call the police!'

Daisy shook her head. 'Sadly, he's ... he's known to us. I don't think he'll come back today, if ever. But I'll settle Mr Pennington and then you can take me home.'

He frowned. 'What, leave the old man on his own?'

'He's very stubborn. I'll ask him to come back with me but I doubt if he will.'

Ten minutes later Daisy climbed back into the taxi alone. In spite of his fright, Albert had insisted that he could not run away from the confrontation indefinitely and would stay at home and await events.

'There has to be a reckoning,' he told Daisy, his tone resigned. 'I think I've known for many years that this might happen. It's just a matter of time.'

If his son intended to kill him there would be no escape.

★ ★ ★

Just after eleven the following morning, Hettie hung up the telephone and marched back into the kitchen where Dilys waited to hear the results of the conversation which Hettie had been having with Montague. Unable to await the expected answer to her letter she had decided to telephone instead.

Now Hettie's face was bright with annoyance and her lips were pressed together – never a good sign. 'Ungrateful wretch!' she snapped. 'I should have known better than to try and help him. That's the thanks I get for my letter! A flat "no"! Not even a "thank you" for all the time and effort I've put in on his behalf!' She stood gazing out across the back garden, her back stiff with indignation.

Dilys hesitated. She was still suspicious of Hettie's motives in the 'power of attorney' business but was determined not to say so or to hint at her suspicions. 'Then maybe we can stop worrying about him,' she suggested, her tone carefully neutral.

Hettie swung round and glared at her. 'Stop worrying about him? What, waste all my time? Is that the best you can say? Wait until he is so incompetent that the family affairs become unsustainable and we are all thrown into penury? Really, Dilys, I thought you had understood the significance of what I have been trying to achieve.'

'I'm sorry, Hettie. I didn't realize you had

263

spent so much time...'

'But that's just it. I have. It's a complex matter! I spent at least an hour in the library last week, trying to unravel the different types of power of attorney and exactly what is entailed. It's not an easy subject to master, believe me.'

'I thought it was just a matter of—'

'You never do think things through, Dilys. I'm afraid the law is not an exact science. For instance, there's an ordinary power of attorney suitable for some situations or events and another – a something-or-other ... Ah! yes, an *enduring* one – which lasts longer but—'

'Enduring?'

'Do let me finish what I'm saying!' Hettie rolled her eyes. 'One might cover a specific event such as the transfer of a property. Another might cover the durations of an illness and the aftermath. There are forms to be filled in and signed and no end of decisions to be made on behalf of the donor.'

'Are you the donor? I mean, would you be the...?'

Impatiently, Hettie held up a hand. 'Don't ask, dear! You wouldn't understand. It has not been easy for me and I suspect my mind is a little sharper than yours. A form has to be filled out and signed – before a notary, no less.'

'A notary?' Dilys felt baffled. Was Hettie deliberately making it sound more difficult than it really was?

'I don't expect you to understand.' Hettie gave a disparaging toss of her head. 'You have no idea how much is involved. If I were to be granted Montague's "power of attorney" I would have to—'

'Surely Albert would be the best person to—'

'Albert has enough to think about right now, Dilys! If we believe all we hear, his wretched son is threatening to kill him! Of course, he will do no such thing but Albert will hardly be in a fit state to worry about his older brother who is becoming senile and needing help.' She drew in a long breath. 'I'm prepared to take it on but I don't pretend that it will be easy. Far from it. There are the tax details to consider, I shall be paying his bills, making decisions about this and that—' she waved a vague hand – 'even selling his property.'

Dilys frowned. 'But Montague doesn't have any property – except his house. He's not going to sell his own house, Hettie. Where would he live?'

'I said *if* he were to sell it,' Hettie said hastily. 'Who knows what might happen to him in the next few years?' Hettie shrugged her shoulders. 'He might have to move in with you if he could no longer manage alone.'

'With me?'

'Why not? You have plenty of room and you're his sister.'

'But he has a housekeeper – or will have, when we find someone. Daisy cannot stay there forever – she really is not suitable for such a responsibility.'

Seeing that this scenario had worried her sister-in-law, Hettie changed direction. 'Montague might become seriously ill and I would have to make a decision about his medical care. I might have to engage a full-time nurse ... Or he might end up in hospital and never come out again and I would have to oversee the sale of his house. We might need the money to pay for the nurse.'

For a long moment neither spoke.

Dilys was struggling with Hettie's gloomy view of her brother's future prospects. She said slowly, 'So you are suggesting that either you, or Albert, would be a sort of executor.'

'No, Dilys.' Hettie raised her eyebrows in mock despair. 'An executor is the person named in a will. Your brother isn't dead. We're talking about someone being granted power of attorney.' She shook her head. 'I don't think you'll ever grasp this, Dilys.'

Dilys sighed heavily. I don't think I will, she agreed silently. And frankly, I don't think I want to.

On Friday Mr Desmond arrived back in the office looking very pale and drawn. He asked for a tray of tea and sent for Steven.

'So how did you manage, Mr Anders?' he asked. 'Any problems?'

'No sir.' Steven smiled with quiet satisfaction. 'I dealt with a few minor things and wrote them up for you, and rescheduled your more serious appointments. How are you, Mr Desmond? You've had a rather nasty few weeks.'

'I'm afraid I have to agree with you. My wife didn't want me to come back today but the status of the Pennington child's adoption is coming to term shortly and I don't want any problems. It has to be handled very delicately.' He sighed heavily. 'I would always prefer to see what is in the sealed envelope in advance so I can be prepared but, naturally, that is out of the question. The contents are always a surprise – anathema to a solicitor as you will no doubt discover to your cost at some time in the future!' He gave a wry smile, sipped his tea and wished his headache would pass. His wife had been right, he reflected. He did not feel well enough to be back at work. 'Remind me what, if anything, you know about the case, Mr Anders.'

'Er...' The young man ran his fingers through his hair and frowned. 'I did take a look at it, Mr Desmond, because I thought you might not be back in the office and I—'

'Good man! Get on with it.'

'Well, I know that there was a child that Montague Pennington knew nothing about ... and the father is not named on the birth certificate.'

'Exactly. Not unusual but was considered so in this particular case. The Pennington's were, or rather *are,* very well respected in Bath. The whole family goes back a long way and has always given generously to the town's various charities.'

'Then presumably they were wealthy men.'

'Oh yes, very. Some of the wealth gained at the gaming tables much earlier on and later, if my memory serves me well, there was at some time a connection with the Bath stone quarries.' He wished Anders would stop fidgeting with his tie. It looked unprofessional. He would have to mention it some time – but not today. He did not feel up to it.

Steven asked, 'So what exactly happened to the child? Do we know that?'

'We do. She was adopted by a local couple who were provided with an annuity towards the girl's keep. But they, the adoptive parents, had no knowledge of the child's parentage although naturally the father's name was known to the private adoption agency. The truth is to be revealed when the girl reaches eighteen – which will be shortly. I'm led to believe there is a letter to the daughter explaining the background – a letter from the mother, that is.'

'Nothing from the father?'

'Not that we know of. Fascinating, isn't it?' He put a hand to his head. 'I'll check through all the information we have and then Miss Field can arrange the appointment.' His head thumped painfully and he closed his eyes.

'Are you sure you are fit to be here, Mr Desmond? You look very pale.'

With an effort he opened his eyes to find Anders staring at him with concern. 'Actually I do feel a little unwell, Mr Anders,' he confessed. 'In fact I feel slightly dizzy.' He rubbed his eyes. 'Yes, perhaps I should go home again and rest. Will you ask Miss Field to order a taxi.'

'Certainly, sir.'

Mr Desmond watched him go. A nice young man, he thought wistfully. He had always wanted a son but had been given two very nice daughters instead. Yes, a nice young man. Steven Anders would make a good solicitor.

ELEVEN

Sunday came and by eleven o'clock Martha was losing patience with her daughter.

'Daisy! Stop daydreaming and set the cloth – not the checked one, the one your grandmother embroidered. It's in the top drawer ... and smooth it out a bit to get rid of the creases.' She narrowed her eyes. 'What's up? Don't you want him to come to dinner? You said he wanted to come. You said...'

'There's nothing wrong with me. I'm just nervous, that's all.'

'It'll be quite all right, Daisy. There's nothing to go wrong. There's a—'

'The tart's burnt!' Daisy pointed an accusing finger at the tart which was cooling on the window sill.

'Burnt?' Martha stared at it in surprise. 'Only a bit, round the edges. That'll scrape off. Don't fuss so!'

'I thought you were making blackberry and apple.'

'There weren't enough blackberries. You know how they go towards the end of the

270

season. Mushy and a bit bitter – when the witches have got at them!'

Daisy managed a laugh. 'So they say!'

'Anyway, apple and cinnamon's just as nice.'

Daisy's heart was hammering with nervous tension as she set out the knives, forks and spoons, wishing all the while that they had a canteen of cutlery like Monty with silver cutlery set in velvet instead of theirs which had bone handles and lived in a deep drawer in the dresser, mixed up with teaspoons, skewers, a wooden spoon and a cracked pie funnel.

She said, 'Sometimes Dilys likes to have flowers on the table.'

'There won't be room on our table. Anyway, you've already put some marigolds on the dresser.'

'Is the hen all right?'

'It hasn't escaped from the oven, if that's what you—'

'Ma! You know what I mean.'

'Daisy!' Her mother groaned aloud. 'I *have* cooked a hen before! It'll be all right. It will *all* be all right. This is just Steven Anders coming to share a meal with us. He's not royalty or anything.' Her voice softened. 'This is just a friend of yours coming to meet us. He'll get to know us and we'll get to know him. I shall put extra butter in the carrots and add a pinch of nutmeg. I've covered the bird with bacon rashers and I've made some stuffing and I'll do some nice thick gravy.' She smiled. 'It's going to be fine ... Let's hope he has a hearty appetite.'

'Ma?'

'Now what?'

Daisy looked at her imploringly. 'Suppose you don't like him?' The treacherous words burst from her.

Her mother shook her head. 'So *that's* what this is all about!' She drew her daughter close and kissed the top of her head. 'If you like him, I'll like him. If you love him then I will love him for your sake!' Slightly embarrassed by this show of affection, she added, 'How's that?'

Daisy clung to her, burying her face in her mother's familiar apron but after a moment she emerged, smiling. 'Thanks, Ma!' she whispered. With an effort she returned to the job in hand and reached for the cruet which had been given to her parents as a wedding present and which stood in pride of place on the middle shelf of the dresser.

When the table was set to her satisfaction her mother sent her upstairs to get ready. Once in her bedroom Daisy kissed the pink velvet mouse, attacked her ginger curls with a hair brush and coaxed them into some kind of order before tying her hair back with

a green ribbon. On went her best skir
her green sprigged blouse and lastly her
shoes which were light brown leather w
single buttoned strap.

By the time the knocker sounded on
front door she had convinced herself that
looked reasonable and flew down the st
to find her father opening the door to t
visitor.

Looking rather awkward in his Sund
clothes, Tom shook hands with Steven a
said, 'The carrots are from the garden. I li
to grow a few vegetables.'

Steven said, 'Carrots? Oh yes, of cours
'We've got decent soil here.'

'Right.'

Martha hurried from the kitchen looking
little flushed from the heat of the oven. 'S
you're Steven. Come in, please, and make
yourself at home. We don't stand on cere-
mony.'

Daisy, speechless with excitement now the
moment had arrived, simply smiled and
nodded.

Steven said, 'Hello, Daisy.' To her father he
said, 'Where shall I leave my bicycle? Will it
be safe out in the front?'

'Best put it in the shed, lad,' her father
advised. 'Come on. I'll walk you round the
side of the house with it and you can see the
garden.'

'Thanks. I've just got to get something first.' He went outside and Tom, Martha and Daisy waited.

He reappeared a few moments later with a potted geranium for Daisy's mother and a small bag of walnut fudge for Daisy.

Moments later, watching from the landing window, Daisy saw her father and Steven chatting in the garden and let out a sigh of relief. Her ma was right, she thought gratefully. It was going to be fine.

Albert opened his eyes next morning and blinked several times in an effort to clear his sight which was always worse first thing in the morning. He sat up and at once the familiar sense of dread filled him as thoughts of Stanley rushed into his mind. He glanced at the clock. Twenty minutes to nine!

'Better get up, old son!' he told himself. Smiling wryly, he remembered the sound of his father's voice when Albert was around nine years old and the greeting was always the same. 'Better get up, old son!'

Albert had had great respect for his father – a respect which he never lost. In those days it would have been seven o'clock on the dot and the maid would be hovering in the doorway with a jug of hot water, and his father would be pulling on his jacket, preparing to leave for his short walk to the office. Before

he left the room he would ruffle Albert's hair affectionately and say, 'Be good for your mother.' That was what Albert had expected when Monica produced their son – a respectful boy who would run down the hall to meet his father with a smile when he came home at the end of each day.

'But that was then!' he muttered and sighed.

Five minutes later, still in his nightshirt and dressing gown, he entered the kitchen. He gave a strangled cry as he jumped with fright. Stanley was sitting at the table and the pistol was resting on it.

'Morning, Father! Nice surprise, eh? Your favourite son has popped in to say "hello"!'

Albert sat down quickly before his trembling legs gave way beneath him. 'What ... what do you want, Stanley?' he asked, his voice hoarse, his heart beginning to thump uneasily.

'I want to know if you're pleased to see me, Father? Are you?'

'I'd be more pleased if you hadn't brought a gun with you!' Albert felt rather proud of these words. They had taken a considerable amount of courage – but his son looked unimpressed. In fact he looked amused by his father's attempt at a rebuke.

'But you see, I feel safer with the gun. Less chance of you packing me off back to Ceylon to that man you considered a friend!'

'He is ... was a friend! We were at school together.' In fact they had lost touch shortly after Stanley arrived at the plantation and, unwilling to deal with the possibility of bad news, Albert had secretly been relieved. 'No news is good news, Monica!' had been his mantra.

Stanley raised his eyebrows. 'He was no friend to me!'

'Maybe you behaved badly – the way you did at home.' Now Albert desperately wanted to know what exactly *had* happened out in Ceylon but he was afraid to ask because that would mean facing up to an unpleasant truth. Maybe it was best that he did not learn the truth because it might be unbearable. He had managed to stifle his conscience over the intervening years and he now felt too old to cope with unpleasant revelations and consequent guilt.

Now he said, 'We thought it for the best, Stanley. You know what you were like – quite unmanageable. Your poor mother was afraid of you, to be frank.'

'And now *you're* afraid of me! I like that!'

'I'm not afraid of you,' Albert lied, 'but I am fearful for you. I don't know what sort of havoc you intend to create, apart from what you've already done. It was heartless to frighten your Aunt Dilys.'

276

Stanley shrugged. 'Just her bad luck to be born a Pennington. We've not been blessed as a family, have we.' It was not a question.

Albert regarded him with growing despair. 'If you think I deserve to die then shoot me, Stanley, but you will pay for it with your own life and I should not care to have that on my conscience.'

'On your conscience?' The question was a sneer. 'If I shoot you, you will be dead and will no longer have the luxury of a conscience!'

Albert shook his head. He wanted this encounter to end but he saw that it could only end one way and he felt obliged to make a last desperate attempt to justify his actions. 'I'm truly sorry it turned out this way, Stanley. I thought that the discipline of life abroad would help you. I was at my wits' end.'

'That made two of us!'

'I wanted to send you away to school earlier but Monica refused to even consider the idea.'

'It seems that your one aim was to get rid of me. Out of sight, out of mind!'

'No!' cried Albert although he knew in his heart there was a germ of truth in Stanley's interpretation. He stiffened as Stanley picked up the gun, studied it almost absently, then dropped it back on to the table. 'But

277

Mother thought I needed *understanding*,' he reminded his father. 'I heard her say so. She wanted me to see a doctor but you refused.'

'I thought they might lock you up in a mental home!'

'I expect they hoped to set my head to rights but you couldn't face the shame, could you, Father? The humiliation! Friends and family whispering behind your back. Because you're a weak man.'

'I was strong enough to get my own way!' Albert snapped. 'Strong enough to send you away!' He took a deep breath, regretting the harsh words. He must not let Stanley upset him, he told himself. He must stay calm and in control. Lowering his voice a little he said, 'You must recall how you were at that time. Out of control and possibly dangerous. You fired an arrow through the neighbour's window! Poor Mrs Gladwell. You might have killed her. No wonder she took against you. It's a wonder she didn't report you to the police, then and there.'

'She shouldn't have called me a hooligan.'

'You broke a bough off her cherry tree!'

'It was overhanging our garden! Mother asked her to trim it back but she refused.'

Albert sighed. 'Monica thought you would end up in prison!'

'I did end up in prison – but not in this country! But you don't want to hear about my problems, do you, Father?' He leaned forward. 'But you have to, because here I am with no money and no home and no job – and with a gun which I intend to use ... on my ever-loving father!'

Albert heard the words with a weary acceptance. He had somehow known for so many years that there would be what his son had called 'a reckoning'. Maybe he deserved it. Maybe he didn't. But it was coming. Albert told himself he would not utter a word of pleading. He would not give Stanley that much satisfaction. He looked his son in the eye and said, 'Go ahead. Do it. It might make you feel better to know that you have revenged yourself.'

'Oh I will – go ahead, I mean! I don't need your permission!' He reached for the gun and levelled it at Albert's head. 'Head or heart?' He said. 'You can choose.'

'Don't play games, Stanley. It's cheap!' His voice shook but he kept his gaze fixed on his son's face.

'But that's fitting, Father, because I am cheap. Dirty, starving, shabby, worthless. Can't get cheaper than that!' He glanced round the room. 'Maybe you should kneel on the floor ... or stand against the wall over there! Yes!' He pointed with the gun. 'On your feet, Father! Stand over there. And close your eyes.'

'No! I won't close my eyes! I need to see you pull the trigger!' He stood unsteadily and stumbled forward to take his position against the wall, his arms held stiffly by his side. Please God, send me a heart attack! he begged silently. Then whatever happens, my son will not be hanged for murder!

Stanley stood up and levelled the gun. 'Any last thoughts?' he asked. 'Any last words?'

Albert heard himself say, 'I loved you once! I'm so sorry!' He didn't close his eyes but they filled with sudden tears so that his sight was immediately blurred.

He heard Stanley say, 'Goodbye, Father!' and then the shot rang out. Oh God! Albert waited for the pain or whatever it was he should expect. Or had Stanley missed! He waited.

There was a heavy crumpling sound. Brushing the tears from his eyes, Albert saw Stanley lying on the floor. The gun was still in his hand and blood was oozing from a hole in the side of his head. The wall to his left was spattered with blood and soft tissue.

'Dear God in heaven!'

Slowly Albert approached his son. He lowered himself to his knees and steeled himself to look more closely. Despite the bullet hole in his son's head, Albert couldn't quite believe that he was dead. Stanley's face showed no sign of anger or grief – no sign of anything, in fact. He looked peaceful, thought Albert with a rush of mixed emotions. The tense mix of anguish and anger, so plain to see before the shot, had been replaced by an expression of calm acceptance. Acceptance of his fate?

'Oh Stanley. My poor angry little boy!' The tears returned to Albert's eyes as he knelt down beside the body of his son and took the limp right hand between his own and kissed it. 'I didn't want any of this to happen,' he whispered. 'I didn't want everything to go so terribly wrong. Monica was right. I should have listened to her. I should have helped you instead of...' He began to sob in earnest, deep, painful tears full of regret and guilt. Awkwardly, he pulled his son up and cradled his head in his arms. This was how it should have been, he thought. I should have 'loved him' back to health and sanity. We did love each other once, when he was small and biddable but then...

With an effort he pushed the unpleasant thoughts from his mind. There was no point in dwelling on past mistakes because there was no way to put them right. Perhaps there never had been.

He caught sight of the gun and for one glorious moment he saw a way out for himself – a way out from the years of remorse that awaited him.

'Shoot yourself, Albert!' he whispered.

But no! He couldn't take the easy way out. That would mean ruining Hettie's life, too, and he must not do that. He'd done enough damage. When his wife discovered what had happened here, she would be devastated and that would be bad enough. He would spend the rest of his life trying to help her recover from this tragedy.

He hugged his son more tightly as time passed, until the clock in the hall struck the hour and he knew he must let Stanley go. He kissed him and gently laid him down where he had fallen.

Time to telephone his wife and begin the long journey of painful contrition which lay ahead. Then he must notify the police. Breathing heavily, he clutched at the edge of the table and began to haul himself to his feet.

Forty minutes later Hettie and Dilys sat in the taxi in a bleak silence. They were on their way to Hettie's home but had decided to call in on Montague and break the news in person. Then they would leave him in the care of Daisy Letts and continue to the chaotic scene they could expect at the scene of the shooting.

Arriving, the two women hurried inside and Montague was fetched from the summer house to sit with Daisy in the sitting room and hear the bad news.

Stumbling a little over her words, Hettie managed to inform them that Stanley was dead. 'I have to be with Albert, and Dilys has agreed to accompany me,' she told her small but seriously shocked audience. 'I can't face it on my own. The police will be there and Albert will be in a terrible state.' She dabbed her eyes with a handkerchief. 'It could have been worse, I know. It could have been Albert who was shot.'

Daisy said, 'They might both have been shot! He could have shot his father and then turned the gun on himself!'

All heads turned in her direction.

Hettie said, 'I'll thank you, Daisy, to keep such terrible thoughts to yourself! What has happened is a family matter.'

'I'm sorry. I only meant—'

'You are here to listen, Daisy! Nothing more. None of this is your concern.'

Montague said, 'That poor boy! What a sad ending to a troubled life. But at least he spared his father. That must count for something.'

Stunned by the realization that there might have been a double tragedy, Hettie's self-control faltered and she blinked furiously.

Daisy said, 'Is Albert all right? It must have—'

'What a stupid question!' Hettie cried. 'How can he be all right? He's just seen his son die!'

'I meant, he must be badly shocked and will need you. Now that we know what has happened, we shouldn't keep you any longer. You could get along to your home. I can look after Mont— I mean Mr Pennington.'

Dilys said quickly, 'Daisy's right, Hettie. Albert must be our first concern.'

Hettie bridled at her sister-in-law's words. 'Albert is *my* husband, Dilys! I'll be the judge of what's best for him!'

Montague intervened. 'I agree with Daisy. We won't keep you talking here. Telephone us when you know more about what is happening. I expect the police are waiting to speak with you and they may want to remove Stanley's body to the mortuary.'

Hettie flushed with annoyance. 'My husband is there,' she pointed out. 'Stanley is his son, not mine. Albert is apparently unharmed and has his wits about him so can no doubt deal with the police and sign whatever forms are necessary.'

Dilys glanced helplessly at her brother.

Daisy said, 'If I could be of help and Mr Pennington doesn't mind, I could come with you.'

Dilys said, 'That's very kind of you, Daisy.' and looked at Hettie.

'What do you think you could contribute?' Hettie demanded.

Daisy ignored her tone of voice. 'Answer the front door, make pots of tea, fetch and carry – that sort of thing. You probably won't feel up to it.'

Montague nodded. 'You go with them, Daisy. You'll be invaluable.'

Hettie finally recognized the value of Daisy's offer and gave in grudgingly and soon the three of them were on their way to Widcombe Hill.

It was even worse than Daisy had expected. As the taxi drew up outside, a man and a police sergeant were talking together on the front step and they glanced up at the new arrivals.

'And you are?' the policeman asked.

'I'm Henrietta Pennington, Albert's wife and this is Dilys Maynard, Albert's sister.' She did not bother to mention Daisy.

'We came as soon as we could.'

The other man said, 'I'm Doctor Woods. I was called to the scene in time to find your husband suffering a minor heart attack brought on by shock. A relatively mild attack and nothing to worry about, I'm pleased to say. He has—'

'Oh no! Oh God!' Hettie blanched, one hand to her heart.

'He has returned to bed, Mrs Pennington,

and I have given him a sedative to help him relax and hopefully sleep.'

'I must go to him!' she gasped and hurried into the house before anyone could stop her.

The policeman addressed himself to Dilys. 'The deceased has been taken to the mortuary but his body will be released after examination. Your brother will be asked for a statement about what occurred here, but not until he is well enough to deal with it. We are assuming, from what he was able to tell us, that the victim first threatened him but then shot himself. We have taken possession of the gun and that will be examined for fingerprints.'

Dilys said, 'So, sergeant, you are not bringing any charges?'

'I have not said so but it seems unlikely. However, suicide is itself a crime and there are certain procedures.'

The doctor pulled out his watch and tutted. 'I shall have to be on my way.' To the policeman he said, 'You know where to find me if necessary.' To Dilys he said, 'My condolences, Mrs Maynard. This has been a terrible tragedy.' He raised his hat and walked briskly to his motor, started the engine and climbed in.

The police left also, promising to be in touch and asking to be advised of any further relevant developments.

Daisy and Dilys watched the two men drive away then turned, and without a word, went up the steps with heavy hearts, and into the stricken house.

Left to his own devices Monty realized he was shaking from the shock and he felt alone and vulnerable. He poured himself a glass of malt whisky and, carefully considering his options, made his way into the summer house, taking *The Times* with him. He hoped to relax and read the paper and hopefully distract himself from the terrible news and all that would follow. He was glad his brother had not been shot but did not envy him the gossip which would follow Stanley's suicide.

He tried to think sensibly and sent up a short prayer of thanks for the fact that the family need no longer live in fear, wondering where poor misguided Stanley would strike next. Children could prove a great disappointment, he told himself. Maybe it was as well that he and Cressida had had no family although, at the time it had been a cause of considerable heartbreak.

It was sheltered in the summer house, the afternoon sun was comforting and the familiar smell of warm wood soothed his jangled nerves. He settled himself on the cushions, sipped his drink and wondered about the future – his own and that of everyone else. A hopeful robin hopped close and Monty smiled.

'Nothing for you here,' he said. 'Unless you drink Famous Grouse!'

He watched the few clouds that moved sedately past, finished his drink and dozed off.

When he opened them again he was startled to see a visitor dressed all in black, walking towards him across the grass. He rubbed his eyes and stared at the approaching figure which looked vaguely familiar.

'Miss Dutton?' he whispered. 'Is that you?'

'It is, sir. I hope you'll forgive the intrusion. May I sit down?'

Without waiting for his answer she made herself comfortable on an upright chair, took a handkerchief from her bag and blew her nose.

He regarded her through narrowed eyes. She looked a little thinner than he remembered and definitely less jolly. Her eyes, peering out from beneath the black felt hat, lacked their old sparkle. He wondered if she were ill ... or perhaps it was her sombre outfit. He had never seen her in black and now decided it didn't suit her.

She said, 'I rang the bell but no one answered. Then I thought you might be out here. I still can't get used to your being up and about.'

'It's been a trying day. I find it very restful here.'

'I've been asking around in the village,' she confessed, 'and I don't think you have found my replacement yet.'

'Not yet,' he agreed, 'but we have interviewed a few people and will be considering others. Miss Dutton forgive me, but ... are you in good health? I don't mean this harshly but you do look a bit peaky. Under the weather, as they say.'

She sighed. 'I'm in perfectly good health, sir, but my mother is not. She died two weeks ago.'

Now he understood. Miss Dutton had lost her mother and was grieving. 'My dear Miss Dutton, I'm so terribly sorry!'

'Thank you. I'm pleased to say she died with me beside her and resting in her own bed. It was very peaceful.'

Montague thought of Stanley's angry and emotional death but said nothing. This was not the time.

'I'm sure she died happy,' he said. 'She was very lucky to have such a devoted daughter.' Suddenly a great hope rose in him as he put two and two together. Miss Dutton wanted her old job back – and she could certainly have it! What luck that they had not settled on anyone else in the few weeks she had been gone. Daisy had done her best to fill the void but she, too, would be pleased to see her friend return.

'I suppose you wouldn't consider returning to me, would you, Miss Dutton?' he said. 'I think we were a happy little household and could be again.'

Her face lit up. 'Well I'm blowed! I was about to ask you if it would be possible! Well! What can I say? I would consider it, Mr Pennington. Yes. Thank you!'

They beamed at one another. Montague lifted his glass. 'Suppose you refill this for me, and pour yourself a sherry. We could toast the future!'

'We could indeed. Thank you, sir.'

Montague watched her pick her way across the grass and his smile persisted. 'Well,' he said softly, 'this is a turn-up for the books and no mistake!' And felt deeply comforted.

Steven was greeted by shocking news when he entered the office on Tuesday the fourth of November. Miss Field, proud to be the bearer of bad news, explained that Mr Desmond's wife had had a serious fall and was temporarily bedridden. She would recover in time but while she waited for her sister to sort out her affairs and come to her aid, Mr Desmond would stay at home with her.

'So we'll be one short,' she told Steven.

'We'll be extra busy. Not much free time for you to study for those exams.'

Steven did not know whether to be pleased or sorry. He hated studying but he knew that with each examination he passed, his salary would improve. A mixed blessing, he thought.

Miss Field elaborated. 'Fell down the stairs in the middle of the night in her nightdress. Must have tripped.'

'Perhaps she was sleepwalking.'

She shrugged. 'Or gone down to the kitchen for a cup of Ovaltine or cocoa. I don't care for Ovaltine, myself.' She eased paper and a sheet of carbon into her typewriter. 'If Mr Marsh is away again, you may have to deal with that adoption case that's coming up shortly.'

'Ah!' Steven frowned. He would never admit that the idea made him nervous. He said, 'Can you run through the details with me?'

'What do you mean? Now?'

'Just a rough idea. In case I have to deal with it on my own.'

Miss Field sighed loudly then leaned forward. 'The letter and records from the adoption society have to be opened in the presence of the adoptee and the adoptive parents. Hopefully they will have told the daughter in advance so there should be no sense of shock.'

'And that's all there is to it?' Steven was reassured.

'That's the basic idea but this case will be a little tricky because the child's real mother has been paying for her upkeep and now the daughter will inherit whatever is left in the mother's account.'

'And how much is there?'

'I don't know. I'm just a secretary.'

'Not just a secretary,' he corrected. 'A very good secretary!'

Her plain face lit up at the compliment. 'Thank you, Mr Anders! I do my best.'

'So—o ... we send for this adoptee and the adoptive parents, read them the contents of the letter and wait for the fireworks to start!' Steven spoke lightly but he was somewhat daunted by the prospect of having to possibly deal with the problem alone and made up his mind to check through his various text books to find something helpful. It would be a coup to deal with it satisfactorily but a rather large blot on his early career if he failed in any way.

'Have you ever been involved with a similar case?' he asked her.

'Only one. It was the first year I came here and I didn't understand much about it – too busy trying to type Mr Desmond's letters without too many errors!' She laughed. 'But it must have been traumatic. The boy concerned was twenty-one years old and was told that the woman he thought was his mother was actually his grandmother–' she frowned – 'and the young woman he thought was his cousin was his mother! I think that's right.'

'Good lord!' he stared at her, appalled. 'Poor young man!'

'Indeed!'

'And do we have an inkling of the name of Cressida Pennington's daughter?'

'Not yet.'

'But the adoptive parents know, of course.'

'Of course they don't. They only know the girl was put up for adoption and the mother was a wealthy local woman – and there are plenty of those in Bath! The town must have other wealthy women who keep the name of a child's father from their elderly husbands!' She laughed at the expression on Steven's face. 'You're an innocent, Mr Anders!'

It didn't sound like a compliment and he at once denied the accusation but he was shocked nonetheless. Adoption. What a minefield, he thought, and he was at once repelled and fascinated by the complexities of the subject, and the idea came to him that once he was fully qualified, he might specialize in this particular aspect of the work.

★ ★ ★

When the telling could no longer be put off until the next day, Martha and Tom asked Daisy to come home for another Sunday dinner, So Daisy had arranged for Monty to go to dinner with Dilys. Hettie was still in her own home where, having refused Dilys's offer of help, she was dealing with the various matters that always arose after a death.

Martha and Tom waited until they had finished their Sunday dinner – a more homely ham casserole instead of a roast hen – and then, at a sign from his wife, Tom cleared his throat and began the little speech he had prepared for the occasion.

'Your ma and me have got something to say to you,' he began, 'and you needn't fret yourself because it's not bad news. Not really ... at least we don't reckon so.'

He glanced at his wife for support.

'That's right,' she said. 'Nothing to worry about.'

At these words Daisy was immediately alarmed and stared from one to the other until her gaze finally settled on her father. Her mind began to search for possible disasters. 'They've bought a tractor! You've lost your job. You're...' She tried to swallow but her throat was dry. 'We're going to lose the cottage!' Daisy was stricken by the imagined news. Firstly on their own account and secondly because of Steven Anders. Whatever would he think when they were thrown out on to the street? It was every family's worst nightmare and the shame it brought was only part of it.

But to her surprise her father tutted with annoyance. 'They've done no such thing!' he told her. 'And don't go guessing like that. Now you've put me off what I was going to say.'

'I'm sorry, Pa.'

'Where was I?' He looked at Martha.

'You were saying as it's nothing to worry about.'

He frowned. 'Oh. Right ... The thing is that it's to do with you, Dais, and me and your Ma.'

Daisy clasped her hands nervously. Now she *knew* it was something bad. Forcing herself to stay calm she watched him as he struggled to form the words which she knew would turn her world upside down. Suddenly it came to her. 'You're ill!' she cried. 'One of you is ill! Oh, don't tell me! I can't bear it!'

Martha said, 'No, Daisy. We're both well. It's nothing like that. We told you – it's nothing to worry about.' She turned to her husband. 'Get on with it, man! You're making things worse!'

Daisy covered her face with her hands, her heart rate quickening. What could be worse than one of her parent's getting ill and dying?

Tom cleared his throat for a second time and took a deep breath.

'The fact is, Daisy, that you are our daughter and always will be.' He had forgotten what he had rehearsed so diligently and now he simply plunged in regardless. His wife was right. She had to be told. It wasn't the 'being told'. It was the way it was told. That's what Martha had said. She had offered to do the telling but Tom, as head of the household, had insisted it was his responsibility although, when she had finally agreed, the enormity of the task had frightened him.

Daisy slowly uncovered her face.

Her father continued. 'But a long time ago there was a kiddie born...' He closed his eyes, unable to go on.

Martha seized her chance. 'Out of wedlock...' she began.

Daisy felt quite faint as the truth dawned. She had been born the wrong side of the blanket! She knew what that meant. How could that have come about, she wondered. Her mother had been expecting a child out of wedlock ... and her father had rescued her by marrying her? For a moment she could hardly breathe but then she understood how difficult it had been for them all these years.

'It doesn't matter,' she told them. 'Truly, it

doesn't.' She looked at Tom. 'I'll always think of you as my father. I'm not upset, Pa.' Was she upset? She didn't know. Perhaps she was. She searched for helpful words. 'These things happen!' She smiled shakily. Yes. 'These things happen.' That sounded wise. That sounded as if she had accepted the news.

Tom groaned.

Her mother reached across the table and took hold of her right hand. 'We're trying to tell you that we ... that we adopted you. You were someone else's child and the mother didn't or *couldn't* keep you and we wanted a baby so we...' It was her turn to fall silent.

Daisy blinked. She had been adopted. That meant that her real mother and father were two other people!

Martha hurried on. 'Your real mother left some money to help bring you up and then she died but she left a letter for you which you can open when you are eighteen. And I expect she will tell you all about how it happened.'

A letter ... was that good or bad? 'So who is she, this mother person?' she asked in a voice that she did not recognize.

'We were not allowed to know any details, Dais. That was part of the agreement. It was all kept very private. Secret, almost.'

Tom was recovering. 'We hoped you would

not blame us for anything. We've tried to do the right thing. We had no children and you had no parents that wanted to keep you. Do you see, Dais? It seemed like a blessing in disguise.'

Daisy nodded. 'Did my ... my other father die too?'

'We don't even know who he was or is.' Martha's voice trembled and she blinked back the first tears. 'We don't know if he knew about you being born. Your mother might have kept it from him for some reason. As you say, Dais, these things happen.'

Daisy tried to imagine what she ought to be feeling. Questions crowded into her mind. How was she supposed to behave now that she knew the truth? Who was she, exactly? And how would Steven think of her when he knew all the facts?

As the silence lengthened Martha began to cry and Daisy sprang from the chair and ran to her. 'Don't!' she cried. 'As you said, Ma, it's nothing bad. Nobody is dying and we aren't going to be thrown out of the cottage. It's a shock, that's all, and I'll get over it. I'll ... I'll just get used to the idea. I know I will – at least, I'm ... Yes, I will. As long as I don't have to go with this other father. I can stay here, can't I? They can't make me...' Her heart hammered.

Tom said hoarsely, 'No one can take you away, Daisy, and we want you to stay – don't we Ma? A hundred per cent. You can bet on that! Martha, do stop crying. You'll upset Daisy.' And you might set me off, he thought nervously.

'It was all legal,' Martha told her, between sobs. 'You are legally our child.' She took a deep breath to steady herself, and then another and another until the fear began to subside. 'Our daughter,' she repeated. They watched her until she dried her eyes and returned the crumpled handkerchief to her apron pocket.

Daisy, suddenly weak with emotion, sat down heavily and they looked at each other warily. Was the worst over?

Tom said, 'Well, I reckon that's sorted *that* out!' He beamed with sudden relief. 'I think we all need a nice cup of tea! What d'you think, Martha?'

'I could do with one!' she said. 'And I'm sure Daisy needs one. She's been wonderful! Very brave.' She threw her arms around Daisy and they hugged long and hard, then she headed for the kettle and the tea caddy and found three mugs.

As they sipped the comforting brew, Tom said, 'Here's to the future, Dais! May it be a happy one!'

'And here's to the past!' Daisy added. 'That

was happy, too!'

Martha, choked by her daughter's generous words, reached once again for her handkerchief.

TWELVE

Daisy lay in bed later that night trying to come to terms with what she had been told. She hoped that her parents did not think that she blamed them in any way for the shock they had given her and she had also been rather quick to say that 'everything was all right'. Maybe it was but maybe it wasn't and she now had time to ponder the unknown and that was making her uneasy. Daisy decided she would stay calm and consider the various aspects of what she now knew. Maybe tomorrow she would write it all down. But for now she would simply mull it over in her mind.

'First,' she whispered, 'I had a mother who has died so how will I ever know anything about her? Maybe I never will ... in which case she will be a mystery mother!' She rolled her eyes. 'I'll know roughly what she looked like because I must take after her in some ways so she may have had my hair colour and maybe a few freckles but she might have had dark hair and I may have inherited my hair from my father.'

She thought about Tom and Martha and it dawned on her for the first time that she did not resemble either of them.

'Not that it matters,' she reminded herself firmly. 'Because it doesn't matter who I look like – I'm just *me!*'

She thought about her parents – the one's who had brought her up – and smiled. She had been so lucky. She might have been handed over to a couple who would not really love her but her mystery mother had carefully chosen Tom and Martha Letts.

'Or I might have stayed with the mystery parents who didn't want me or who might not have been very good parents.' She frowned into the darkness. She had probably had a lucky escape. Suppose her father had been a criminal! Or he might have been a very famous man who was already married ... And her mother might have been a very young innocent woman and he had taken advantage of her! That would have been a scandal.

She closed her eyes, confused but not disheartened. It was all rather exciting in a way but there were so many missing details. How was she supposed to understand and accept everything when she did not yet know everything and might never know it? A new thought intruded. Who could she tell who could keep a secret?

Steven? Startled, she sat up suddenly and said, 'Oh no!' What would Steven think about it?

A gentle knock on the door interrupted this train of thought and her mother's head appeared in the doorway.

'I thought you might be awake and worrying,' she said. 'Would you like a mug of Ovaltine?'

Daisy shook her head. 'Were *you* awake and worrying?'

'Yes – but your pa's fast asleep. It would take a hurricane to wake him! He's lucky like that.' She crossed the floor and sat on the end of Daisy's bed. 'Nothing's changed,' she said earnestly, 'except that now you know about it. Your pa reckons you've got a sensible head on your shoulders. He says you'll be fine.'

'Suppose the other father was ... a murderer?'

'If he was he'll be dead by now, Dais. Hanged by the neck and all that.'

'Ah! I hadn't thought of that!' Daisy grinned. 'Or he might have been a handsome prince...'

'...who fell in love with a woodcutter's daughter! Sounds more like a fairy tale!'

Daisy's expression changed. 'Ma, when I know all the details ... Do I have to do anything or can we just keep it to ourselves? What I mean is, I don't want anything to be different once I know. I like things the way we are. We're happy, aren't we?'

'Of course we are.'

'So I don't have to meet my father. I don't want to know him. If he doesn't know about me then I don't have to tell him, do I? Can it be exactly the same afterwards as it was before?'

'Of course it can. You can tell people or not tell them. It's going to be up to you, Dais.'

They sat for a few moments in a thoughtful silence.

Daisy said, 'I might tell Steven ... if anything happens between us, like getting married, I wouldn't want to keep things from him.'

'Quite right. Certainly you could tell him.' She patted her daughter's hand. 'If he was worth his salt, he'd still love you, Dais. Any man would.'

'So, in a nutshell, everything's the same as before.' Relieved, Daisy drew in a long breath.

Martha hugged her. 'Everything's fine,' she promised.

To Daisy's surprise, however, she was soon of the opinion that, contrary to expectations, everything was *not* fine and this was because she learned on Friday morning that Miss Dutton was to return as Monty's housekeeper. Her employer broke the news while she was serving up a lunch of sausages and mash.

She stared at him, baffled, a forkful of sausage arrested halfway to her mouth. Slowly she lowered the fork. 'Coming back here?'

'Yes. You don't look very pleased, Daisy. I thought you'd be...'

'When did you decide ... that is, what about her mother? Who is looking after her?' Her thoughts reeled at this unexpected betrayal.

Surely she had proved herself capable of looking after him. She had rescued him from his bedridden state and brought him back to life! Now he was bringing back Miss Dutton.

'Miss Dutton's mother died, Daisy. Miss Dutton came here the day Stanley died and you were all over at Albert's place. Maybe I didn't mention it. Everything was at sixes and sevens. Miss Dutton asked if she could have her old job back. I thought you two were on friendly terms.'

Daisy struggled with her feelings. She had enjoyed seeing herself as a 'trainee housekeeper' and now she would be demoted. 'But I thought ... I was hoping to become your housekeeper at some time.'

He hesitated. 'We did toy with the idea but Miss Dutton needs a job and it seemed only fair. You have a long way to go yet in the ... the culinary arts, Daisy.' Seeing her puzzled expression he said, 'Your cooking is slow to improve, Daisy. I think that's fair, don't you?'

'You didn't complain.'

'No. I knew you were doing your best and Dilys and Hettie were trying to find a replacement housekeeper for me.' To avoid seeing the hurt on Daisy's face, he took another forkful of mashed potatoes and gravy.

Slowly and with deliberation, Daisy put down her knife and fork.

'You said you liked my cooking.'

'I said you were improving and you are but–' he took a quick breath – 'Hettie has asked us to feed the mourners here after Stanley's funeral which is now planned for next Wednesday. Albert may not be fit enough to attend and he doesn't want what he describes as a "houseful of people". There will be a funeral lunch for the family and a few friends and acquaintances, with a menu which Hettie has planned and which would be beyond you.'

'Such as what?' Daisy's tone was steely.

'Such as a game pie, salmon in aspic, a vegetable terrine ... Need I go on?'

Daisy rolled her eyes but was forced to

acknowledge defeat. A game pie would be beyond her, she had never cooked a salmon and she had no idea what a vegetable terrine looked like. It sounded like one of the dishes soup was served in but that couldn't be right. Discouraged, she began to finish her food, dismayed to notice that the mash was lumpy and her second sausage a little burnt. Distracted of late in various ways, she had neglected to attempt new menus.

'Miss Dutton will start here again on Monday,' Monty told her, 'in time to accomplish all that has to be prepared but I've told her about the progress you've made. You will be a great help to her, Daisy.'

Suddenly Daisy imagined herself confiding in Miss Dutton about her newly discovered mystery past but almost as abruptly she knew it was out of the question. Miss Dutton would be an unsafe 'confidante'. She was an inveterate chatterbox and knew too many local people. Daisy's secret would leak out.

For a few moments they ate in silence but then Daisy began to look forward to the notion of a funeral lunch – with game pie, salmon and whatever else he had listed. She could help Miss Dutton make it all and improve her own knowledge.

She promised herself that when the time came for Steven to propose to her – if he ever did – she would be a superb cook.

307

The day of the funeral dawned wet and cold and Miss Dutton sighed gloomily as she and Daisy carried crockery and cutlery into the dining room and set it on the sideboard alongside a pile of white damask serviettes.

'Aren't we going to lay the table?' Daisy asked. 'And what about place names. We went to a wedding once and—'

'No.' Miss Dutton ran a finger down the stack of plates to count them. 'We don't know how many people are coming so we'll bring in a side table for the food to go on and people can help themselves and then find a chair at the table. It's easier that way. Folk can sit next to whoever they want to.'

'Is it all right to smile? I mean, it is a sad occasion.'

'If you don't overdo it. A polite smile rather than a cheerful grin, if you see what I mean.'

Back in the kitchen Daisy glanced at the clock. Ten past two. The funeral service would have started. She tried to imagine the pews full of people, sombre in their best black. Would the church be full or empty, she wondered. Since poor Stanley was to be buried in unconsecrated ground, there might not be very many mourners. Would there be a choir? Was music allowed?

'Stop daydreaming, Daisy, and carry the glasses into the dining room.'

She had just reached the dining room when Monty appeared. He was dressed in a black suit and a shirt with a stiff white collar and looked very uncomfortable.

'You look very nice, sir,' Daisy told him.

'Damned lot of fuss!' he grumbled sheepishly.

Miss Dutton darted a look in his direction. 'A funeral's a funeral, however you look at it,' she reminded him. 'You should be there. You're his uncle. You're family.'

'I didn't feel up to it and Dilys insisted I should stay at home. Thought I'd catch my death of cold – you know how chilly that church can be at this time of year – and then there'd be another funeral!' He sat down on the chair at the top of the table.

Miss Dutton frowned. 'You'd best let Albert sit there,' she suggested. 'He was the boy's father, after all.'

'For all the good it did either of them!'

He received another sharp look. 'And don't you go talking like that if the vicar comes back with the others.' She turned to Daisy. 'Fetch the flowers, Daisy, will you. We'll put them in the middle of the table to cheer things up.'

'But Mrs Pennington said they were to go in the hall.'

'I'm in charge here. Not Mrs Pennington.'

'But I thought—'

'Don't think, Daisy. Just do it, please.' She frowned. 'And while you're in the kitchen take a look at the salmon. If it looks as if it's drying out, put a clean damp cloth over it.'

Daisy retired to the kitchen, halfway to a sulk. She didn't envy Miss Dutton the responsibility of the funeral feast but, since her return to the household the previous day, Daisy felt that Monty had been snatched away from her. And this morning, Dilys had arrived and *she* had started making decisions for him.

Daisy considered the salmon, glorious in its slices of cucumber and radish curls and decided that when she married Steven they would serve a similar salmon. After helping herself to a couple of slices of cucumber she rearranged the rest to hide the gap, found a clean tea towel, dampened it under the tap and laid it over the fish. The large game pie contained chicken, ham and pheasant and Miss Dutton had grumbled that it had been 'a bit of a swine' to make! The vegetable terrine, with its neat layers, would be turned out at the last minute so that the aspic jelly did not melt.

Daisy smiled, picked up the flowers and carried them along the passage to the dining room. Whatever she might think about the Pennington family, there was no doubt she was learning a lot from them.

An hour later, the funeral repast had been enjoyed somewhat cautiously. The fact that Stanley had committed a sin by killing himself had meant a restricted service in the church and his coffin had been lowered into a grave dug in an area of unconsecrated ground. Now eleven people sat around the table, including two neighbours who had been recognized by the vicar as inveterate mourners.

Most had drunk a little more than was good for them and Hettie was watching Albert like a hawk in case he decided to make a speech. She was trying to persuade Montague to do the honours but he refused point blank, insisting that he and Stanley 'had never really got along'.

'Someone should say something!' Dilys agreed. 'Whatever he did, he's a Pennington. You're his stepmother, Hettie. You say something about him.'

'Say what? I didn't even meet him. Really Dilys! He was long gone when I married Albert! You knew him better than I did!'

Daisy and Miss Dutton, hovering in the doorway, tried not to show too much interest in the proceedings. The latter, however, was bathed in relief that the food had been well received. Miss Dutton had hoped that there might be plenty of leftovers that she and

Daisy might enjoy in the privacy of the kitchen after everyone had gone but was disappointed to see that despite any reservations about the occasion, the mourners had made serious inroads into the pie and had demolished the salmon.

Daisy was busy with her own thoughts which centred around Steven and a possible future together but which she felt might now be complicated by the traumatic revelations about her past.

Suddenly Albert struggled unsteadily to his feet and someone tapped on the table with a spoon and called for silence. Hettie muttered 'My Godfathers!' and closed her eyes.

'He wasn't the best son a man could have...' he began, 'but then I wasn't a very good father!'

Hettie sprang to her feet but Dilys, sitting next to her pulled her back into her seat and hissed, 'Let him have his say, Hettie!'

Albert leaned forward, his hands resting on the table in front of him. His voice shook as he went on. 'Things could have been better ... *should've* been better but they weren't...'

Miss Dutton pulled Daisy out of the doorway into the passage and whispered, 'We can hear it all from here. Best they needn't see us listening.'

'...Something wrong in his mind, poor

312

boy...' Albert's voice was low and several people inclined their heads in an effort to hear what he was saying. 'He went wrong but ... but he didn't deserve that miserable grave.'

The vicar, obviously embarrassed, said something about 'God's will' but a few dark glances in his direction reduced him to silence.

Hettie, her face flushed, stood up and hurried towards her husband. 'That's enough, dear. You're not really up to this. We know what you're trying to say.'

She tried to ease him back into his chair but he pushed her away so that she stumbled and almost fell.

'Stanley was ... We didn't know how to help him and he...' Tears filled his eyes and ran unchecked down his faded cheeks. 'He wasn't happy ... I wish things had been different ... I'm so dreadfully sorry!' He sat down abruptly, weeping noisily, gulping for air and rubbing at his eyes.

Hettie glanced round in desperation but nobody moved until Daisy darted back into the room. To Hettie she said firmly, 'Let me help you get him up to the spare room. He can rest on the bed.'

'To rest? Oh ... yes!' Hettie took one arm and Daisy took the other and they gently hauled him on to his feet and half carried

313

him out, to sympathetic murmurs of understanding.

The vicar stood, put his hands together and muttered an incomprehensible prayer before murmuring a 'goodbye' to everyone. Then he made his way slowly out of the room, nodding apologetically to Miss Dutton as she saw him out.

That evening, Albert and Hettie had been taken home by taxi and Monty had retired early to bed. Miss Dutton and Daisy had cleared the table and washed up and sat together at the kitchen table sharing what was left of the pie, drinking what was left of the sherry and saying little.

Several days later Daisy and her mother sat in the office at Marsh & Desmond, staring at each other in shock. The name of Daisy's mother had been revealed and she now knew that she had once been Dorothea Pennington – Cressida's illegitimate daughter. More of a shock still was the news that Albert was her father.

Daisy leaned back in her chair and closed her eyes and tried to sort out the confusion that swept through her. So ... Monty was Albert's brother so that made Monty her uncle. But maybe not ... Maybe because Monty was married to Cressida at the time

314

of her birth, he was her legal father *before the adoption*. Or was he her stepfather? If Albert was her father then Hettie was her stepmother ... and was Dilys her aunt?

Her mother put a hand to her mouth and whispered, 'The Penningtons! Of all people!'

Mr Desmond said soothingly, 'I know this has come as a great shock, Miss Letts, but the Penningtons are a very well respected family. Very well known in Bath.'

'Do they know about me?' Daisy asked, dreading the answer.

'No. They are quite unaware of the—'

'Do they have to know?'

Her mother said, 'There's nothing to be afraid of, Dais.' And put out a hand to rest it on her daughter's arm.

Mr Desmond said, 'I'm sure they would be delighted to know that...' He broke off, frowning.

'To know that Albert and Cressida were ... were lovers?' Daisy blinked. Albert and the wonderful Cressida who everyone admired?

Completely at a loss, Martha tutted. 'It would certainly set the cat among the pigeons.'

Mr Desmond shrugged. 'Presumably Albert knew nothing about his child. It will cause quite a stir if you wish him to be told. Or decide to confront him.'

Daisy struggled to see the ramifications of

315

such a disclosure. 'But then they would all know about Cressida not being so perfect ... and Hettie would be upset and furious with her husband.' She put a hand to her head which felt as if it were somehow spinning out of control. 'Monty would never forgive his brother ... Oh Lord!'

Martha shook her head. 'I hate to think...' she began. 'Listen Dais, they don't have to be told anything. If Cressida wanted to keep it all a secret and she obviously did ... Well!' She shrugged. 'You can keep the secret and so can I and so can your pa. You can think it over for a while.' She turned to the solicitor. 'Mr Desmond won't say anything, will you?'

'Most certainly not. That would be quite unethical.' He looked at Daisy over his spectacles and cleared his throat. 'There is a small amount of money left for you – a little over four hundred pounds. Unless you wish otherwise we can open a bank account for you and transfer the money which we have been holding in our account on your behalf.'

'Four hundred pounds?' It was a fortune, Daisy thought dazedly.

'And this letter is for you, Miss Letts.' The solicitor handed her a slim envelope. 'From Cressida Pennington. I suggest you have had enough shocks for one day so why don't you take it home with you and read it when you feel calmer?'

Before Daisy could answer, her mother said, 'Good idea. What d'you think, Dais?'

Daisy took the envelope and swallowed hard, suddenly unable to speak. Finally she said, 'Maybe, Ma, when we get home and Pa is back from work, you could read it aloud for us – one mother for another.'

Martha brushed tears from her eyes and smiled at her daughter. 'Thank you, Dais. I'd love to.'

The letter was short and to the point.

Dear Dorothea,
This is to tell you that I love you and to say how sorry I am for any hurt my actions and this revelation might bring you later. Please forgive me. I know that you have had loving parents and for that I am deeply grateful. God bless and keep you.
Your loving mother, Cressida Pennington.

Daisy shared the letter with Steven next time they met, as they walked alongside the river, and he marvelled at the convoluted series of events which had brought him and Daisy together.

'Do you think it was meant to be?' Daisy asked him, relieved by his positive attitude towards the Pennington history.

'Of course it was meant!'

'So everything is the same ... between you and me?'

'I certainly hope so!' To prove it he gave her a quick kiss on the cheek.

Daisy, lost in her own new and bewildering world, missed the significance of the first kiss. 'I shall stop working for Monty,' she told him. 'He has Miss Dutton and he does not need me and I can't bear to see them all, day in, day out, knowing what I know about them.'

'Are you sure that's what you want, Daisy? It can't be an easy decision.'

She nodded her head firmly. 'I've talked to Ma and Pa and they agree it's up to me – and that's what I think is best. I don't want the Penningtons to know anything about what happened.' She hesitated. 'I'm still Daisy Letts. I don't want to be a Pennington. The truth is, Steven, that the Penningtons aren't a very nice family – not nearly as nice as mine! And I can easily get another job.'

'But you have a lot of money now, Daisy.'

'I know but I don't want to think about that just yet. It's a bit of a worry, in some ways.'

'A big responsibility, I'm sure.'

'Yes.' She regarded him earnestly. 'You may think me very odd but I'd like to be a house-maid for a few more years. I'm happy as I am and I don't want big changes in my life.

Does that make any sense to you?'

Steven smiled. 'You might want to marry one day – that would be a big change!'

Daisy laughed. 'That big change I could manage!' she told him, 'When the time is right!'

'And the man is right?' He looked at her hopefully.

'And that!' She squeezed his hand.

He slipped an arm round her shoulder and kissed her again and this time she *did* understand the significance of it – and kissed him in return. As they walked on in a happy, thoughtful silence, Daisy was overcome by a deep sense of gratitude. She had been born a Pennington and brought up as Daisy Letts but would one day she would change her name again. To Anders? It certainly had a very nice ring to it, she decided, smiling.